Friend
Monkey

by the same author

Mary Poppins

Mary Poppins Comes Back

Mary Poppins Opens the Door

Mary Poppins in the Park

Mary Poppins and Mary Poppins Comes Back
(Combined edition)

Mary Poppins from A to Z

Maria Poppina ab A ad Z
(in Latin)

A Mary Poppins Story for Coloring

(all published by Harcourt Brace Jovanovich, Inc.)

I Go by Sea, I Go by Land
(published by Dell Publishing Co., Inc.)

The Fox at the Manger
(published by Grosset & Dunlap, Inc.)

P. L. TRAVERS

Friend
Monkey

Harcourt Brace Jovanovich, Inc.

New York

Frontispiece by Charles Keeping

To Emily and Arthur
and
All at Tripoly

CONTENTS

PART I

Friend
Monkey

1

All night long the wind and the rain went roaring through the jungle. The trees tossed and bowed and tumbled. Branches snapped off and were blown away. Never before had there been such weather; never such a tempest.

The small jungle creatures trembled—the lizards, the magus, the spotted mice—and crept into holes or under logs to wait for the storm to pass.

But the monkeys were not so patient. They sprang up out of their nests in the treetops and fled away, shrieking and wailing. Head over tail, tail over head, they swung themselves from branch to branch, swooping through rainy darkness. Wild oranges bounced on their sodden shoulders, nuts and twigs blew into their eyes, as they swung along their switchback trail seeking for a warm dry place out of reach of the storm.

Soon they were far away in the distance. Only a faint chattering echo told which way they had gone. The rain beat down on their forest city. The wind blew their leafy nests apart. Nothing remained, no sign, no footprint, to say that they had been there. You would have thought that in all that tossing jungle world there was not a monkey left.

But you would have been wrong.

For early in the morning, when the storm had blown over and the rain was no more than one leaf emptying its load of water with a plop on to another, a monkey pushed aside the jungle curtain and came out into the clearing.

He stood there, blinking at the scene, half as tall as a tall man, his wet fur edged with light. Upon his brow was a white spot. And round his neck, like a circle of flowers, were patches of white amid the brown.

He was young. You could tell it from his rounded body and the downy fur on his arms and legs; the softness of his large ears, the plump pouches of his cheeks, and the suppleness of the long tail that was wound about his waist. You could tell it, too, from his expression. It was candid, friendly, and defenceless, as though the world had been always kind and he trusted it not to hurt him.

His dark glance, at once inquisitive and mild, darted eagerly here and there, taking in the scene. He examined the little grassy clearing. He stared at the line of cocoanut palms standing up to their knees in sand. And beyond them he spied an enormous lake on which lay a large white bird. He did not know that the lake was the sea and the bird a sailing ship.

The morning brightened. He turned his head. And his glance took in the distant hills. Behind them, something round and red was rising into the sky. Up it came, glowing and swelling, filling the world with the day. The dark monkey-eyes widened. The furry figure trembled. Then, with a bound, he was in the air, leaping towards the shining thing, with his arms flung out before him and his tail unfurled behind.

And the next moment—plop!—he was down in the grass

and the sun as far away as ever. He did not know that the golden ball was not a large wild orange.

"That was excessive," said a voice. "Excessive and uncalled for."

Monkey looked up from the damp grass and found himself face to face with a tiger.

"Moderation in all things, remember. That is the Golden Rule. No one can pluck the sun from the sky. Far less make a meal of it. You had better take a fig."

The tiger broke a fig from a branch and tossed it into the air.

Monkey caught it in one quick paw and stretched the other out palm-downward in a shy, appealing gesture.

The tiger regarded the paw with interest. It was young. It was tender. It would doubtless make a juicy mouthful. So would the arm, so would the shoulder. Indeed, when he came to think of it, the whole body, as it bent so courteously before him, would make a succulent meal.

And yet—the tiger hesitated. In his experience—which was large—the first thing a monkey did when it saw him was to scurry up the nearest tree and hide away in fear. But this monkey was not afraid; indeed, it was offering, trustfully, the eager paw of friendship.

The tiger came to a quick decision. He took a purposeful backward step and put himself out of temptation—a gesture made easier by the fact that recently he had eaten a pig and the edge had gone from his hunger.

"All alone?" he enquired with interest. Monkeys, he knew, went about in packs. Where one was—it was common knowledge—another would be at hand.

Monkey stared. His dark eyes grew darker still. The word

"alone" had a lonely sound. For the first time, or so it seemed, he realised his position. Was he, indeed, all alone? Yes, indeed he was.

He nodded.

"Very well, then," said the tiger, grandly. "You can live with me and be my servant. Take notice, everyone!" he roared. "This monkey is under my protection!"

The clearing trembled but no voice answered—except for the cackle of a mynah bird who, when she caught the tiger's eye, turned the cackle into a cough.

"*Under my protection,*" the tiger repeated. "He will fetch me water when I need to drink and pluck out the burrs from my coat."

The tiger, of course, was not speaking English, nor even using words. Animals do communicate but not in human language. They roar, they squawk, they bellow and squeak, they mew and hiss and whistle. They practice, too, a kind of silence—the blink of an eye, the lift of a tail, a nose wrinkling up, perhaps, or, best of all, perfect stillness. But if a story is to be told, words are what it chiefly needs. It cannot do without them.

Monkey's heart beat gratefully. He could never, he felt, do enough for the tiger.

But as it turned out, he did too much.

The time arrived when the tiger was thirsty. And Monkey came running with a palm-leaf, its wavy edges gathered together as though it were a handbag.

Then—splash! The palm-leaf burst with a popping sound and the tiger was nearly drowned. He sneezed, he wheezed, he coughed and spluttered; the water ran into his eyes and ears.

"You've forgotten the Golden Rule," he roared. "I ask for

a drink and you bring me a rainstorm. And, what is more, it's *salt!* If *you* cannot pluck and eat the sun, *I* cannot drink the sea!"

Monkey sighed. Serving a tiger, it appeared, was not an easy task. The only thing to do, he thought, was to try a little harder.

So he sat himself down on the tiger's back to comb the stripy fur.

"Ouch! That hurts! Take care, I say!" The tiger jerked his head around. Tufts of black and tufts of gold were swarming through the air, like bees.

"It won't do. It will not DO!" The tiger let out a throaty growl. "I asked for the burrs to be removed. And what happens? You remove my coat. Bare patches everywhere! You have made me look ridiculous. Out of my sight, you wretched monkey! Out—before I change my mind and make a dinner of you!"

And flinging his servant off his back, he stalked away, offended and proud, his striped coat moving in folds about him as though it were rather too large for him or he a little too small for it.

Monkey eyed the retreating back. What had gone wrong, he asked himself. He had done his best to serve the tiger and the tiger had not been pleased. The world outside the jungle, it seemed, was chancy, full of pitfalls.

Now he was all alone again. And again the word had a lonely sound . . .

17

2

"Lost your friend?" a voice enquired, apparently from the air.

Monkey looked up. There on a branch stood the mynah bird, busily preening her wings.

"Well, it's no good sitting there and moping. You'd better come and live with me and help to take care of my nest. Here! Mind what you're doing!" She let out a shriek. "You nearly knocked me off my perch."

For Monkey, with a great leap, had landed in the tamarind tree and was swaying at the end of the branch, extending his paw, palm-downward.

"Goodness, you gave me quite a turn! Well, there's the nest. Take care of it. I need a change from time to time. All work and no play turns mynah birds grey, so they say!" And laughing at her own joke, the mynah bird flew off.

She was noisy, awkward, undignified. Her voice was harsh, her manners lacked polish. But to Monkey she seemed the queen of birds. She had offered him a home.

He swung along the branch to the nest and examined it with interest. It was built untidily of twigs and lined with strips of rag. Even so, it was draughty. A few of the holes had been stuffed with grass and others with tufts of black-and-gold fur that Monkey had plucked from the tiger. And within this seedy, tattered dwelling lay four blue shiny eggs.

Monkey regarded them with affection. One day those eggs would become his brothers. And since he was, by nature, neat, it seemed to him that his family should have a more orderly home.

And so, he set to work.

In went his careful, exploring fingers. Out went the bits of faded rag, out went the tiger tufts. He stopped the holes with fresh green moss; he threaded the twigs with strips of palm and added, simply for decoration, a flower from an orange tree.

There! It was finished. The rubbish heap had become a mansion. And within it lay the four blue eggs—silent, not a cheep among them—unaware, apparently, of the change in their situation.

Monkey surveyed his handiwork. Had he left anything undone?

Yes, he had—one thing!

He knew, from his jungle experience, that a nest needs to be kept warm. So he sat himself down upon it.

There he brooded contentedly, glad, after the busy morning, to take a little rest. His head nodded. He slept. He dreamed.

He dreamed of his friend, the mynah bird, who seemed, in the dream, to have gone mad. She was standing on his hand, shrieking, and pecking at his eyes.

He woke with a start and leapt up. The dream, he found, was true!

"Villain! Monster! Murderer!" The mynah bird danced with rage.

"Can't you do anything by halves, you good-for-nothing creature? Take care of my nest, was all I said. I didn't ask you to sit upon it. Where are my lovely dirty rags? Where are my tiger tufts? Oh, my chickens!" She stared at the eggs. "I counted you before you were hatched—and now you're cracked, all cracked! Viper!" she shrieked. "You have done enough. First for the tiger and then for me. Out of my tamarind tree!"

She rushed at Monkey, flapping her wings. And Monkey took a flying leap and landed in a palm tree.

"Good riddance!" squawked the mynah bird, as she pulled her elegant home to pieces. Out went the moss and the strips of palm. In went the rags and the tiger tufts. And when at last it was sufficiently dilapidated, she huffily turned her back on Monkey and settled down amid the mess to lay a new clutch of eggs.

Monkey sighed. He had done his best for the mynah bird. And the mynah bird had pecked at his eyes and ordered him out of her tree. Life outside the jungle, it seemed, was not to be depended on. And he himself, apparently, had still a lot to learn.

He leaned his cheek, perhaps for comfort, on the cheek of a cocoanut fruit. And it seemed to him that, once again, he was all alone in the world . . .

3

The wind from the sea blew through the palm trees. And after a while the cocoanut, unable longer to bear the strain, broke away from its stem. Down it went, crashing through the leaves. And from below came a shout of pain and the sound of a body falling.

There, stretched out on the sand, was a man. One arm lay across his breast. The other cradled a bundle of sacks. The cocoanut, apparently, had knocked him, senseless, to the ground and pushed the cap off his head. It lay beside him, flat and blue, with the two words *London Exporter* printed in gold on the rim. There was cocoanut milk on his blue trousers and scraps of broken cocoanut on his blue-and-white sailor collar.

After a time, he moaned a little and put up a hand to his brow. But another hand was there before it, busily patting and rubbing.

Hurriedly, the sailor sat up. And there, crouching at his shoulder, was a small brown furry shape.

"Blimey, a monkey!" the sailor gasped, nervously backing away. You never knew with wild beasts. Better to take no chances.

But Monkey, never doubting his welcome, merely scrambled after him and offered his paw, palm-downward.

The sailor took it gingerly. "Friendly, are you? That's a relief! All right, all right! Give over, do! You've shaken my hand and smoothed my brow, you don't have to take my skin off, as well!"

For Monkey had returned to his labours and was trying to rub away the bruise.

"ENOUGH, I said!" the sailor protested, scrambling nimbly to his feet in an effort to get away. But Monkey insisted on dusting him and wringing the cocoanut milk from his trousers.

The sailor gave a long-suffering sigh. "Look here, chum. Don't overdo it. I'll clean myself up when I'm back at the ship. You whistle off to your monkey pals. I've got to get on with my work."

21

He gathered up his bundle of sacks and surveyed the waving palm trees.

"Cocoanuts!" He laughed aloud. "The Captain sends me for cocoanuts. 'Hawkes,' he says, 'get away off to that starboard island and bring back some fruit against the scurvy.' And what happens? A cocoanut clonks me on the noddle and I go out like a candle. How's that for an able-bodied seaman?"

He asked the question of the air. But the air made no reply.

"Well, heave-ho and here we go!" The sailor put his arms round a palm trunk and gave it a hearty shake.

Nothing happened.

He tried again. Not a cocoanut budged.

He took off his cap and scratched his head. "That's queer! Cocoanuts hanging up there in dozens and I can't get a blinking one. Hey! Mind what you're doing. Lay off, can't you? I don't want another knock-me-down."

For the tip of a brown furry tail had struck him sharply on the nose as Monkey, with one of his great leaps, whizzed past into the branches.

And then the hullabaloo began.

From tree after tree the cocoanuts came thundering down like cannonballs. And the sailor ran in and out among them, sheltering his head with his arm, grabbing at the round green fruits and stuffing them into his sacks.

"All right, old pal, that'll do!" he shouted. "I've got enough and to spare. As if a dumb beast could understand!" he said, as he tied up the sacks.

But, oddly enough, as soon as he spoke, all the hubbub ceased. No cocoanuts fell. No palm leaf rustled. There was

22

not a sound along the shore but the rocking of his little boat as it swung to and fro in the water.

The sailor cocked his head and listened. "Maybe he understood, after all. Rum things happen—of that I'm sure."

Sailors are simple and superstitious. They find it easy to believe the things that landsmen laugh at. They live their lives between two worlds, the deep of the sea and the deep of the sky, both mysterious. The possible and the impossible are, for them, not far apart.

But where, in this silent scene, was Monkey? The sailor's blue eyes raked the foreshore. Somewhere, amid that froth of green, a furry shape lay hidden.

"Ah, well," he murmured. "He's gone his way." He humped the heavy sacks to his shoulders, staggered to the waiting boat, and stowed them in the stern. Then he settled himself and took the oars.

The sacks sat upright, lumpy and solid, screening the shore from his eyes. He peered around their enormous bulk, first to one side and then the other, hoping for a glimpse of Monkey.

But there was nothing.

"Well, so long, matey!" He brandished his cap. "You did me a good turn and I'm grateful. Thanks—wherever you are!"

"And that's the end of him," thought the sailor, as he feathered his oars and made for the ship.

Little did he know!

4

The ship swung to and fro on the water, her white sails flapping in the breeze, like washing on a line.

"Ahoy, there!" bellowed the sailor's mates, as his laden boat drew nearer.

"Ahoy, yourselves, and let down the rope! My cargo's about to sink the boat."

A rope ladder came snaking down, and up it, hand over hand, went the natty navy-blue figure. Two fat bundles were tumbled aboard, and the sailor began to huff and puff as he laboured up with the third.

"Funny," he thought, as he heaved and panted. "I'd have said they all weighed about the same, but this one—whew! —it's a blooming millstone. Out of my way, Young Napper," he warned. "If this load falls on top of you, we'll be short of a cabin-boy!"

But the skinny, gangling lad at the rail made no attempt to move. He was staring over the sailor's shoulder.

"W-what you got there, Mr. Hawkes?" he stammered, pointing towards the sack.

"Yes, Barley," echoed Fat Harry, the cook. "What you been up to now, mate? I thought you was sent for cocoanuts."

"And cocoanuts, Harry, is what I got. Round green fruit off a cocoanut tree, in case you never saw one!" Barley Hawkes was sarcastic.

24

"Well, take a look behind you, mate. You'll find you've got more than nuts."

"More than nuts?" He turned his head. "Well, I'll be—" But what he was going to be no one knew, for as he lowered the sack to the deck, Monkey came sidling from behind it, extending his paw palm-downward.

"So that's where you were!" said Barley Hawkes. "And me thinking you'd hopped it! Well, you've got a cheek, I must say, boarding my boat without a ticket. And who requested your company, if I might be so bold to ask?"

Young Napper thrust himself between them.

"Don't go hurting him, Mr. Hawkes! He's only a beast. He knows no better!"

"Yes, Barley. You let him be!" Fat Harry grabbed him by the arm. "He's not done anyone any harm. Give him half a chance!"

"Hurt him? Me?" roared Barley Hawkes. "You gone crazy, the two of you? Why should I hurt him? He's my pal!" He flung Fat Harry and Napper aside and bent to receive Monkey's proffered paw.

But Monkey was there no longer.

He was busily emptying the sacks and tossing cocoanuts into the air. Fat Harry caught one in his apron. Napper tucked two inside his blouse. The rest of the crew came running up, and Monkey darted about among them scattering nuts in all directions. One fell into the sea with a splash, another was caught in a coil of rope, and another tripped the Captain up as he entered on the scene.

"What's going on?" the Captain demanded. "This is a ship, not a football field." He glanced round disapprovingly at the litter on the deck. Then his eye fell on the furry

25

shape, a whirling thing with a long tail and a cocoanut in its arms.

The Captain's face was a sight to see. He was both surprised and indignant.

"I sent you for cocoanuts, Mr. Hawkes, not apes! You know the company's regulations. No pets allowed on the high seas!"

"Ay, ay, Captain, I know the rules. And I went for nuts, just like you said. It was him—" He jerked his head at Monkey. "It was him that got them for me."

"What? That hairy creature?" The Captain frowned.

"He did, sir, honest and hope to die. Shook the cocoanuts down from the trees when they wouldn't budge for me. But I never meant to bring him aboard. He must have stowed away on the boat when I turned my head away."

"Well—" The Captain bent down to stare at Monkey and touched the outstretched paw. And Monkey, taking this for a welcome, thrust the cocoanut into his arms.

"Hurrrumph! Well, the thing seems to be tame enough. I'll make an exception just this once. But he'd better behave —I warn you, Hawkes—or he'll find himself stowed away right there!" He pointed downwards with his thumb. "Right there in Davy Jones's Locker."

Davy Jones's Locker is down at the bottom of the sea. All drowned things go there at last, men and ships and chests of gold. There is nothing deeper in the world than Davy Jones's Locker.

"Cross my heart," said Barley Hawkes. "He'll be helpful, sir, I promise!"

Oh, the rash promises of sailors! But how could Barley Hawkes have known—no tiger was there to bid him heed,

26

no cautionary mynah bird—that the time would come when he would wish that Monkey had helped a little less?

5

Meanwhile, Monkey was all agog and delighted with his new world. Fat Harry searched through his dwindling stores and found him a ripe banana. Young Napper sewed him a blue serge cap with half the name of the ship round the rim. *"London Ex—"* was all it said. For Monkey's head was far too small to accommodate the whole word. Not that it mattered, the men agreed. An animal, since it could not read, would never know the difference.

"There you are!" Young Napper exclaimed, as he set the cap at a jaunty angle. "Now you're one of us. You're a sailor!"

Monkey, overwhelmed with joy, was about to reward him with half the banana, when the Captain's voice called from the stern and Napper was hailed to more pressing duties.

"Anchors aweigh!" the Captain ordered. And at once there was a rattle of chains, the pounding of feet along the deck, the thunder of sails as they took the wind—the usual orderly confusion of a vessel resuming her voyage.

But where was Monkey?

Everywhere!

The new sailor worked with a will, hiding things that everyone needed, dragging out others that nobody wanted.

Once, he got under the Captain's feet, but the Captain mistook his leg for a rope and pitched him into a corner.

The ship moved, giving herself to the sea, her timbers creaking rhythmically like the sound of somebody breathing.

"Take a last look at your island, pal," said Barley Hawkes to Monkey. "We shan't get another sniff of land till we dock in London River."

He turned to gaze at the sandy shore, edged with its shawl of jungle green and the hills rising behind it. But, to his surprise, he could not see them. There was nothing but endless ocean.

"Captain! There's something wrong to starboard. That cocoanut island—it's disappeared! Take a squint through the spy-glass, sir! Maybe you can see it."

"Disappeared? Ridiculous!" The Captain put his glass to his eye. He took it away, rubbed the lens, and peered through it again.

"Preposterous! It must be there! And yet—" The Captain's voice was quiet. "You're right! That island's gone."

"But where would it go, sir? It couldn't just blow away—like smoke!"

"Wherever it's gone, I don't like it. It wasn't on the chart, remember. We came on it unexpectedly. I used to hear tales," the Captain brooded, "of islands that came and went. But I took them simply as sailors' yarns. It's a bad omen, Hawkes," he said, as he swung his glass in a wide circle, searching the empty sea. "Great stars!" he cried. "What's that up there!"

"Not the island, sir, surely?" An island in the sky, thought Barley, was as useless as one that disappeared.

"No, no!" said the Captain, testily. "There's something up there on top of the mast."

It was Monkey.

He had seen Young Napper run up the rigging and—anxious, as always, to render assistance—had scrambled after him. Now he was hanging, feet over head, apparently urging his sailor friend to work in the same position.

"Stop it! Let go!" Young Napper yelled. "You'll have us overboard!"

But Monkey clasped him around the waist and swung him away from the mast. Together they dangled aloft for a moment, with only the sea beneath them. But Napper, alas, was too heavy.

"I'm gone! I'm lost! Oh, me poor old mother!" He slipped from Monkey's circling arm and hurtled towards the water.

The Captain and Barley Hawkes waited, helplessly flinging out their arms, for the end of their cabin-boy. But just then the ship gave a lurch to starboard, a sail swung out in a puff of wind and caught him in its lap.

With a horrible screech of tearing canvas, Napper slid down the slope of the sail and landed on the deck. Monkey, with a single leap, was waiting there to greet him.

"Oh, let me die," Young Napper moaned. "All me bones are broken!" He pressed himself against the deck, grateful for its solidity after the nothingness of air.

"Well—if there's a bone that isn't broken, I'll break it myself, Young Napper!" The Captain, relieved of anxiety, could now give vent to his anger. "Look at that sail, all ripped to ribbons! Bully beef and water for you, until it's properly patched. And don't let me find you wasting time playing

29

with that ape. Get a rope and tie him up or we'll have him wrecking the ship!"

"Oh, please, sir, not to tie him up! Wild beasts don't like it. They pine away."

"That wouldn't worry me," said the Captain.

"But he's not to blame—it was me, Captain!" Young Napper searched for a plausible phrase. "I was trying to be a monkey."

"Then try to be a cabin-boy." The Captain turned away.

"Ay, ay, then, sir," Young Napper snivelled, scrambling to his feet. He searched through the treasures in his pocket and fished up a piece of string. Then he put out his hand for Monkey.

But Monkey had left the scene of disaster and was now perched on the ship's side, gazing at the sky.

"Leave it loose," whispered Barley Hawkes, as they tied one end of the string to the rail and the other to Monkey's ankle. "Don't let him think he's a prisoner."

Monkey, however, had no such thought. The string, he assumed, was another gift. And since his friends were tying knots, it was clearly his duty to help them. So, in spite of their efforts to dissuade him, he lashed his own foot to the rail as though his life depended on it.

Having done that to his satisfaction, he turned to the sky again.

"What's he staring at?" said Napper, tilting back his head.

A shadow was moving over the ship, blotting out the sun.

"An albatross!" The sailors cheered. For to meet an albatross at sea is considered great good fortune.

"A lucky omen!" the Captain cried, his anger visibly melting.

"An omen with a catch though, sir. It's lucky, they say, unless you feed them. Once they've eaten the food of land—" Barley Hawkes gave a shudder. "They follow and follow after the ship, till somebody from the land joins them. I know it, Captain! I've seen it happen."

"Nonsense, Hawkes! That's an old wives' tale." The Captain believed in old wives' tales, but he did not like to admit it. "And who would feed it, anyway? An albatross gets its food from the sea."

The great bird glided over the ship, dipping and swerving above the sailors in a kind of skiey dance. Now and then he would turn away as though he had seen enough. But each time he came winging back, swooping lower and lower. Then, suddenly, with a determined movement, he folded his black and white wings together and landed on the rail.

"He's looking for someone!" said Barley Hawkes, as the bird turned his head from side to side.

Fat Harry gave a sudden cry. "He's looking for me! I know him now. It's my old mate, Sim Parkin! We lost him overboard in a gale, down by Santiago."

Albatrosses, seamen believe, are really the souls of drowned sailors. The bodies of men who are lost at sea go down to Davy Jones. But the rest of them, their own true selves, fly up to the air as birds. How this happens nobody knows. And sailors, being superstitious, do not like to enquire.

"It *is* you, Sim—isn't it?" Fat Harry lumbered towards the rail.

"Of course it's not Sim Parkin, Harry!" The Captain stamped with impatience. "Nor Tom Smith, nor anyone else. Now, all of you, get back to work. You're sailors, men,

31

not bird collectors. I tell you, this will bring us luck. Fair winds. Smooth waters. You'll see." He strode off down the deck.

The Captain had spoken no more than the truth, at least as far as he knew it. He had met with many an albatross. And each time the meeting had brought him luck.

But he had not reckoned with Monkey. There he sat, lashed to the rail, his dark glance moving back and forth from the cook to the brooding bird.

"I know you, Sim!" Fat Harry whispered. "I know the squint in your left eye."

The bird's slanting eyes flickered, and he reached out with his beak.

"No, no! You keep off, boy!" Fat Harry took a step backwards. "If I let you touch me, that's the end. I'll find myself down there." He nodded darkly at the sea.

The albatross withdrew his beak and hung his head on his breast.

"Don't take it hard," Fat Harry pleaded. "I can't help liking my bit of life. You did, too, remember, mate? But if you're lonely—well, I'm here. You can always drop in when you're passing. Hi! Hold off! You leave him be!" Fat Harry let out a warning yell.

Monkey—having decided, apparently, that the albatross was in need of help—was now helping the albatross. One paw was stroking the drooping head, the other pressing upon the beak a morsel of banana.

"Don't eat it, Sim!" Fat Harry wailed. But the warning came too late.

The albatross had sniffed the fruit and was gobbling it down. It seemed to satisfy something in him, for his head went up with a lordly toss. His squinting eye fell on Fat Harry with a dark, significant glance. His beak, half open, seemed to smile. Then, with a lift of his great wings, he gave himself back to the air. Once more he circled about the ship, his shadow falling on every face. And then he turned away. The sailors watched, half bewitched, as his shape grew small in the distance.

"He's had what he came for," Fat Harry moaned, blubbering into his apron. "A bit of food from the land he wanted. And why? Because he wants me, too."

"Shut up, Harry, you're not dead yet. And maybe it's just a seaman's yarn." Barley Hawkes tried to reassure him.

"No, no, it's only a matter of time. And it's him!" He shook his fist at Monkey. "It's that dumb thing as who's to blame. Him and his old banana!"

"You won't tell the Captain?" implored Young Napper.

"Of course he won't tell," said Barley Hawkes. "Harry's a gentleman."

"What? Me split on anyone to the Captain?" Fat Harry was deeply offended.

So they buttered him up and smoothed him down, and soon he was laughing again. Fat Harry was an optimist. His mate, Sim Parkin, would surely get him—of that he had no doubt. But not today. Tomorrow, perhaps. And tomorrow, he reminded himself, is something that never comes. So he waddled off to the ship's galley, planning a new kind of stew for supper—salt-beef, hard biscuits, and cocoanuts.

It was a success. Everyone had a second helping.

There was even a saucerful for Monkey, which he picked at, not because he liked it, but simply to gratify Young Napper.

They sat together in companionable silence, Monkey secure in his knots of string, Young Napper untidily sprawled beside him.

The constellations were out in the sky. The North Star, that brings all sailors home, was shining in the Great Bear's tail. A following wind filled the sails, and the labouring ship creaked and groaned as she thrust the waves behind her. It was a moment—such a one comes in every voyage—when sea and sky, ship and men were part of a single whole.

As for the Captain, he was full of high spirits. Up and down the deck he went, shouting important orders. "Trim the sails! Square away! Put the helm down! Put the helm up!" and other nautical expressions.

"You see, Hawkes, I was right!" He laughed. "The bird has brought us luck!"

"Ay, ay, sir," answered Barley Hawkes, exchanging a glance with Young Napper and hoping that this was indeed the case.

The Captain had forgotten—if he ever knew—that luck, like fruit, takes time to ripen. It doesn't happen all at once.

With ill luck it is just the same . . .

6

Hour by hour, on their steady course, the constellations moved. The sailors alternately slept and watched, as they ran before the wind.

But towards morning the wind fell. There was not a

pocket of air in the sails. The ship lay becalmed upon the water, motionless as a model ship inside a whiskey bottle.

And to make matters worse, a thick mist rose up out of nowhere. No man could see his own hand. The sailors spoke to each other in whispers, like ghost talking to ghost.

The Captain took this sudden change as a personal affront. He had praised the weather and called it lucky, and the weather, far from appearing grateful, had turned and flouted him.

He stumbled along the invisible deck giving orders in a loud voice that the mist absorbed and muffled.

Once, something moved swiftly by him, brushing against his arm.

"Is that you, Hawkes?" he called sharply.

"No, Captain, I'm up in the bow."

And again, as he passed beneath some rigging, his glass was knocked from his hand.

"Is that you, Napper?" the Captain bawled.

"No, sir, I'm in the galley with Harry."

"Then who keeps bumping me, confound it?"

Barley Hawkes made a move in the mist. He would have to go and help the Captain. He put out a hand to feel his way and found in it a small warm paw.

And within the paw was the Captain's spy-glass.

Monkey had wearied of sitting still, gazing at the sea. It was all very well when the stars were out. But now it was dark and misty. He knew—he had learned it in the jungle—that mist was tricky, not to be trusted. And where were his friends? In danger, perhaps? If so, they would surely need his help. So he quickly untied the string from his ankle and went to look for them.

Up and down the ship he hunted, using his tail as a sounding line. He banged into this and knocked down that. And at last, after a long search, he came upon one of his cronies.

"So it was you! I might have known it! Don't you ever know when to stop? How can I save you from Davy Jones if you gallivant about like this?" Barley Hawkes, exasperated, felt around in the dark with his foot and came on a coil of rope. He seized Monkey by the scruff of the neck and dumped him down inside it. "Now you stay there!" he whispered hoarsely. "Or I'll scalp you—that's a promise!"

The coil of rope was like a nest, cleaner than the mynah bird's, and not a sign of an egg. Monkey settled himself serenely, taking it for granted that, as he had helped the mynah bird, he was now helping the sailor. All that could be seen of him—if any eye could have pierced the mist—was the flat top of his blue serge cap and the letters *London Ex—*

Barley Hawkes felt his way forward.

"Your spy-glass, sir!" he said smartly, as the Captain loomed up beside him.

"Great heavens, Hawkes, a glass can't fly! How did it get up here?"

"Dunno, sir." Barley Hawkes was stolid. "Funny things happen in the mist."

"Far too many funny things, if you ask me, Mr. Hawkes."

"But it's lifting, sir. I can see you clear."

And, indeed, the mist, having done its worst, was now giving way to the dawn. Ship and sailors appeared again as though from a conjuror's hat.

"And about time, too." The Captain grumbled. "Now we must whistle for a wind."

Landlubbers find it hard to believe that a wind may be called as one calls a dog. But for sailors it is a fact.

36

Barley Hawkes pursed his lips and whistled. And it seemed that the sky sent back the sound—a high, shrill, screaming echo that ended in a loud bang as something hit the deck.

It was a cannonball.

"Steady, lads!" the Captain shouted, as the seamen set up a wild commotion. "Somebody's making a big mistake. They can't do this to us, men. We're not armed, we're a trading ship. Run up the white flag—that'll show them!"

"Shippa ahoy-a! Heave-a to-a!" Voices were calling across the water.

"What do they mean—Heaver Toer! We're hove to already! Where's my glass?"

"There's a ship standing off on the port side, sir. By the look of the crew, I think they're pirates."

"Pirates, Hawkes? Have you gone mad? This is eighteen hundred and ninety-seven. There haven't been pirates in these seas for over fifty years!"

"Well, they're flying the Skull and Crossbones, sir. And they're putting off a boat—"

"You're right! It's unbelievable! My thundering stars, they're boarding us. All hands on deck!" the Captain roared, as a dozen pirates, brandishing knives, came swarming over the side.

"At 'em, boys!" the Captain ordered, seizing a pirate by the waist and sending him sprawling across the deck.

"Ay, ay, sir!" willing voices answered. And then the rumpus began. Bumps, bangs, curses, groans—all the pandemonium of a hand-to-hand shipboard battle. And the sailors got the best of it. They were all unarmed, but their blood was up. Pirates, indeed! They'd pirate them!

So the raiders were flung this way and that, into the scup-

37

pers, against the masts, moaning and sobbing and rolling their eyes. Daggers and cutlasses slipped from their hands, the deck resounded with falling bodies. At the end of the fray there was not one pirate standing upright. The sailors tied their hands with rope, propped them against the ship's side, and regarded them triumphantly.

They were, indeed, a poor lot—shabby, toothless, and skinny. A tatterdemalion remnant, perhaps, of the buccaneers of long ago.

The Captain eyed them with contempt. "Well, what have you got to say for yourselves?"

"Notta spikka Angliss," a pirate muttered, dejectedly shaking his head.

Not speak English? Great gods! Bad enough to be a pirate, worse to board a British vessel lawfully plying her proper trade, but not to speak English—! What could the world be coming to, the Captain clearly wondered.

"We'll deal with this riff-raff later, lads! In the meantime, we must celebrate. Harry, splice the mainbrace!"

Splicing the mainbrace on board ship means doubling each man's ration of rum. The custom is highly esteemed by sailors.

And soon there came from the ship's galley such a sound of junketing, such roars of laughter, such jollification, that a passer-by, had there possibly been one, would have said that the mainbrace had been spliced many times more than once.

"Down with all pirates!" the Captain was shouting. "We'll take their ship in tow, hearties. It's treasure-trove and prize money for every man of the crew." A loud cheer greeted the good tidings.

"Well, fill up once more and then to work!" The Captain

38

held out his pannikin. And something that looked like a very small sailor filled it with rum from a keg.

The Captain stared. Was it possible? Apparently, it was.

"It's that ape again!" he said, wrathfully. "I thought I gave orders to tie him up! How did he get in here?"

Nobody knew—except Monkey.

Sitting in his coil of rope, he had heard the panting battle cries and assumed that the sailors and their friends were playing a rowdy game. Such things happened daily in the jungle. And so he joined the fun. He was here, he was there, he was everywhere. But in all that skelter of arms and legs no one had noticed an extra pair. And later, amid the jubilation, no one had noticed the extra sailor. So the extra sailor had busied himself with pouring out the rum.

"Well?" said the Captain, ominously.

"He *was* tied up, Captain, sir! I did it myself," Young Napper declared.

"It's true, sir," put in Barley Hawkes.

"Cross my heart," Fat Harry added. "Trussed him up like a roast duck."

"Then it must have been those damned pirates. They'll have set him free as they came aboard." Napper, Hawkes, and Fat Harry glanced at each other but said nothing. There was nothing to be said.

"Well, he seems to be making himself useful. And he'd jolly well better, or there'll be trouble!" The Captain's voice sounded ferocious, but for once his bark was worse than his bite. He was far too full of his own good fortune to be worried by a mere monkey.

Think of it! He had captured a gang of bloodthirsty villains—not single-handed, but that was a detail—the last

39

pirates, perhaps, in the world. And now he was a hero. Maybe, as well as the prize money, someone would give him a silver medal. They might even make a waxwork of him and put him in Madame Tussaud's.

This rosy vision so cheered the Captain that he burst into a sailing song and held out his cup again.

But Monkey was no longer there to fill it. He was now searching through the ship, looking for other friends to help.

And very soon he found them.

They were sitting on the deck in a row, each with his head on the next man's shoulder, dejected and forlorn.

Their eyes brightened when Monkey appeared, for any pirate, like any sailor, knows a keg of rum when he sees it. And since, to Monkey, a pirate was as thirsty as the next man, their spirits were shortly as bright as their eyes. Up and down the row he went, tipping the rum to every mouth until the keg was empty.

The strangers were obviously grateful. They nodded and smiled at him toothlessly and held out their fettered hands. And Monkey, at once, knew what was needed. He had been tied up himself.

So he quickly unloosed the knotted ropes, eagerly glancing from pirate to pirate, hoping to be of further service. But his new friends, it seemed, were about to depart. The only help they needed—or wanted—was a leg-up over the side. One by one, they tottered shakily to their feet and, with Monkey giving a heave and a push, clambered to the top of the rail and disappeared from view.

"Farewell and adieu to you, sweet Spanish ladies," came the Captain's voice from the galley.

"Farewell and adieu to you, ladies of Spain!
Until we strike soundings in the channel of old
  England,
From Ushant to . . ."

The last words were drowned in a burst of applause. "Up with the Captain!" somebody shouted. "Down with the pirates!" cried another. And they clapped the Captain so hard on the back that they pushed him out of the crowded galley and followed him on to the deck.

It was just at this moment that the last pirate, courteously assisted by Monkey, clambered on to the rail.

Suddenly the rumpus ceased. The shouts died on the sailors' lips as they took in the situation. Even the sea was quiet.

For a second that seemed as long as a year, sailors and pirate stared at each other. Then the pirate took off his greasy cap and made a mocking bow.

"Gooda-bye-a! Olly vore! Ta, ta!" He smirked. And with a hearty shove from Monkey, he was over and out of sight.

From below came the clonk and rattle of oars and a cackle of laughter, most un-English, as the pirates pulled away.

"Hawkes!" The word rang out like a shot from a gun.

"Ay, ay, sir," muttered Barley Hawkes, who thought he knew what was coming.

The Captain pointed a trembling finger. His body shook with rage.

"Irons!" he spluttered. "Put him in irons! Get that brute out of my sight. Take him below and clap him in."

"Oh, not irons!" Young Napper wailed.

"It's that or drowning. Take your choice."

"I could sew him up in a hammock, sir. He wouldn't es-

41

cape, I promise." Barley Hawkes reached out his arm for Monkey.

"TAKE HIM AWAY!" the Captain yelled. He was clearly beside himself. "Sew him up, for all I care. Put him in chains! Strangle him! But if I set eyes on him again, you know what will happen, I warn you! He's brought nothing but trouble, trouble, TROUBLE, since the moment he came aboard."

One cannot really blame the Captain. Being spick and orderly himself, he felt he had a right to expect that life should be orderly, too. Yet here it was, all ups and downs, like a game of Snakes and Ladders.

He had found fresh cocoanuts, it was true, but he had lost an island. An albatross had brought him luck in the shape of a gang of pirates, and a wild beast, a thing from the jungle, had set the pirates free. No sooner, it seemed, was he up a ladder than he was down a snake. No one would give him a medal now, nor make a waxwork of him. The ill luck had indeed ripened.

As a last straw, it sent him a wind. Barley Hawkes had whistled for it, and the Captain had confidently expected a well-behaved, dependable breeze that would blow him gently home.

But what he got was a tornado.

It rose up out of nothingness, bellowing rudely through the rigging, ripping the sails into tatters. It flung the waves on top of each other till the sea, like a great watery whale, alternately swallowed the *London Exporter* and spat it out again. It even broke off the top of an iceberg and sent it into the Bay of Biscay, just where the ship was passing.

And always at the edge of the weather, round and round

tirelessly, a dark shape flew and hovered. The sailors knew it was watching and waiting. But they did not tell the Captain.

Then, just as they entered the English Channel, the wind broke open the door to the galley where Fat Harry, bouncing from wall to wall, was trying to make a pudding. It sucked him out of his warm shelter and swept him on deck, shrieking for help. Then it picked him up, pudding and all, and tossed him into the sea.

"He should have been lashed to the stove," said the Captain, as the waves closed over his body.

But no rope on earth, the sailors knew, could have lashed Fat Harry tightly enough to save him from his fate.

They were silent, staring down at the water. And the sea was suddenly silent, too. The wind changed from a roar to a whisper, the watery mountains flattened out, the iceberg turned tail and floated away. And the flying shape that had watched and waited lifted its wings triumphantly and flew towards the horizon.

"He knew it would happen, Harry did." Young Napper wiped his nose on his sleeve. "That there banana it was, what done it. And now Sim Parkin's got him." He had no chance to finish what was evidently intended to be a long lament, for Barley Hawkes's hand was over his mouth.

"Hold your gob or I'll spiflicate you! Do you want the Captain to hear?"

He was thinking, of course, of Monkey and trying to save him, if he could, from Davy Jones's Locker.

But what was Monkey thinking?

There he lay, sewn up in his hammock, looking like an Egyptian mummy, with only his head uncovered. All through the storm, as the ship rolled over on her side or spun like a merry-go-round in the waters, he had seen the sailors tossed hither and thither and had longed to rush to their aid.

But no amount of twisting and turning could set him free from his canvas shroud. Barley Hawkes had done the job well. He couldn't even bite his way out, no matter how hard he tried.

Why had this happened, he asked himself. He had thought he was helping his new friends, and those same friends, far from being pleased, had sewn him up like a parcel.

He had never heard of Snakes and Ladders. But, nevertheless, it seemed to him that life was full of surprises. Up one minute and down the next with no one to tell him why.

So, since there was nothing else to do, he lay quite still and wondered.

And while he was busy doing this, the ship, egged on by a kindly breeze, came safely into port . . .

7

"Dear me!" thought Mr. Alfred Linnet, staring at the *London Exporter* as she lay in her berth in the Port of London. "That ship has undoubtedly been in trouble!"

She was all stains and dents and bruises, like somebody come from a nasty brawl. And because he was an imaginative man, Mr. Linnet felt his heart quicken. In his mind's eye he saw the prodigious seas, heard the wind moaning among the sails, and felt within him the shake and shudder as she fought her way through the storm.

But, as well as being imaginative, he was also a stay-at-home man, so he hurriedly thanked his lucky stars that he was not a sailor. His life might be humdrum, he told himself, but at least it was free from great extremes. He had worries, of course. But who hadn't? And, anyway, he was used to them and could tell from one day to the next exactly what would happen.

He would have been surprised to learn that his lucky stars, bored with this commonplace state of affairs, were getting ready to change it.

"Eighteen, nineteen, twenty," he counted, as the bales of cargo swung ashore.

Mr. Linnet was a checking-clerk. He made lists of what came off a ship and checked them against another list of what had been put on. In this way he could be quite sure that the cargo had all arrived. There could be no chance, he was glad to think, of any hanky-panky.

"Twenty-seven, twenty-eight." Mr. Linnet, a small, neat, sprightly man, ticked the items off his list as he leapt over the bales.

There were spices and sugar, tea and silk, come from the ends of the earth. Deserts, oases, and plantations; Eastern cities full of bells—Mr. Linnet thought of these whenever he checked a ship. And at night when he returned home, he would tell his children about the cargo and the places it had come from.

Victoria, he thought to himself—"Thirty-one, thirty-two!"—was never really interested unless he could tell of embroidered muslin or silver earrings or lengths of velvet—the kind of thing, Mr. Linnet supposed, that little girls prefer.

But Edward—perhaps because he was a year younger—would listen, not so much with his ears, as with the whole of his body. Mention China or Timbuctoo and Edward would be already there, all of him flown away from home to the other side of the world. Indeed, Mr. Linnet had often wished—"Forty-four, forty-five!"—that Edward was less fanciful. He was given, alas, to day-dreaming and seeing things that were not there. The red-coated soldier, for instance, who stood behind his bedroom door, limping on a wooden leg and tapping the wall with a pencil. And the two dogs, known as One and Two, clearly visible to Edward, but not to anyone else. Whenever Mr. Linnet thought of his worries, Edward was first among them. With all that wealth of imagination, it looked as though, when he grew older, he might turn into a poet. Mr. Linnet hoped not. It was a fate that he himself had narrowly escaped.

As for Trehunsey—"Fifty-six, fifty-seven!"—he never listened to anything. But then he was only nine months old. It was a pity, Mr. Linnet reflected, as he bounded over a crate of coffee, that any child—much less his own—should be saddled with such a name. But that was because of his uncle. Or was it, perhaps, his wife's uncle? They had forgotten long ago whose uncle Uncle Trehunsey was. But since he lived with the Linnet family, or rather—Mr. Linnet corrected himself—since the Linnets lived with Uncle Trehunsey, it had seemed to them the proper thing to give his name to the baby. Or, to put it more accurately, Uncle Trehunsey, since he ruled the roost, had himself insisted upon it. And whenever Uncle Trehunsey insisted—Mr. Linnet permitted himself a sigh—there was nothing to do but obey.

Mr. Trehunsey Truro, a retired corn-chandler, with a large ugly house in Putney and severe gout in his left big toe, was another of his nephew's worries. But today, Mr. Linnet was quite determined, was not a day for troubles. Here he was, doing the work he loved, counting the riches of the East, with the London morning glowing about him— not exactly sunny, perhaps, but full of soft secret light, like the inside of a pearl. And his breakfast of kidneys and streaky bacon, cooked for him by his wife, Rose, was quietly working in his stomach to produce in Mr. Linnet's mind a feeling of contentment.

And anyway, he told himself, the day would come—at least he hoped so—when he would have a house of his own; a modest, unassuming house that would recognize him as its lord and master as soon as he put his key in the lock. The furniture would be plump and inviting, as different as it could possibly be from Uncle Trehunsey's sofas—which were made of horsehair and blocks of wood and seemed, no matter how tired you were, to dare you to sit upon them.

"Sixty-eight, sixty-nine!" Mr. Linnet sniffed the air. Could it be cinnamon? How delicious! Two crates from Java, a land of spices, where a temple stood at every corner and cows wore garlands of marigolds.

He ticked the cinnamon off his list and continued his cogitations. When his ship came in, he told himself—or rather, when many ships came in and he had checked them carefully and earned a substantial rise—he would have not only his own house but also someone to keep it tidy and help to amuse the children. His wife would be able to take a rest

47

and sit all day in a rocking chair, waving a palm-leaf fan. As things were, she was forever protesting that she only had one pair of hands. It was no use trying to convince her that a single pair was the usual number. She simply refused to believe it. But, if she had had, say, four hands—and this, of course, was only supposing—would his breakfast, Mr. Linnet wondered, have tasted any better?

Impossible, he told himself, with a deep, contented sigh. Besides—"Eighty-one, eighty-two!"—four hands would make an added expense. Think of the extra pairs of gloves! Think of the extra sleeves!

"I couldn't afford it!" said Mr. Linnet. "Dear me," he added, "I beg your pardon!" For, stumbling backwards over a bale, he had fallen against a tall figure—a figure that seemed, from the feel of it, to be wearing a thick fur coat.

Raising his hat, he turned about and found himself staring, eye to eye, with a large brown grizzly bear. Oh dear! Mr. Linnet, losing the use of his legs, sat down on a crate of bananas.

"I must send for the police," he muttered, as he huddled into his jacket. "I'm only supposed to check the cargo. It's not safe, dealing with wild beasts. I must think of my wife and children."

"Nay, he'll not harm ye!" said a voice. "He wouldna discomfort a beetle."

Mr. Linnet, somewhat assured by this, peeped over the edge of his collar. Before him stood a curious figure, a tall, thin, scraggy man with long grey hair that waved in the breeze. He seemed to be a Scotsman, for under his green, voluminous ulster he wore a tartan kilt. He was looking down at Mr. Linnet with a sort of double glance, one eye brown and shrewd and small and the other large and blue—

a bright, innocent, shiny eye that sparkled like a coloured glass. A small cat-basket swung from his wrist, and his hand clasped the paw of the bear.

"Hold on to him!" Mr. Linnet implored.

"Nay, he's a puir, low-spirited creature, more frightened, Ah don't doot, than yersel'. Ah abstracted him from the *Eastern Clipper*. And this wee fellow"—he waved the basket—"is a sickly bit of a leopard cub Ah had from the *Indian Queen*. But let me make so bold, dear sir, as to introduce maself."

The stranger dropped the bear's paw and rummaged in his pocket. He drew out a dirty, crumpled card and thrust it at Mr. Linnet.

Shocked at seeing the bear set free, Mr. Linnet shrank back into his jacket and limply took the card.

The One and Only
Professor McWhirter!
Animal Fancier and Collector.
Zoos, Circuses, and Pet Shops Catered For.
Suitable Situations Found
For Birds, Beasts, Fish, and Reptiles.
Highly Recommended.

As Mr. Linnet read the words, a change came over his face. He was, by nature, a prudent man. If a dog was sleeping, he let it lie. But this card—it was too much! His fear gave way to indignation, and his breakfast began to seethe inside him. Animal fancier indeed!

"So—" he said, witheringly. "You wait on the wharf till the ships come in and then—"

"Right the first go!" said Professor McWhirter. "Ye've hit the nail on the nob!" His brown eye offered Mr. Linnet a

49

confidential wink. "Ah approach the—um—crew as they come ashore—cautiously, ye understand. And if they've smuggled in a beastie or two—Ah try to—hum—negotiate."

"On behalf of zoos and circuses, and yourself, of course, into the bargain!" Mr. Linnet glowed with righteous wrath.

"Mebbe, mebbe." The Professor smiled, this time favouring Mr. Linnet with an artless glance of blue. "One good turrn desairves another. Men and beasts have to live, ye ken."

"But not in cages!" said Mr. Linnet, congratulating himself on the fact that no sailor from the *London Exporter,* or any ship checked by him, had ever smuggled into London so much as a mosquito.

"Well, you'll find no beasties aboard my ship to be sold away to pet shops!" He flung down the card and stalked away.

The Professor, with a gesture of resignation—as though it were something he was used to doing—picked it up from the wharf.

"Ah, man, ye're foolish! Ye may need it!" He held out the card again.

"Keep it," said Mr. Linnet coldly. *"I'm* not an animal fancier! Nor do I sell wild beasts to the Zoo. Keep it and give it to the circus!"

He turned his back on Professor McWhirter and hurried up the slanting gangway of the sailing ship *London Exporter.*

How could he know, as he held out his checking list to the Captain, that one day—thanks to his lucky stars—he would find himself wishing urgently for that dirty piece of pasteboard . . .

8

The Captain stood at the head of the gangway, counting the men as they came ashore.

"Hurry along there, lads," he was saying. "And be sure you get those beards trimmed before you're back aboard."

"Well, Captain," said Mr. Linnet, politely, as he glanced aloft at the torn sails. "You seem to have come through some heavy weather."

"Weather, Mr. Linnet, is what I'm here for. It's something I can cope with. But when it comes to other things—finding islands that aren't there and losing a gang of brutal pirates—"

"P-pirates?" stammered Mr. Linnet. He had thought that the seas had been cleared of pirates fifty years ago. But if they really still existed, shouldn't a captain be glad to lose them? So much safer for all concerned. And as for islands that weren't there—he stole a nervous glance at the Captain. Could he, perhaps, be overwrought? His mind astray after all those storms? He certainly looked dilapidated, with his cap all stained and a button missing.

Mr. Linnet put on a soothing smile.

"Well, at least the cargo's safe," he said.

"Hang the cargo!" the Captain spluttered. "I'd gladly have lost the whole lot if I could have caught one pirate!"

Hang the cargo! Mr. Linnet was shocked. Surely the purpose of any voyage was to bring the cargo home! And where would he himself be if captains went and lost it?

51

"Just one pirate!" the Captain repeated. "And islands properly marked on a map. That's what I asked for, Mr. Linnet. And what did I get? Disaster! And all—" He glared at the passing sailors. "And all because of a wretched ape!"

"An ape?" Mr. Linnet edged away. The Captain was clearly out of his wits.

"An ape, my dear sir! Two legs and a tail and a couple of arms—there's a cargo for you!" He thumped the cargo list with his fist. "You mark my words, Mr. Alfred Linnet—" But the words to be marked were never spoken. The Captain broke off in mid-sentence as a cautious shuffle sounded behind him.

Two seamen were edging past, trying not to be seen—one with a large bulge in his jacket, the other carrying over his shoulder something that looked like a strip of fur. They glanced away guiltily as they caught the Captain's eye.

"Why, it's Barley Hawkes!" said Mr. Linnet, who knew all the names of the crew. "But why has he suddenly grown so fat? And whatever can Young Napper be doing with that curious fur necklet?"

"Well you may ask!" said the Captain, grimly. "Speak up, Hawkes! Answer Mr. Linnet! What have you got to say?"

Barley Hawkes shifted his feet and hitched up his protruding jacket. "Well, nothing, sir—in a manner of speaking—" He was manifestly uneasy.

"Then *I've* got something to say, Hawkes!" The Captain spoke through clenched teeth. "If you want to sail with me again—"

"Oh, I do, sir, truly—" said Barley Hawkes. One captain, he thought, was as good as another, and he had his eye on *The Thread of Gold,* a sailors' pub on the Dover Road, that he hoped, one day, to buy.

"Then you'll have to get rid of that," said the Captain, pointing a finger at the bulge.

"Of course, of course," put in Mr. Linnet, anxious to ease the situation. "A week or two of careful diet. No potatoes, butter, beer, or bread."

"Diet!" The Captain laughed a hollow laugh. "No diet from here to Kingdom Come will cure Mr. Hawkes of that!" He gave the bulge an angry thump, and the bulge slipped out of the blue jacket and landed on the deck.

It was furry, with arms and legs and tail, and on its head was a sailor cap with the letters *London Ex—*

"A monkey!" Mr. Linnet blinked.

"A monster, you mean! A fiend! A devil! A wild beast that sets pirates free and does away with islands. Get him off my ship, Hawkes, or I'll do it myself, I warn you!"

"May I be of sairvice?" said a voice, as a hand came round Mr. Linnet's neck and presented a card to the Captain.

"What's all this—the One and Only? Zoos and circuses catered for! Why, Hawkes, here's the very thing! You can give him away at once."

Young Napper broke into lamentation. "Oh, not the circus, Captain, sir. You wouldn't do that to a friend!"

"He's no friend of mine," said the Captain, grimly.

"And not the Zoo either," said Barley Hawkes, as he took the card from the Captain. "I couldn't let him be catered for, sir. Nor put behind bars in a pet shop."

"Well, it's one or the other—take your choice!"

"Captain, 'ave mercy! 'E didn't mean it!"

"I'll find him a home myself, I promise!"

"Home be damned! Get him off my ship!" The Captain was shouting at Barley Hawkes. Barley Hawkes was shouting at the Captain. Young Napper was sobbing into his collar. Mr. Linnet was murmuring soothing words.

And there, amid the din, stood Monkey, cheerfully glancing from one to another, admiring what he took to be a kind of jungle party.

"I could offer a leetle remuneration!" Professor Mc-Whirter, bear in hand, edged nearer to the group.

"You can have him for nothing!" the Captain bellowed.

"No, no!" Mr. Linnet put up his hand. The words were out before he knew it.

"Now, Linnet, don't you interfere. The beast has got to go!"

Before him the Captain was shaking his fist. Behind him, the Professor's breath was hot upon his neck. And Monkey, happy to find a new acquaintance, was presenting his paw, palm-downward.

Mr. Linnet was seized by a reckless impulse. He bent and took the paw.

"Then he'll go with me," he said calmly. And, amazed at the strength of his own daring, he scooped up Monkey from the deck and wrapped his arms about him.

"Linnet, you're crazy!" the Captain cried. "He'll bring you nothing but trouble."

"You won't regret it, Mr. Linnet! You'll find him neat and clean and helpful." Barley Hawkes's voice was gruff with emotion.

" 'E's a pal, that's what 'e is," said Napper, trying to wring Mr. Linnet's hand.

Professor McWhirter stared at Monkey, taking him in from top to toe. As he peered under the sailor cap and noted the markings round the neck, his blue eye blazed with light.

54

But the brown, as he turned to Mr. Linnet, was shrewd and calculating.

"He's no' a bad wee beast," he said. "Name yer price and Ah'll whisk him away. But remember, sir, Ah'm a puir man. Ah'll ask ye to be reasonable."

Mr. Linnet, who by nature was the most reasonable of men, regarded Professor McWhirter sternly.

"I will not be reasonable," he said. And giving Monkey an upward heave, he safely skirted the grizzly bear and hurried down the gangway.

"Bide a wee!" cried Professor McWhirter, dashing along the wharf in pursuit, dragging the bear in his wake.

But Mr. Linnet was well ahead. He seemed, to his own astonishment, to be flying rather than running. With his arms closely locked round Monkey and Monkey's tail encircling him, they sped along like a single person; through the gates, around a corner, up an alley, and into the street where Mr. Linnet, to his relief, espied a waiting bus.

"All aboard!" the driver cried, mounting behind his horses.

"Just in time," panted Mr. Linnet, as he scurried up the curving staircase and plumped down on to a seat. He glanced about him cautiously, fearful of seeing Professor McWhirter appearing round a street corner. But just then the driver cracked his whip, the horses broke into a lively lollop, and the bus was on its way.

Mr. Linnet mopped his brow and proceeded to peel off his burden. He lifted a foot from his jacket pocket, unwound the tail from about his waist, and edged the weight off his knees on to the seat beside him.

And then—since he now had time to deliberate—he took

a look at Monkey. Up and down, down and up, from the curling toes to the sailor's cap, he savoured his new acquaintance. And the realisation of what he had done came home to Mr. Linnet.

Good heavens, could it really be true? Of course not! It was impossible. And yet, between one breath and another, he had changed from a timid checking-clerk to a man who could kidnap a wild beast. For a moment he thought—indeed, he hoped—that perhaps it was all a dream. He closed his eyes and opened them. The picture remained the same. There was not the smallest doubt about it. He was riding on the top of a bus accompanied by a monkey!

Mr. Linnet put his head in his hands. His mind, usually so neat, was a tangled skein of questions. Why hadn't he looked before he leapt? Waited a moment? Thought it out? How could he break the news to his wife that she now had another mouth to feed? Were monkeys, he asked himself, kind to children? And could he be sure, on the other hand, that children were kind to monkeys? And what—he shuddered at the thought—what, when he saw the new arrival, would Uncle Trehunsey say? The questions went whirling round.

But what of Monkey? What was *he* thinking?

Not of the future, certainly, but perhaps of the fortunate present. He was free at last of his canvas trappings and out abroad in the light of day, where everyone—he had no doubt—was anxious to be his friend. He slipped from his seat and explored the bus top, swinging by his tail from the handrail, accepting a biscuit from a short-sighted lady, who mistook him for a little boy, and offering his paw. But the other passengers were convinced that they saw an apparition. A flash of fur would appear beside them, scatter their bundles and walking-sticks, and then be gone again. They

56

stood up, protesting, and waved umbrellas. Such things were against the laws of nature. They would ask for their money back.

"Now, now, what's all this?" The Bus Conductor came up the staircase as Monkey, standing on the rail, was breaking a sprig from a passing lime tree.

"A ghost! We're haunted! Call the police!" Everyone was shouting.

"Dear little lad, he means no harm," said the kind, short-sighted lady.

"Hey, *you!*" said the Bus Conductor, sharply, rapping on Mr. Linnet's hat.

Rudely summoned from his meditations, Mr. Linnet raised his head.

"That beast over there belong to you?" The Conductor waved his hand at Monkey, who was daintily eating a leaf.

"Catch it! Hold it! Take it away!" the angry voices cried.

"Boys will be boys," said the short-sighted lady.

Mr. Linnet took in the scene— the passengers waving their arms and shouting, the untidy scatter of sticks and parcels. It was the kind of situation that any man would shrink from. And if he denied all knowledge of it, who could really blame him?

But Monkey's arm was around his neck. Monkey's paw— as though Mr. Linnet were another monkey—was trying to press between his teeth a little spray of lime flowers.

And from somewhere deep in Mr. Linnet, the hero who had defied the Professor and rejected the warnings of the Captain, rose up again to the surface. He swallowed the flowers at a single gulp and faced the Bus Conductor.

"Yes, he is mine," he said, stoutly, and put his arm round Monkey.

"Then, hop it!" the Bus Conductor said, pointing towards the ground with his thumb. "Wild beasts not allowed on a public transport! Two tickets—fourpence each!"

Mr. Linnet handed the money over. And, wound together as one creature, he and Monkey went down the stairs, and the bus went off without them . . .

9

It was a long way from London Wharf along the river to Putney. The pavements, Mr. Linnet thought, seemed to be made of iron. Had he been a rich man, he could have hailed a hansom cab. As it was, he had to walk—and he was not a walker. The only exercise he took was a stroll with his family on Sundays to watch the river go by.

Tramp, tramp. He was getting tired. And what was even more important, he was wearing out his shoes. Of course, it wasn't *only* the walking. Climbing trees, for Mr. Linnet, was also quite fatiguing. Three times he had had to swarm up a maple and coax his companion down.

"You are not in the jungle now!" he said, firmly, as he tightened his grasp on the paw. But Monkey, accepting this as a mark of affection, darted into a laurel bush and dragged Mr. Linnet with him.

There were also other complications—the lady, throwing bread to the sea-gulls, whom Monkey, in his desire to help, nearly knocked into the river. And the old gentleman reading a paper who, when Monkey tried to turn the pages, was so incensed at the kindly gesture that he threatened to call the police.

Mr. Linnet trudged on. He could hear the lap and slap of the river, the sneezing of starlings in the trees, and the blare of a barrel organ.

As Monkey and Mr. Linnet drew nearer, it was playing "Ta-ra-ra-boom-de-ay" in a rather dejected manner. And beside it stood the organ-grinder, with a black patch over his eye and a notice hanging round his neck that said just one word—BLIND. He was wearily turning the organ handle and holding out a cup.

Mr. Linnet was filled with pity. He himself had troubles enough, and today—he gave Monkey a rueful glance— today he had even added to them.

But here, in this poor organ-grinder, was someone far worse off. Not to be able to see the sun! Not to be hurrying home as he was—or as he fervently hoped he was—to a welcoming wife and family! What an unfortunate situation!

In no time Mr. Linnet had invented for the organ-grinder a life so full of emptiness that his own eyes brimmed with tears. He hesitated. He knew that he needed every penny. Even so, he had to do it. He thrust his hand into his pocket and tinkled a sixpence into the cup.

"Ah, Godda blessa you, sir, signore!" The organ-grinder stopped playing and felt in the cup for the coin.

An Italian! A stranger in a strange land! Worse and worse, thought Mr. Linnet, and added a penny to the sixpence.

"May angels rewarda you and da monka!" The organ-grinder was clearly grateful.

"But you can't see!" Mr. Linnet exclaimed. "How do you know I've got a monkey?"

"Ah, we blind men, we got sixta sense. I say to myself, 'He

gotta da monka.' I smella heem. I heara heem. And I tink of
my owna littla monka and how I have heem no more—"

"Oh dear, oh dear! What happened?"

"Dead. Dead. Quita dead!" The organ-grinder sobbed.
"So nice, so clever a littla monka, so happy in da good home
I give heem—and now I am alla allonea." He dabbed his
eyes with his woollen scarf.

"How very distressing!" said Mr. Linnet, who was almost
sobbing himself. He wrung the organ-grinder's hand and
hurriedly turned away. If he listened to another word, he
might—and he knew he couldn't afford it—be tempted
to further philanthropy.

He drew his friend close to his side, grateful that *his* monkey, at least, was healthy and alive.

So they walked along companionably, Mr. Linnet's arm
round Monkey's shoulders, Monkey's round Mr. Linnet's
waist. Twilight was falling all about them. They had come
to the end of a long day—a day full of incident and adventure, and Mr. Linnet, unused to excitement and also to
being without his lunch, was feeling its effect. It wasn't
only that he was tired. He was also apprehensive. As he
turned the corner into his street, his courage was ebbing
fast. And the sight of Uncle Trehunsey's house sent a
shudder down his spine.

"What a beautiful sunset, Mr. Linnet!" said a voice
from a nearby garden.

It was Miss Brown-Potter, who lived next door, taking the
air in the early evening with Stanley Livingstone Fan.

Miss Brown-Potter was a female explorer, who now lived
in retirement. Once, on a trip to Africa, she had rescued a
baby from a crocodile on the banks of the River Tooma. He
belonged, she had learned, to the Fan tribe, and since his

family seemed not to want him—perhaps because the child was deaf—she had brought him back to England with her and named him after two famous explorers. For twelve years they had lived together, in harmony and mutual affection, next door to Uncle Trehunsey.

"I see you have found a new friend!"

Oh, blessed, blessed Miss Brown-Potter, standing there in her black bonnet, decked with its flowers and bunch of grapes; her velvet cape studded with jet, and her black elastic-sided boots! She was plain, with rather prominent teeth. No one would have picked her out of a crowd except for her luminous eyes. But to Mr. Linnet, at that moment, she was lovelier than a goddess.

What had she said? Not, "Take him away, he's a wild beast!" Not, "Foolish man, how extravagant!" But simply, "You have found a friend."

His spirits bubbled up within him. He could have kissed Miss Brown-Potter's hand had it not been otherwise employed. She had stooped and offered it to Monkey, and Monkey, ever sociable, had given her his paw, palm-downward.

"We are glad," she said, ceremoniously, "to welcome you to Putney." She might have been addressing the Mayor or perhaps a Member of Parliament. "I am sure Stanley agrees with me."

Stanley said nothing, for being deaf, he was also dumb. But he smiled and spread his arms wide. And Monkey, with one leap, was in them. The black and the brown hugged each other as though they were long-lost brothers.

Miss Brown-Potter regarded the pair with bright, benevolent eyes. Then she gently loosened their embrace.

"You must take him in now, Mr. Linnet. The family will want to see him."

"Will they, I wonder?" thought Mr. Linnet. But Miss Brown-Potter had given him courage. And courage was what he needed.

He took his friend firmly by the paw and walked up the garden path.

At the front door he hesitated. But only for a moment. Then he straightened his shoulders—and also his hat—thrust his key into the lock, and ushered Monkey in . . .

10

"But, Uncle Trehunsey, he won't hurt you! He's as gentle as a mouse, I promise. Please put down that chair!"

Mr. Linnet stood in the midst of his dear ones, holding Monkey to his side and trying to make his voice heard.

"Get rid of him! Call the police! I won't have a wild beast in my house!"

"Would never have thought it of you, Alfred—not to re-member me and the children! What will my poor dear mother say, not to mention my cousin Clara—" Mrs. Linnet, always vague, and very seldom less than flustered, was now, it appeared, distraught.

"Why is he wearing a sailor cap? I want a sailor cap, too!" Victoria was shouting.

Edward was silent, finger in mouth, anxiously watching the scene.

And Little Trehunsey, in his cradle, bellowed with rage and frustration.

Mr. Linnet sighed. The welcome was even worse than he had expected. All of them had turned against him. He began to think it would have been better if he had not been born.

"Bring me the bread knife!" roared Uncle Trehunsey, thrusting the wooden chair before him as though fending off a lion.

And Monkey, assuming that he was taking part in some rowdy family entertainment—such as often happened in the jungle—sprang upon a leg of the chair and offered a paw to his new acquaintance.

Uncle Trehunsey, with a howl of terror, flung himself, bandaged foot and all, behind the horsehair sofa.

"Don't you touch me, you hairy ape!"

And the hairy ape, taking this as part of the game, sat himself down on the arm of the sofa, patted Uncle Trehunsey's head, and from there took off for the cradle.

"He'll kill him!" Uncle Trehunsey roared. "He'll kill my only namesake!"

"My baby, my baby!" shrieked Mrs. Linnet, dashing towards the cradle.

A sudden silence fell on the room. Even the clock stopped ticking. Had Little Trehunsey fainted away? Not at all. Far from it. In a rare moment of winsomeness, he had seized on Monkey's proffered paw and put it in his mouth.

"You see, my dear!" said Mr. Linnet, as Monkey stretched the unoccupied paw, palm-downward, to Mrs. Linnet.

She put out her hand reluctantly.

"Well, maybe all right—one never knows—only hope his paws are clean—the baby seems to like him." Privately, she had to admit that anything that Little Trehunsey did not actively dislike could be reckoned as a blessing.

"But, of course, another mouth to feed—prices always going up—wages always staying the same—I suppose you've thought of that, Alfred—"

"Oh, that's no problem." Mr. Linnet was airy. "Just nuts and fruit and a leaf or two—I'm sure we can manage, Rose—"

"Well, he can't eat my geranium plant!" Victoria, who, not for nothing, was her great-uncle's great-niece, thrust aside Monkey's proffered paw, plucked the sailor cap from his head, and put it on her own.

"Bother! It's too small for me. Mamma, Mamma, let him stay. Then you can make me a cap like his." She tossed the cap back to Monkey who received it from her gratefully as though she had given him a present.

Edward, with a plopping sound, pulled the finger from his mouth.

"I like him, Papa!" he said, with conviction. "And so do One and Two!"

He took the paw that Monkey offered and held it out sideways and down, as if giving something, or someone, a chance to take a sniff.

"One and Two!" Victoria scoffed. "Those dogs aren't real, are they, Mamma?"

"Of course not—just imagination—" As she spoke, Mrs. Linnet lost her footing, and her skirts went swirling round her ankles.

"You were caught in their leads," said Edward calmly, making passes in the air as though to unwind two obstreperous dogs.

"Do I understand you intend to *keep* him?" The outraged face of Uncle Trehunsey rose up from behind the sofa.

"Well, he's neat and clean and very helpful." Mr. Linnet

quoted Barley Hawkes, devoutly hoping, as he did so, that what he said was true.

"Then, you'll have to master him, do you hear? Or else you'll be out on the pavement. I won't provide for you *and* an ape. Master him! That's what animals need!"

"Yes, of course," said Mr. Linnet, meekly. After all, he was only a poor relation, a guest in Uncle Trehunsey's house. And what could a poor relation do except say, meekly, "Yes."

But could he—even if he wished to—could he master Monkey? And would Monkey, on the other hand, allow himself to be mastered?

"And the extra work—" Mrs. Linnet was saying. "May be last straw on the emu's back—always have to remember, Alfred, I have only one pair of hands—"

"I know it, my dear," said Mr. Linnet, shaking his head for the hundredth time at this unhappy affliction. "But that is where he will come in useful. He'll be able to give you a helping paw." He smiled at her appealingly, hoping that she would share the joke.

But Mrs. Linnet was too upset.

"Well, with me working day in, day out, I only hope he does—that's all—"

And Monkey did—as we shall see . . .

11

Nothing was too much for him. There was never such a willing worker. Whatever anybody did, Monkey was there to help him do it.

When Mrs. Linnet washed the dishes, Monkey stood at her side and dried them, cheerfully breaking a cup or a plate as though they were nothing but jungle twigs. Mr. Linnet spent a lot of time glueing the pieces together.

When Uncle Trehunsey's toe was dressed, Monkey helped with the bandages, winding them round himself and the chair—even, at times, the table leg. And Mr. Linnet, apologising, would undo Monkey's careful work and bind the foot again.

When Mrs. Linnet swept the floors, Monkey would rush to her assistance, wielding the broom so vigourously that the carpets were almost worn away.

And when anyone started to light the fire, Monkey was always at hand to help, throwing on anything made of paper —bags full of biscuits, packets of tea, even *The Times* and *The Evening Mail* before anyone had read them.

"Really, Alfred—" said Mrs. Linnet, as she tripped, one day, on a hole in the carpet.

She was by nature a kindly woman and as pink and pretty as her name. She could not be persuaded, however, that the many troubles of the world had not been designed, by an adverse fate, expressly for Mrs. Linnet.

"Really, Alfred—" She picked herself up.

Mr. Linnet thought he knew what was coming and hurried to forestall it.

"We must always remember," he said quickly, "that he's very good with the children."

It was true. The change in Little Trehunsey was remarkable. Whenever Monkey was anywhere near, he not only ceased his bellowing but even condescended to smile.

If Victoria happened to have an earache, Monkey would curl his tail round her head, as a sort of muff to keep her warm. He tidied the dolls' house with delicate fingers and cared for the dolls as tenderly as any domesticated father cares for his newborn child.

As for Edward—he and Monkey would sit together, silent and companionable, while Edward nibbled a sugar clock—the pink-and-white sticky kind that could then be bought for a farthing. Edward had a collection of these, all of them saying Ten Past Five and all nibbled round the edges.

"If I ate the whole clock," he told his parents, "I would never know the time."

They shook their heads at each other and sighed.

But Monkey seemed to understand. When Edward held a clock to his lips, he, too, nibbled carefully round the edge. And when Edward walked among his tombstones—a set of white cardboard shapes planted in the grass of the lawn—Monkey would tiptoe after him, never disturbing a single grave. Joe Tip, R.I.P.; Bessie Tip, Much Regretted; Mrs. Tip, Lost For Ever, were safe in their resting places.

But there were more people in the world than the Linnet family and Uncle Trehunsey, as Monkey soon discovered—all of them unaware, as yet, that a friend was at hand to help them.

He began to wander further afield. Over the next-door

fence, for instance, where Miss Brown-Potter and Stanley Fan would always give him a welcome.

But his visits to other neighbouring houses, while full of interest for Monkey, were not so happy in their outcome.

There was the lady along the street who, not having heard of the new arrival, was shocked to find she was seeing things —things that clearly could not be there—and urgently sent for her doctor.

"What kind of things?" he wanted to know.

"Monkeys," she said, "in sailor caps, peering in through the windows."

And the doctor, knowing that there were no monkeys nearer than the Zoo, and none at all wearing sailor caps, decided she was astray in her wits and sent her into a hospital so that he could keep his eye upon her. This was a blow to her family. She had been a loving wife and mother and also an excellent cook.

Then there was the Lamplighter. He complained to the authorities that each night, when he lit the streetlamps, a shadowy something ran beside him, taking the pole out of his hands and touching it to the gas mantle. No, he admitted, it didn't harm him. But it made him feel creepy. He couldn't stand it.

So the Lamplighter, whose name was Smithers, was sent to work in another street, while a man called Cooper took his place. And the same thing happened to Cooper. Luckily, he didn't mind. It saved him work, he told the Inspector, and he liked the companionship.

It was just the opposite with the Milkman. He did not care for companionship. Nor did he approve of wild beasts, particularly when they tried to help him by pouring the milk on to the pavement instead of into a jug. He was sorry, he said, but there it was. He wasn't going to deliver milk—never no more—to Mr. Truro.

This created a difficulty. For it now appeared that Mrs. Linnet, as well as only one pair of hands, had also a single pair of feet. She could not, under the circumstances, be expected to fetch the milk.

So the burden fell on Mr. Linnet. Each morning when he went to work, he took with him an empty jug. And each night it came back full, with Mr. Linnet behind it.

One evening, as he and the milk were coming home, a dog in one of the gardens barked—an angry You-Keep-Out bark that made Mr. Linnet look up.

Across the street was a shadowy figure. It was tiptoeing along the pavement, stopping every now and again to peer over a gate. Was it, perhaps, a burglar? Mr. Linnet shivered. He stood there, holding his jug and his breath, watching the flitting figure. Where had he seen that shape before—the flowing cloak, the long legs, the swinging skirt—no, the kilt! Of course! Professor McWhirter!

Mr. Linnet's back stiffened. The milk jug trembled and spilt a drop. Professor McWhirter in *his* street, stealthily prowling among the gardens, looking for beasties to put in a pet shop! His thought at once flew to Monkey. And Monkey in his imagination became a maiden in distress and he a knight on a noble charger hurrying to the rescue.

Hark! What was that? A battle cry? Another knight rattling his sabre?

No. The sabre was Uncle Trehunsey's stick being banged upon the floor. And the battle cry was nothing less than Uncle Trehunsey's voice.

The good steed neighed and disappeared. The knight's helmet transformed itself into a bowler hat. And Alfred

Linnet was again himself, scurrying round to the back of the house in order to creep in unnoticed.

What had Monkey done now? He silently asked himself the question and thought of possible answers.

"I'll report you!" Uncle Trehunsey was shouting. "I'll have you dismissed from the service!"

Mr. Linnet peeped round the kitchen door.

A small, thin man in uniform, looking as though he were out in a storm, was standing on the hearthrug.

Behind him Mrs. Linnet hovered, looking pink and anxious.

Monkey was peacefully rocking the cradle.

"Er—what is the Postman doing here? Has he brought a telegram? I hope it is not bad news." Mr. Linnet put the jug on the table and prepared himself for the worst.

"He has NOT brought a telegram, my good Alfred. He has not brought anything at ALL and he owes me TWENTY POUNDS!"

"Oh, no, really, Mr. Truro! I don't owe no one a penny piece." The Postman wrung his hands.

"Then where is it? Where's my pension? It always comes on the third of the month."

"I know, sir. Regular as daylight. In a yellow antelope. Very neat."

"Then why isn't it here TODAY?" Uncle Trehunsey's face was purple.

"But it *did* come, I tell you! First thing this morning. I delivered it myself."

"Then WHERE is it NOW? Answer me that!"

"How do I know?" the Postman cried. "All I can say is it come as always. And I gave it to the little feller."

"Edward?" asked Mr. Linnet, quickly.

70

"Not Edward. The one in the fur coat. Him over there."
The Postman pointed, and edged towards the door.

Oh, no! Mr. Linnet groaned within him. What had Monkey done with the letter? He glanced round wildly for a clue. His eyes met Monkey's, bright as stars—or was it reflected firelight? And suddenly, with a pang, he knew.

The evening fire popped and sparkled, the flames stretching up to the logs, away from the mass of kindling paper. With a cry, Mr. Linnet ran to the hearth.

"Oh no, Alfred—you'll burn your fingers—not a scrap of butter in the house —not even bicarbonate of soda—" Mrs. Linnet protested.

But Mr. Linnet thrust in his hand, brought out a yellow envelope and the charred remains of banknotes.

A terrible silence fell on the room. It was broken only by the rock of the cradle and Uncle Trehunsey's panting breath as he struggled for suitable words.

"My PENSION!" he blurted out at last, shaking his stick at the fire.

"I know, I know, Uncle Trehunsey. But I'll make it up to you, I promise. I'll put in extra time at work. I'll sell my overcoat—and hat. It won't really take me very long—"

The words tumbled out of Mr. Linnet, anxious, beseeching, reassuring. The Postman hurriedly slipped away.

"That ape! That savage brute! That monster! He lit the fire with MY pension!"

"He was really only trying to help. It's just that he doesn't understand. It's not his fault," Mr. Linnet pleaded. "Now, what's the matter, Victoria? There isn't any need to shout!" Shouting, Mr. Linnet thought, should be left to Uncle Trehunsey.

"There is, there is!" Victoria shouted, as she noisily clattered down the stairs, waving a doll in the air. "He's been giving a bath to Arabella—I saw him with Trehunsey's sponge—and he's washed her face right off!" She flung the faceless doll on the floor and stamped her foot at Monkey.

And Monkey—delighted, as usual, at any rumpus—showed his happy appreciation by swinging the cradle harder.

"There, there!" Mr. Linnet was soothing. "I'll paint Arabella another face—prettier than the first—you'll see! Now, Edward, what are you crying for?"

If only, Mr. Linnet thought, troubles would greet you one by one instead of in battalions!

Edward, weeping bitterly, was slowly coming down the stairs, dragging the two dogs at his heels and holding in his free hand the remains of a sugar clock. Someone had taken out of it a large semi-circular bite.

"He's eaten Ten Past Five, Papa! And now I'll never know the time." He turned a tragic face to Monkey. And Monkey swung the cradle harder.

"He stole my pension, the hairy ape!"

"He washed off Arabella's face!"

"He ate the time out of the clock!"

"Oh dear, oh dear—never expected to live with a monkey —not as though we were in a jungle—why not a cat or a dog, Alfred—or a white mouse in a cage—"

Voices were shouting. Feet were stamping. The party, or so it seemed to Monkey, grew merrier every moment.

He danced, he capered on his toes, sharing the general frenzy. And out of this plenitude of joy he swung the cradle so forcefully that Little Trehunsey flew out of it and landed on the sofa.

Mrs. Linnet let out a cry of anguish and flung herself on her child.

Mr. Linnet and the children stared in silence. So did Uncle Trehunsey.

But Little Trehunsey did not like being smothered, even by his mother. He seemed to have enjoyed his flight, for he now was kicking with all his might and holding out his arms to Monkey.

And Monkey, happy to be needed, leapt across the room towards him, knocking over on the way a large blue china vase.

Crash!

"My great-aunt Hester's jardiniere! Alfred, can really stand no more—it's not as if I were a camel—"

Mrs. Linnet stood among the shards, holding her protesting child and pointing a shaking hand at Monkey.

Mr. Linnet turned away. "I know," he said. "You needn't tell me."

After all, he reasoned to himself, he had to think of his family. A sugar clock he could replace; he could paint a face on a faceless doll; he could even repay the Twenty Pounds. But he couldn't replace Trehunsey. After this, he could never be sure—if Monkey continued to rock the cradle— that the child, when rocked out of it, would land on a suitable object. Next time it might be the mantelpiece. Or Uncle Trehunsey's foot!

Of course Monkey would have to go! As a father, and also as a husband, he was utterly determined. Monkey would have to go! And yet— Those two words ached in Mr. Linnet.

"I told you to master him, didn't I? And now look what

he's done! Twenty Pounds gone up in smoke and my name-sake practically brought to his death. That's what comes of not mastering!"

Uncle Trehunsey, still fuming, was shaking his fist alternately at Monkey and Mr. Linnet.

Mr. Linnet sighed. How pleasant it would be, he thought, if Uncle Trehunsey, just for once, would try to master himself.

"Well, he's going away, Uncle Trehunsey. He won't disturb you any more."

"And about time, too! You should never have brought him."

"Papa, Papa, where is he going?" Victoria's eyes were bright with interest.

Mr. Linnet stared at her. He hadn't thought of that. Where, indeed, he asked himself. And the prowling shape of Professor McWhirter slipped stealthily into his mind.

"It would be a way out," something in him whispered. "After all, you've done your best. Nobody could do more. And the world is full of kindly people. The old man may not be so bad."

Kindly people! The *London Exporter*'s captain kindly? The passengers on top of the bus? The Milkman? Uncle Trehunsey?

"No!" said Mr. Linnet, aloud, closing his ears to that cunning whisper, at the same time ruefully regretting that his better feelings once again had got the better of him.

And then, like a flash, the solution came. There *was* a home waiting for Monkey. How could he have forgotten? It was not in a zoo, not in a circus, not in any other place where Professor McWhirter plied his trade.

"I know where he's going," he said firmly, as he buttoned on his coat.

He reached out for his bowler hat, and Monkey gave it to him.

He then reached out a hand for Monkey and found Monkey's paw within it.

Mr. Linnet's heart faltered.

"If only," he silently said to himself, "if only he wasn't so willing!"

And without a word to anyone, he marched away out of the house, hand in paw with the willing creature, to find him another home.

Monkey, as usual, was happy. He was off, it seemed, on a new adventure. And a friend was walking by his side. That was enough for Monkey.

12

The clock ticked on the mantelpiece. The fire died down to its embers.

Little Trehunsey, refusing all his usual comforts, had cried himself to sleep.

Uncle Trehunsey dozed in his corner, snorting and wheezing like a grampus, his foot propped up on a stool.

Mrs. Linnet sat on the edge of a chair, feeling at odds with herself. It was not because the chair was hard, though that was undeniably true. She was haunted by her husband's face and the look it had worn as he marched away. She had seen it troubled—all men have troubles—but never so unhappy.

"But what else could I have done?" she argued. "Three young children and Uncle Trehunsey—cooking, washing, mending, shopping—everything falling on my shoulders—and me with only one pair of hands—can't be expected to do more, can I—?" But whoever she was arguing with said nothing in the way of comfort.

Victoria was sprawled on the floor, clapping her heels together.

Edward, hunched up on the sofa, alternately patted and stroked his knees, trying to comfort, apparently, a pair of unhappy dogs.

Tick-tock, said the clock on the mantelpiece, taking no notice of any of them.

A key turned in the front door lock, and Mr. Linnet came in. He put his hat on its proper hook. He took off his coat and hung it up.

His family watched him in silence.

He sat down on a horsehair chair—which creaked at him ungraciously—leant his head upon his hand, and stared into the fire.

"Alfred—?" Mrs. Linnet began. The question hung in the air.

"Yes," said Mr. Linnet. "Yes. I have given him away."

"Who to?" Victoria demanded.

"Whom, Victoria, not who. I gave him to an organ-grinder, whose own monkey had died."

"What did the organ-grinder look like? What tunes does his organ play?"

Mr. Linnet heaved a sigh. Why did his daughter always insist on asking irrelevant questions?

76

"He's an Italian. And he's blind. I don't know what the organ plays."

"I hope—" Edward patted the dogs. "I hope he'll have a good home, Papa."

Mr. Linnet gave him a grateful look. "That is what I hope, too, Edward. The organ-grinder seemed glad to have him."

He turned his head away again. And a lump rose up from his heart to his throat. It burst out in a rush of words.

"I am ashamed!" said Mr. Linnet. "We have given away a friend!"

Yes, they had given a friend away. Each one of them knew it.

They were all silent, thinking of Monkey—Monkey with his helpful paw, ever ready and willing; Monkey whose only weakness was that he couldn't help helping too much.

A loud rap-tapping broke the silence.

"I'll go!"

Mrs. Linnet ran to the door and came back, looking shy and flustered, with Professor McWhirter behind her.

He was carrying a cage of canaries. And the heads of rabbits and guinea pigs peeped out from his various pockets.

Mr. Linnet sprang to his feet.

"Nay, dinna let me distairb ye, man. Ah just looked in on ma way by. The Captain gave me yer address. It's just a friendly visit, ye ken, to see how the beastie is keeping."

The Professor's eyes raked the room, the brown and the blue both searching.

Edward slipped quickly under the sofa, dragging his arm behind him. The strange man in the cloak and kilt was not going to get the two dogs, not if Edward could help it.

"Well, you won't find any beastie here. He's gone," said

Mr. Linnet. He glared at the furry well-filled pockets and the feathered crowd in the birdcage.

Professor McWhirter seemed surprised—surprised and not too pleased.

"Ah'm sorry, indeed, to hear that. If ye'd just slipped me a wee worrd, Ah'd have found him a home masel'."

"Thank you, but he already has one—better than any you could give him!" A home in a pet shop! A home in a zoo! Fine homes, thought Mr. Linnet.

"Oh, Ah wouldna be sayin' that, at all." The Professor's brown eye glinted. "Ah've a large number o' clients, ye ken, and the verra best connections."

Yes, thought Mr. Linnet, grimly—the best connections in circuses!

"Weel, Ah mustna keep ye, Mr. Linnet. Ah'm glad to have had a glimpse of ye. Yersel' "—he glanced at Mrs. Linnet—"yersel' an' yer bonnie lassie. Oh, bye the bye"—he was casual, as he sauntered toward the door—"would ye have his address, perhaps, aboot ye? The wee beastie's, I mean."

"I would not," said Mr. Linnet, sternly, flinging the door wide open.

"H'm—a pity, that. A grreat pity! Weel, Ah'll bid ye good night, the lot o' ye!" And, folding his cloak round his pocketed creatures, the Professor took his leave.

"A pity, indeed! Bonnie lassie, indeed!" Mr. Linnet was fuming.

But Mrs. Linnet prinked and bridled. She liked being called a bonnie lassie, even by strange professors.

"Thought he was rather nice, Alfred—curious to look at, of course—like an old untidy stork—but dear little rabbits and things in his pocket—he's probably very kind and sweet—"

"Sweet! He's an animal fancier! All those birds and animals were going to be sold to pet shops. What do you think he came here for?"

"Well, he *said* he had just looked in—oh, NO!" Mrs. Linnet stared, aghast. Professor McWhirter had come for *Monkey*! He had wanted *Monkey* to put in his pocket! Were there really such villains in the world?

She had no time, however, to ponder this question, for Victoria was shouting.

"Mama, there's a face at the kitchen window!"

A loud wail came from under the sofa. "Without a body? It must be a ghost! One and Two will be frightened!"

"Nonsense, Edward—can't be a ghost—no ghosts around here, are there, Alfred?—all faces have bodies, haven't they, Alfred?" Mrs. Linnet waited for her husband's answers. Edward's fancies were infectious. She almost believed them herself.

But Mr. Linnet had flown to the kitchen. He had recognised the face.

Mrs. Linnet and Victoria followed, but Edward watched from a safe distance, not taking any chances.

"What is it? Where is he? Why isn't he with you?"

The face, which indeed was possessed of a body, took on an unpleasant leer.

"Where is he, guv'nor? You tell *me!* He's come back here or I'll eat me cap." The cap was a checked one, dirty and torn. It did not look worth eating.

"But—" began Mr. Linnet, staring. "How did you manage to find this place? It's such a long way—and you can't see!"

"Carn't see? 'Oo said so? Not me, I never!" The face was now belligerent.

"But the placard hanging round your neck! BLIND, it says. So I thought it was true."

"Ar, that's becos ye're soft, mate. You believe whatever yer see." A crafty smile spread over the face. "And you thought I was Eyetalian, din'yer?"

Mr. Linnet nodded, mutely.

"Well, I ain't. And I'm not blind, neither. It's just to catch the pennies, see? People come by and look at me placard. 'Spare a penny for da blinda man and Godda bless you, sir,' I say. And they thinks, 'Dear me, the pore chap, a strynger in a strynge land!' And then they out with the spondulicks. Tinkle, tinkle, into the cup! Cor, it makes me laugh!"

Mr. Linnet was all a-blush. Such had, indeed, been his own emotions, and now he felt cheated of them. Never mind! Why bother about it? The only thing that mattered was Monkey.

"But what have you done with him? Where is he?"

"You mean—you ain't got him yourself? Not hidden away in a cupboard?"

"Of course I haven't. I gave him to you. And you promised—crossing your heart, remember?—you promised you'd take care of him."

"Well, *he* didn't take no care of *me!*" The organ-grinder was surly. "Of course, I'd have give him a bit o' tucker and a sack on the floor to sleep on—"

A sack on the floor! Mr. Linnet shuddered. Monkey had always slept on the sofa.

"But he never gave me 'arf a chance. Just took the cup and passed it round—there was quite a crowd sayin' 'Ooh!' and 'Ah!'—and as soon as someone put something in, he would snatch it out with that paw of his and give it to somebody else. Sixpence here, a shillin' there, even, once, 'arf a crown. *I* never saw a penny of it!"

Mr. Linnet could picture the scene—Monkey, with his friendly paw, pressing the organ-grinder's money on every passing stranger.

"Oh, I was mad!" said the organ-grinder. "Who did he think he was, then, givin' away my hard-earned cash? And when I kicked him, you should have seen him—"

"You *kicked* him?" Mr. Linnet stiffened.

"Well, you got to master 'em, haven't you? Anyone knows that. But you should of seen the look he gave me! Not fierce, mind you, nothing nasty. But sad and proud, just like a human. Really, I had to laugh!"

"Oh, so you had to laugh, had you?" Mr. Linnet could hardly contain his wrath.

"I did!" said the organ-grinder, laughing. "It's funny, a monkey seemin' human. And then, very quiet and dignified, he puts the cup by me on the pavement and disappears - like that!" He gave a snap of his grimy fingers. " 'Gone up a tree,' I thinks to meself. 'He'll be down, he knows where his bread is buttered.' So I waited, but he never came. And then—well, you'd given me your address, so I thought I'd come and fetch him. Him—" The face under the cap was crafty. "Him or the money he took from me. Take your choice, which. It's up to you!"

"But he isn't here!" cried Mr. Linnet, who was now in a state of panic. Where *was* Monkey? How could he set about finding him? Would he have to search the whole of London?

"Then it's got to be the money, mate! I took him to do you a good turn, but I can't let meself be out of pocket. Stands to reason, don't it?"

81

"How much?" asked Mr. Linnet, quickly. "How much would you say he gave away?"

"Well—" The organ-grinder was calculating. "The crowd was thick, and they seemed to like him. I'd say—and I'm being generous, mind, but I'm like that, never think of meself—I'd say it was all of thirty bob."

Mr. Linnet blenched. Thirty bob, indeed! He knew quite well he was being diddled. But he reached up to the kitchen shelf and took down a china jar.

"But, Alfred—that's the housekeeping money—and the grocer not paid for the last two weeks—" Mrs. Linnet protested.

"I know, but I'll pay it back, my dear. I shall give up smoking a pipe."

"That's the ticket. You're a genelman, guv!" The organ-grinder greedily watched as the money was counted out. "Well, Godda blessa you, sir, signore. I'll letta you know if I finda da monka."

"You will not find him," said Mr. Linnet, as the organ-grinder, guffawing loudly, lurched away into the darkness. "Victoria, will you get my hat?"

"Papa!" called Edward from the sofa.

"My coat, too, please, Victoria!"

"Papa! Do listen to me, Papa!"

"Not now, Edward. Another time. I must go and look for him."

"But I've seen him, Papa! So have One and Two."

"Well, I can't worry over the dogs now, or ghosts at the window or—*what* did you say?" Mr. Linnet broke off and stared at Edward.

"I'm trying to tell you. So are the dogs. Look, Papa! He's come back!" Edward pointed triumphantly.

And there, creeping in through the front window, was a furry, familiar shape. It paused for a moment on the sill. Then it leapt through the room to Mr. Linnet, flung out its paw in an eager gesture, and presented him with a penny.

There wasn't any doubt of it. Monkey had come home . . .

13

"A penny! He's brought me a lucky penny!"

Mr. Linnet, laughing and crying, caught Monkey in his arms. They were both beside themselves with joy.

"Rose, my dear? My darling dear?" He flung a questioning glance at his wife. "I could take the rockers off the cradle. I could mend Aunt Hester's broken vase! Put a new face on Arabella! Buy another sugar clock! I could do anything, if only—" He left the rest of it in the air, anxiously, eagerly, waiting.

And Mrs. Linnet, to his delight, drew a long breath and smiled.

"Vase not really important, Alfred—it was just that everything seemed too much—so many troubles all at once—and me with only a single pair—"

"Yes, dear, I know." His voice was tender.

"And rockers off a great improvement—always making somebody trip—my grandmother never approved of rockers —if we got some paint for Arabella—"

"She doesn't need another face!" Victoria picked up the doll by a leg. "I like her just as she is."

"He can eat the rest of the sugar clock. I don't think I'll mind—at least, not much—" Edward broke off, uncertainly. He had said a very brave thing and he needed to digest it.

Mr. Linnet flung out his arms and tried to embrace them all.

And then—how it happened, nobody knew—they were dancing in a ring. Round and round, all joining hands, Edward careful not to step on the dogs, Mrs. Linnet flustered and gay and looking like a full-blown rose.

And Monkey ran in and out among them, rejoicing in the family joy, quite unaware of the reason for it. In the jungle, nobody needed reasons. They danced for the sake of dancing.

It was a moment such as seldom comes—a moment when everyone was happy. The room seemed to spin like a spinning top and the Linnet family with it. Little Trehunsey's waking protests sounded amid the merriment. But nobody took any notice. All he wanted—they all knew—was simply to make himself heard.

But the waking protests of Uncle Trehunsey were a different kettle of fish.

Wheeze! Snort! Cough! Splutter! He opened his eyes and stared.

What on earth were the Linnets doing—playing Ring-a-Rosy? That in itself was bad enough—disturbing the peace, like barbarians—but what was that brown thing dancing with them? Could it be? Yes, it could—the ape!

A dreadful noise filled the room. It was like an erupting volcano.

"WHAT IS THAT CREATURE DOING HERE? WHY HAS HE COME BACK?"

The words brought the Linnets to a standstill. But to Monkey, used to the ways of the jungle, where monkeys beat

84

their breasts and shouted, this seemed to be just another welcome— louder, perhaps, but no less sincere. He leapt across the room.

"Don't you dare touch me!" cried Uncle Trehunsey, throwing his footstool at Monkey's head. And to show that he knew this was part of the game, Monkey went scrambling up the curtains, hung by his tail from the curtain rod, and waved at Uncle Trehunsey.

S-w-i-s-h!

The curtains came billowing into the room, curled round the oil-lamp on the table, and swept it to the floor.

At once there was a burst of flame. It ran in a trail along the carpet, licked with its fiery tongue at a cushion, and began to swallow the tablecloth.

Mrs. Linnet screamed. Victoria shouted. Edward stood still with his thumb in his mouth. Little Trehunsey railed.

The flames ran greedily through the room. They pounced upon the mantelpiece and gobbled all the letters; raced each other up the walls; plunged into wastepaper baskets.

"Quickly, Rose!" cried Mr. Linnet. "Get yourself and the children out. I will go for the fire brigade. Hurry! It's spreading fast."

"*Am* hurrying, Alfred, as best I can—not a female spider, however, only one pair of—come, children—!"

She frantically scooped up Little Trehunsey and hustled the others in front of her, like a hen with a brood of chickens.

"Be careful, Mamma! Don't step on the dogs!" Edward did not like being hustled. It was dangerous for One and Two.

"He's silly, isn't he, Mamma? He knows there aren't any dogs."

"Now, Edward, now, Victoria—Trehunsey, do be quiet!

—must get into the garden quickly—don't want us all to be burnt to ashes—"

"And what about me?" yelled Uncle Trehunsey. "Fuss, fuss, fuss over women and children! Nobody thinks of me!" He shook his walking-stick at the flames, and the flames caught hold of the end of it and turned it into a torch.

"I'm coming to get you, Uncle Trehunsey!"

Mr. Linnet came rushing back, full of shame and remorse. In his anxiety for the others he had quite forgotten his uncle.

"Take my arm! There we are!"

"Ouch! Look out! Don't touch my foot! Well, Alfred, I hope you're satisfied. This will probably be the death of me. And all because of a beastly ape."

Uncle Trehunsey, groaning and swearing, was carefully eased out of the house and planted on a garden seat.

Mr. Linnet darted away.

The living room was now ablaze. Neighbours were crying, "Fire! Fire!" Strangers were running along the street. A crowd of interested spectators had collected at the gate.

At the edge of it, quietly watching, stood Miss Brown-Potter and Stanley.

Mrs. Linnet, her arms full of her younger son and all his many necessities, came dashing wildly past them.

"Give him to Stanley, Mrs. Linnet. Please let us help you," said Miss Brown-Potter.

"Oh, thank you—such a trouble—thank you—!" Mrs. Linnet thrust the child at Stanley. "One or two things—no flames in the kitchen—thought I would rescue the—very kind, thank you—"

She darted into the smoking house, pulled some drying

86

clothes from a line, gathered up various pots and pans and the jar of housekeeping money.

Back and forth went Mrs. Linnet, rescuing all her valuables and piling them on the lawn. And Monkey, pleased with this new sport, helpfully carried them back.

"Oh, what shall I do?" moaned Mrs. Linnet, as she watched the frying-pan, through the smoke, returning to its shelf.

Stanley gave her his large smile and handed over Trehunsey. He seemed to know just what to do, for he dashed away across the lawn, seized the frying-pan and Monkey, wordlessly gathered the two children and brought them all to a safe place at the side of Miss Brown-Potter.

"Fire! Fire!" voices were shouting.

"Ring-ting!" came the sound of a bell.

Then with a clatter of horses' hooves and the stertorous hissing of the engine, the fire brigade rattled into the street.

"Hooray! Hooray!" The crowd cheered. The horses flung up their heads and snorted. The firelight shone on the firemen's helmets.

What a spectacle! All that scarlet! All that polished, shining brass! The handsome faces under the helmets! Brave men dashing into danger!

The crowd felt proud and rich and important. "Hooray! Hooray!" They cheered again. There was nothing like a fire, they said. A fire was a terrible thing, they said. But splendid, too—they had to admit it.

"Save my furniture! Save my house! I won't be ruined by an ape!"

High above the shouts and cheering came Uncle Trehunsey's voice.

"Apes on the brain!" the spectators said and soothed him with comforting words.

"Don't you fret. It will all come right. You can always trust the fire brigade."

This, indeed, was no more than the truth. The firemen were living up to their legend, hoisting ladders, unwinding hoses, sending up fountains of water.

And among them now was an extra fireman. Mr. Linnet, in a borrowed helmet, was working with the rest.

Hose-pipe in hand, he was everywhere—not so much saving his uncle's house as putting out the Great Fire of London; preserving Rome while Nero fiddled; rescuing highborn Russian ladies from Moscow's smoky ruins.

One extra fireman? No! There were two!

No one had given Monkey a helmet. But neither had he been prevented from seizing one of the hoses.

As usual, he worked with a will, pulling the hose through the wheels of the wagon, looping it round the horses' legs, hosing the firemen so spiritedly that they nearly fell off the ladders.

Hiss, crackle, sizzle! Crackle, sizzle, hiss! The jets of water were doing their work. The flames could not withstand them. The roar of the fire died away. And at last there was not a spark left, only a black vapourous cloud that covered the house like a veil.

"There!" said the crowd, triumphantly, as though by its own personal efforts the fire had been put out.

Mr. Linnet, minus the helmet, rejoined his wife and children. He had several doughty deeds to his credit, and he felt the better for it. The Fire of London had been halted. Rome had been saved from sack and pillage. And all the high-born Russian ladies were asleep in their flouncy beds.

"Well, sir," said Fireman Number One, saluting Uncle Trehunsey. "I think we've got it under at last. There hasn't been such a deal of damage. Mostly curtains and furniture—and there's quite a lot of those left. No, no! I'm wrong. I spoke too soon." The Fireman looked again at the house.

There, in the yellow glare of the streetlamps, one lonely figure could be seen, still steadily hosing. The sofa in the living room was collapsing beneath a jet of water, its insides spilling out of the frame in a froth of wire and horsehair. The chairs were in a similar plight, drunkenly leaning against each other with nothing at all inside them. Never again would anyone—no matter how hardy his constitution—be able to sit upon them.

Suddenly, the hose went flat. Someone had turned off the water.

Monkey stood still and gazed about him, surveying his handiwork.

The Fireman looked at him and chuckled. "That's a great little feller you've got there, sir."

Uncle Trehunsey turned his head. Little feller? What little feller? He knew no little feller.

"Done a lot to help," the Fireman went on. "Though inclined, perhaps, to overdo it. What's it like above, Number Two?"

A fireman came briskly down the ladder. "No beds or chairs left, Number One. Somebody's turned the hose right on 'em. All ruined by water."

"Hm. So he's been up there as well, has he? Well, I'm sorry, Mr. Truro, sir. We've managed to save the house intact. But you'll need to be getting new furniture. There's not a stick of it left!"

Uncle Trehunsey glared at the Fireman.

"Not a stick? All my beautiful horsehair?"

Mr. Linnet exchanged a glance with his wife, a glance of mutual satisfaction. Monkey, indeed, had overdone it. He had overdone it completely. The furniture that had so long defied them, refusing to let them be comfortable, was now beyond repair.

Their eyes shining with gratitude, they turned to look for Monkey.

And there he was, standing beside them, mutely asking— or so it seemed—what next he could do to help.

"Here, you! Fireman! What's your name!" Uncle Trehunsey made a jab with his stick. "If my furniture's ruined, it's your fault. I'll make you pay for what you've done. You see if I don't!"

"You can't do that, I'm afraid, Mr. Truro. We did what we came for—put out the fire. We're not responsible for more. Now, men—ready?" called Number One.

The firemen in their smoke-stained helmets were crowding on to the wagon. The horses, having done their share, flung up their heads and neighed. One of them—feeling peckish, perhaps—helped himself to a calico rose from Miss Brown-Potter's bonnet.

"All aboard? Well, giddup now!" The driver cracked his whip.

"Stop!" yelled Uncle Trehunsey. "Stop! Where am I going to sleep tonight?"

"Not our business!" said Number One, as the wagon clattered away.

"No house! No bed! What shall I do? Nobody ever thinks of me!"

Mrs. Linnet hugged her baby closer. Mr. Linnet put his arms round the children. Uncle Trehunsey, inevitably, was anxious about himself. But they were anxious about Little Trehunsey and Edward, Victoria and Monkey. The question of where they would all sleep had now to be confronted.

A quiet voice solved the problem for them.

"Do not be anxious," said Miss Brown-Potter. "You will all come and live with me . . ."

PART II

Friend Monkey's Friend

1

Miss Brown-Potter's house next door was more commodious than Uncle Trehunsey's and, if anything, uglier. It had turrets and pinnacles everywhere, plastered on just for decoration like feathers on a hat.

Attached to it on one side was a grandiose conservatory, where flowers and trees and tropical creepers grew in great profusion.

At the back of the house was a large garden running down to the river; and a broad, rather muddy lake where water-lilies bloomed in the summer and where, in winter, when it froze, the ice was thick enough to skate on.

Miss Brown-Potter had been born in the house, her mother, too, and her mother's mother.

As a child, she had lived on the attic floor, first with a nurse as her companion and later with a governess. Up there, it was quiet and remote. She had been like a bird in a high tree, listening to the sounds of laughter that floated up from below. Horses and carriages every day came clop-petting up to the front steps, disgorging ladies in lacy dresses and men with black shiny hats and swinging, waisted coats.

Miss Brown-Potter remembered the time when the house

had seemed like a living person, happily humming to itself. In those days there was always music—a clarinet piping an old tune, somebody playing the drawing-room piano, somebody else standing beside it, singing a song or a ballad.

Very often there would be parties, with the swish of taffeta on the stairs, a quartet playing the "Blue Danube," the tinkle of silver on glass or china, the hubbub of talk and laughter.

On these occasions, Miss Brown-Potter would be brought down—a shy child in a long white dress—to stand by her father or her mother and receive a nut or a piece of ginger.

After that, the treat given, her parents would feel they had done enough and would sign to the nurse or governess to take her away again. And the guests, having wondered stealthily why such a handsome pair of parents should have produced so plain a child, would continue the talk and the laughter.

The child had a quick ear for such remarks but had never been troubled by them. To her, they were simple statements of fact. Indeed, she was so convinced of their truth that when one elegant gentleman had protested, laughingly, to her mother—"But, May, she has really beautiful eyes!"—Miss Brown-Potter had been displeased. So much so that she hurriedly returned the peach he had given her from the table. He was either mocking her, she felt, or disparaging her mother. Could he not see and understand—it was clearly seen and understood by each of the three Brown-Potters!— that the two parents had all the beauty and that she, far from being jealous, was content that it should be so.

So Miss Brown-Potter had lived and grown, isolated in her treetop world, gazing out on the River Thames and thinking of all the far-off places its waters were heading for—Cyprus, Africa, Cathay, the Bering Straits, Australia.

And at last she came to realise that what she wanted most in the world was to go and explore those places. She would have to approach her parents, of course, and ask for their permission. They would think it a very odd idea, even unsuitable, perhaps. But eventually they would agree—and never miss her, she was sure. They needed only each other.

However, as it turned out, neither of them was ever to hear their daughter's strange request. They were killed one sunny afternoon when their carriage suddenly overturned on the way to a brass-band concert. All that remained of their lives and their laughter, the elegant friends and the dreamy music, was a faint echo that sometimes sounded when the house was very still. That, and the portrait in the drawing room, next to the one of their only child, painted at the age of ten, looking mumpish and forlorn.

It showed them skating on the lake, arm across arm, furred and rosy, sharing together a bunch of cherries—he tall, poetic, graceful, she like a creature from fairy-tale.

And now their daughter, home from her various explorations, was older than they had ever been. She thought of them with tender pride, as a pair of long-lost children, and saw them, as though through a telescope, continually skating away, forever young, forever fair, needing nobody but each other.

She was not lonely. She had too much inside herself for that. Besides, there was Stanley Livingstone Fan. Since their return from Africa they had lived in the old echoing house in perfect amity—two good, trusty friends mutually caring for each other.

Three others shared their frugal household—Louis, a sulphur-crested cockatoo, a badger called Tinker, and a dog called Badger.

Tinker had a badger-sett in the garden, but he liked to sleep on the eiderdown on Miss Brown-Potter's bed. So, unfortunately, did Badger.

At bedtime there was always a rush to see who could get to the eiderdown first. After a series of noisy scuffles the winner would burrow into the quilt, and the loser would have to content himself with a rug in Stanley's tent. This was pitched by a turret window and made of two blankets and a broomstick. The broomstick served as a perch for Louis, though he sometimes slept on a wardrobe.

Louis was difficult to please. He was bad-tempered, selfish, autocratic, and finicky over his food. He didn't like this and he didn't like that. Miss Brown-Potter and Stanley Fan were forever trying to tempt him. At last they discovered that what he chiefly preferred was candles and a sip or two of beer.

He was also extremely talkative and always wanted the last word. His knowledge of swear words was extensive. He sang hymns, all of them gloomy. And now and again he would heave a sigh and declare in a fainting, feminine voice, "It is all too much for me!"

Miss Brown-Potter had concluded, if language was anything to go by, that, before he joined the Putney household, Louis, in turn, had belonged to a soldier—probably one in the cavalry—a pessimistic clergyman, and a lady unable to cope with the world.

But Stanley came to no conclusions, for he never heard what Louis said. Indeed, he never heard anything. He inhabited a world of silence. But in spite—or, perhaps, because—of that, he understood a lot. Between himself and Miss Brown-Potter there was never any need of words. They read each other's thoughts. And with everyone else it was the same. He lost the sound but caught the mood, which was just as good, and perhaps better.

People, of course, stared at him, not merely because of his black face and his naked legs and feet; but also because of his curious clothes—yellow breeches with bows at the knee, a waistcoat with shiny silver buttons, and a blouse of fine white linen. These had been found by Miss Brown-Potter in an old chest in the attic. They had once belonged—so she supposed—to her great-great-grandfather as a boy, and she thought them just the thing for Stanley.

So they were. And Stanley liked them. The word "fashion," if he had heard it, would have seemed to him quite meaningless, as, indeed, it was to Miss Brown-Potter.

As for his face—well, even if strangers stared, they liked it. It was quick to smile and full of contentment. Few people are satisfied with their faces. They feel there is something wrong somewhere—the eyebrows or perhaps the mouth—unworthy of the self behind it. But this was a face that had all it wanted. The outside exactly matched the inside. It seemed to be glad to belong to Stanley and Stanley glad to belong to it.

It was this face, smiling from ear to ear, that was at the door with Miss Brown-Potter to welcome the Linnets and Uncle Trehunsey as they straggled up the path.

They were all grimy with smoke and soot and shaken by their adventure. Edward looked shy, Victoria glum, Little Trehunsey was crying loudly, and Uncle Trehunsey hobbled along, muttering imprecations.

Mr. Linnet brought up the rear, laden with various bundles. And Monkey, with the frying-pan, tripped along beside him. Anyone watching would have seen a small man in a bowler hat accompanied by a jungle creature. Mr. Linnet saw it otherwise.

In the distance between one house and the other, the man who had been an assistant fireman had become a Bedouin chief, and Monkey was his faithful camel. Robbers had recently set upon them, and now, with a remnant of their possessions, they were trudging across the Sahara Desert to a distant green oasis.

So deeply was he involved in this story that Mr. Linnet was surprised when Miss Brown-Potter gave him her hand and not a handful of dates.

"Welcome!" she said in her calm voice.

She stood there with the light behind her, a tall statue with shining eyes, and Mr. Linnet woke up.

He tossed his Bedouin garb aside and decided to be Sir Walter Raleigh flinging a velvet cloak in the mud for Miss Brown-Potter to step on.

"Thank you," he said, with dignity.

"So kind," Mrs. Linnet was murmuring. "Trehunsey, dear, do be quiet—such a lot of us, Miss Brown-Potter—sorry to be such a burden on you—and my uncle, no, my husband's uncle—and only one pair of hands—so awkward—"

Miss Brown-Potter drew them in. "The house is large enough for us all. I am glad to have Mr. Truro here and to get to know him better."

Uncle Trehunsey grunted. He was by no means glad to be there or to know Miss Brown-Potter better.

"Gitt on! Gitt up! Gitt out, can't yer? Hell's bells! Gitt

100

out of here!" Louis, on his perch in the drawing room, was shouting in his trooper's voice.

It was hardly a friendly welcome.

And Tinker and Badger, taking one look at the new arrivals, made a hurried dash for the stairs. Any one of this horde of intruders might be after the eiderdown.

"Badger? Tinker?" called Miss Brown-Potter.

But neither of them answered.

"Why are they named Badger and Tinker?"

Mr. Linnet sighed as he put down his bundles. More questions from Victoria!

"Well, my great-grandmother," said Miss Brown-Potter, "and for all I know, *her* great-grandmother, always had pets called Badger and Tinker. So had my grandmother, so had my mother, and so, of course, have I." Such a line of reasoning seemed clear enough to Miss Brown-Potter, if not to anyone else.

"I hope," said Edward, anxiously, "they won't hurt One and Two!"

"Oh, I'm sure they won't hurt anyone. They're really very gentle."

"One and Two!" scoffed Victoria. "Edward pretends he has two dogs. But they aren't real. He's making them up."

Miss Brown-Potter seemed not to hear.

"What colour are they?" she enquired.

"One is black and Two is white, like the dogs on the whiskey bottle."

"How suitable! Tinker and Badger are sure to like them."

"Gitt on! Gitt up! Gitt out! Gitt off!" Louis shook his wings at the guests. And, when this did not have the desired effect, he dug into his repertoire and came up with a hymn.

101

"The day thou gavest, Lord, is ended," he croaked in a gloomy voice.

"That will do, Louis," said Miss Brown-Potter. "He is right, however, Mrs. Linnet. I'm sure you are longing for a rest."

She and Stanley exchanged glances, and at once, working as one person, they set about getting bowls of soup, gathering up the scattered bundles, lighting lamps, making beds.

And Monkey, as usual, was helpful.

He tidied away the housekeeping money to a place under the grand piano; hung Mr. Linnet's bowler on top of a chandelier; took away Uncle Trehunsey's rug, which he needed for his bad foot, and tried to wrap it round Miss Brown-Potter, who did not feel the cold. He folded Mrs. Linnet's apron and hid it behind a row of books, and was narrowly prevented by Stanley Fan from tidying Little Trehunsey away into the drawer of a chest.

The house began to ring with voices. "Here, not there! This room, not that! Where are the matches? Bring me a candle!"

Footsteps were hurrying everywhere. Little Trehunsey's cries of displeasure repeatedly rent the air. Uncle Trehunsey cursed his fate as his nephew helped him up the stairs and Monkey kindly tried, but failed, to carry the walking-stick.

Tinker and Badger, for once sharing the eiderdown, grumbled together at the noise.

And downstairs, in the drawing-room, came a fainting, feminine wail from Louis—"Oh, dear, I'm really worn out! It is all too much for me."

But eventually the house was quiet. The Linnet family and Uncle Trehunsey fell into the sleep of exhaustion.

Miss Brown-Potter went the rounds, locking the doors, putting out the lights.

Stanley, with Louis on his shoulder, followed her with a lighted candle.

"Through the night of doubt and sorrow," sang Louis gloomily.

"Hush!" said Miss Brown-Potter, softly.

They had come to the conservatory and found that something new had happened. The rubber trees at either end, brought from Burma long ago by one of Miss Brown-Potter's uncles, were bending over towards each other, their branches twined together. And, within the leafy bed they made, lay Monkey, quietly sleeping.

Having seen his friends to their proper places, he had neatly tidied himself away. In one paw lay a half-eaten lily. The other clasped the frying-pan.

For a long time Miss Brown-Potter stood there, gazing at the sleeping figure. His cap, with its letters *London Fx—*, had fallen a little sideways. She could clearly see the blaze on his brow and the small white patches round his throat.

At last she turned and smiled at Stanley, putting her finger to her lip and sending the candle a sidelong glance.

Stanley Livingstone Fan nodded, cupping his hand round the flame.

And quietly, anxious not to wake the sleeper, they went upstairs to bed . . .

2

"And how did you sleep?" asked Miss Brown-Potter, as the family straggled down to breakfast.

"Bed too soft. I'm used to horsehair."

Uncle Trehunsey, carefully choosing the best chair, sat himself down upon it. Stanley came forward with a stool.

"I didn't sleep very well," said Edward. "Neither did One and Two."

"Now, Edward, don't be difficult." Mrs. Linnet sent him a warning glance. Why couldn't Edward be like the others? She had many times asked herself the question.

"I'm not being difficult, just telling. My soldier was tapping behind the door."

"Then try and think of something else. Why not angels?" asked Mr. Linnet.

He himself often thought about angels. They sat beside him on top of the bus and walked with him along the docks, trailing their plumy wings.

"I don't like angels. They're always prying. In at the window or over your shoulder."

"Not like angels? Whatever next?" Mr. Linnet was disappointed.

"So I thought of the dogs," continued Edward. "And I came downstairs when I heard the music."

"What music?" asked Miss Brown-Potter, quickly.

"It was the piano." Edward pointed. "Two people—a

lady and a man. One was playing and the other singing. A song about eyes drinking."

"How could eyes drink?" Mrs. Linnet demanded. "Couldn't be anyone playing and singing—all of us asleep in bed—Edward fanciful, I'm afraid—seeing things that aren't there—very like my cousin Claude—better when he gets older—odd man out, in a manner of speaking—but children will be children—"

Flustered and apologetic, she pleaded for Edward with Miss Brown-Potter.

> *"Drink to me only with thine eyes*
> *And I will pledge with mine,*
> *Or leave a kiss within the cup*
> *And I'll not ask for wine—"*

sang Miss Brown-Potter softly. "Was that it, Edward? Was that the song?"

"Yes!" cried Edward, delightedly. "They were singing and smiling at each other—the way they are in the picture." He nodded upwards at the portrait. "They weren't wearing their fur hats, but I saw some cherries on the piano."

He looked across at the grand piano. There was not a cherry to be seen.

"Silly! Those aren't real cherries." Victoria was scornful. "They're only paint, aren't they, Mamma? And the people are skating—so it's winter. You don't have cherries in winter-time."

"Some people do," said Miss Brown-Potter. "I'm very glad you saw them, Edward."

Mrs. Linnet looked round for her husband. Was Miss Brown-Potter fanciful, too? She hoped not. What a predicament!

But Mr. Linnet had taken his hat and was off to catch the bus. He was working extra time now to repay the Twenty Pounds. So Mrs. Linnet, inevitably, had to make what she could of the situation.

And, indeed, apart from the possibility that her hostess might be fanciful, it was not so very hard. The household went its way serenely, no more disturbed by the Linnets' arrival than the sea is disturbed by a few more fish. Miss Brown-Potter and Stanley Fan took life, like the weather, just as it came. If it rained, they put up the umbrella. If it was fine, they were grateful.

Mrs. Linnet, always in need of hands, had now two extra pairs to help her. And the children seemed to be happy. Little Trehunsey, it is true, persisted in his noisy habit of demanding everyone's attention. But that was his way of enjoying himself.

And since the house was full of treasures, collected by Miss Brown-Potter's mother and all her other ancestors, Victoria could indulge to the full her tireless curiosity.

"What is this? Where did it come from? Who gave it to you? Why?"

Things that could be seen and touched were what Victoria liked. She needed names and labels. Everything had to be this *or* that, black *or* white, up *or* down, with nothing in between.

But with Edward, all was in between. The only black and white things were his two invisible dogs. Time, for Edward, was still a problem, no matter where he lived. And the soldier was still behind his door, tapping the wall with his pencil.

The only thing that was different now was that somebody seemed to understand.

"Are you sure he's there?" asked Miss Brown-Potter, flinging wide the bedroom door and disclosing absolutely nothing, not even the ghost of a soldier.

"Of course I am!" Edward replied. "He's there inside my head!"

"Ah, yes, I see!" said Miss Brown-Potter. "I should have thought of that."

But in spite of the soldier, he liked the house. It was full of curious pockets of laughter; music that nobody else heard; rustling ladies on the stairs who were gone as soon as he saw them.

It must also be said that Mr. Linnet, in spite of having to work so hard, was happy in his new home. Monkey was a welcome guest and therefore safe from Uncle Trehunsey. And he had a friend in Miss Brown-Potter.

When he tired of being Sir Walter Raleigh, he would bravely rescue Joan of Arc—looking exactly like this friend —from a cruel death at the stake; or snatch away Boadicea — again the image of Miss Brown-Potter—from troops of Roman soldiers.

There was only one difficulty, it seemed—but that was a major one, Uncle Trehunsey.

Mr. Truro did not like the house. He did not like Stanley Livingstone Fan, and there weren't enough words in any language to say what he thought of Miss Brown-Potter.

He was used to being cock of the walk. And what was he here? Merely a guest! A guest who wanted nothing more than to rid himself of his hosts.

They had turned his whole life upside down. Nothing was certain any more. Where he had hectored, ordered, hounded, he now had to ask and be polite. Not that they required it of him. Neither of them had any requirements.

They simply made it impossible for him to do anything else. When he ranted at Mr. or Mrs. Linnet for not bringing something that he wanted, he would find Stanley Fan beside him, with the object in his hand. When he snarled at Edward or Victoria for coming within a yard of his foot, Miss Brown-Potter would take them away and explain that gout was a painful illness and ask them to make allowances.

Make allowances! *Them!* For *him!* He'd give her allowances—if he could!

And if he attempted to rail at Monkey, call him an ape, order him out, Miss Brown-Potter would gravely remark that animals were hard to rear and a great responsibility.

"I well understand how you feel, Mr. Truro!"

Oh, indeed! She dared to understand him—did she? He who had never been understood or felt the need of it!

She was ready for him at every point. If he wanted anything, he got it. If there was something he did not want, nobody pressed it on him. She was kind, courteous, and friendly. She surrounded him with every comfort. And Uncle Trehunsey, constantly seething with inward rage, was brought to the brink of madness. All he wanted was to get back home, order some new horsehair chairs, and return to his proper way of life, as king of his own castle.

"How you must long for your home, Mr. Truro! And to be in charge of things again!" Miss Brown-Potter beamed at him, as she spread the rug over his knees.

Uncle Trehunsey glared at her, unable to say a word. She even knew what he was thinking!

But what of Monkey?

Did anyone know what *he* was thinking?

And was there only one fly in the ointment? No, there were two! Though Monkey was not the second fly.

As usual, he was helpful and busy, putting a finger in every pie. And his two hosts were also busy, saving the pies from Monkey's finger.

They did not mind. They even liked it.

"It is better to do too much than too little," Miss Brown-Potter declared. "Much can always be whittled down. But little can be done with little."

So she calmly accepted Monkey's help and took the consequences.

For instance, when they went shopping, he would help by carrying the bag and giving away to passers-by eggs, ink, buttons, pepper—anything, everything. And Miss Brown-Potter would either have to buy more or ask the recipients to return them. It was no good trying to stop Monkey. Whatever language he understood, it certainly was not English. Moreover, he lived by his own rules.

On one occasion, a pretty lady, all furbelows and feather boas, was accosted by what seemed to her a small boy, clad in fur and wearing a cap, who handed her a package.

"What is this?" she said, haughtily.

"A pound of butter," said Miss Brown-Potter.

"But I don't *need* a pound of butter! What do you think I am—a pauper? I shall get my husband to make a complaint."

"To whom?" asked Miss Brown-Potter, with interest.

To whom, indeed? It was a puzzle. Could one complain to a court of law? Judges don't deal in pounds of butter. A policeman? Definitely not. He would probably laugh in a rude way and say, "Go home and eat it!"

The pretty lady was cornered. And the pretty lady knew it.

"Tuh!" she said, exasperated. She flung the butter at Miss

109

Brown-Potter, tossed her feather boa about her, and hurried into a nearby house, where the door was opened by a butler.

Miss Brown-Potter, the butter, and Monkey proceeded on their way.

And presently Stanley Fan joined them. He had taken a written list to the market and was bringing home vegetables and fruit.

Monkey leapt at him at once. He already had Miss Brown-Potter's bag, and now he wanted Stanley's. He was even willing, it appeared, to carry Stanley, too. At last, after some skirmishing, where everything from both bags was scattered on the pavement, Monkey agreed to carry a cabbage while Miss Brown-Potter and Stanley Fan gathered up the parcels. The three turned into their own street, amicably silent.

Suddenly, from far behind them, came the sound of running footsteps.

"Stop!" cried a voice. "Stop! I beg you!"

Miss Brown-Potter turned about. A man was hurrying after her, holding up his right hand as though she were traffic and he a policeman. His eyes had a wild and feverish look. His body trembled like grass in a breeze.

"Madam," he panted, pointing his finger. "Do you see what I see?"

Miss Brown-Potter looked about her. She saw nothing extraordinary—nothing but Stanley Fan and Monkey.

"I'm afraid," said Miss Brown-Potter, kindly, "that I don't know what it is you see. Has anything upset you?"

"I see—oh, no! Of course I don't! It's a figment of imagination. But I thought, for a moment—no, it can't be—"

The man buried his face in his arms and leant against a fence.

"Please let me help you," said Miss Brown-Potter. "What is your name? What did you see?"

"Beaver," the man groaned. "Timothy Beaver. I was coming out of my garden gate and, as you went by, I thought I saw—alas, alas, what shall I do? First my wife and then me! Oh, my poor young children!"

"Mr. Beaver, try to be calm. What is the matter? Your wife, you say?"

"Yes, yes, they've taken her away. They had to. She was seeing things." His sad eyes filled with tears.

Stanley put his hand in his pocket, drew out Miss Brown-Potter's great-great-grandfather's handkerchief, and gave it to Mr. Beaver. It was made of fine white cambric, with lace around the edge.

"Thank you," muttered Mr. Beaver, and hurriedly blew his nose.

"What kind of things?" asked Miss Brown-Potter.

"You'll think it strange—so did the doctor. It was monkeys wearing sailor caps, looking in through the windows."

"But, Mr. Beaver—"

"All right, I know what you're going to say. Monkeys never wear sailor caps and they're all in the zoo—the monkeys, I mean. That's the proper place for monkeys—not looking in at people's windows or walking with ladies along the street—"

"*Mr. Beaver!*"

"Oh, it's all a terrible delusion. You don't have to tell me, my dear lady. And yet, as you passed, I distinctly saw it—at least, I think, or I thought, I did. That's how you know your mind is going. You see things that aren't there—monkeys with tails and sailor caps. And this one—yes I must be mad! —was carrying a cabbage!"

111

"MR. BEAVER! Please *listen!* Look at what is beside you!"

There stood Monkey, with arms outstretched, offering him the cabbage.

"What is this?" Mr. Beaver demanded, brushing the tears from his eyes.

"It is a cabbage," said Miss Brown-Potter.

"A cabbage?" Mr. Beaver stared. The thing was heavy in his hands, warm from the sun and solid.

"You—you mean—?" He stammered wildly at Miss Brown-Potter. But her eyes directed him to Monkey who was now bending shyly before him with his paw held out, like an olive branch.

Mr. Beaver fell to his knees. He looked at Monkey, anxiously. Then he took the paw.

A look of relief flooded his face.

"It's real!" he cried, triumphantly. "You're true, you're alive!" he assured Monkey. As if there had ever been any doubt! "Oh, everything has come right, at last! I must go at once and tell the doctor. My wife's not mad. Neither am I. We shall all of us be together again, and apple-pie for dinner!"

Mr. Beaver sprang to his feet, took off his hat, and rushed away.

"Thank you!" he called back over his shoulder. "Thank you, madam, thank you!"

They could hear his "Thank yous" growing fainter as he disappeared round the corner. He had taken the cabbage away with him, as well as Stanley's handkerchief.

"Never mind," said Miss Brown-Potter. "I will make you another, just as pretty. And instead of cabbage, we'll have carrots." She pointed to one of the paper bags.

Stanley grinned from ear to ear. He much preferred carrots to cabbage, and he knew that Miss Brown-Potter knew it.

They sauntered homewards contentedly, each of them taking a monkey paw while Monkey swung along between them as though they were walking trees.

He would never know that—because of him—a good wife, mother, and cook had been reft from her loving family; or that now—again because of him—the good mother, wife, and cook would shortly be restored to them . . .

3

No, Monkey was not the second fly. The second fly was Louis.

"What has happened to him, I wonder?" Miss Brown-Potter looked the words at Stanley. And Stanley flung out his arms and shrugged. He was wondering, too.

Was it the arrival of the Linnets or some frustration within himself that made Louis, day by day, increasingly resentful?

He had always been a peevish bird. But that was just eccentricity. A word or a look from Miss Brown-Potter was enough to smooth his ruffled plumage. Her grey eyes would outface his blue—the forget-me-not eyes with the red centres that were like two ladybirds—and Louis would lower his voice.

And then, after a little while, he would bend his crested head towards her to have its feathers scratched.

He had been like an old curmudgeonly colonel whose troops, in spite—or because—of his temper, had a strong affection for him.

But now he was actively unpleasant. He swore at them all, even Miss Brown-Potter, whose eye he now refused to catch. He allowed Stanley, though grudgingly, to carry him on his shoulder. But none of the Linnets dared to approach him. And, for some unfathomable reason, he would now have nothing to do with Monkey.

Of course, Monkey overdid things. That was to be expected. Louis was used to candle ends, and Monkey brought him a packet of candles. He liked his beer in a mustard spoon, and Monkey brought him a gallon jar.

"My dear, it's all too much for me!" Louis would wail in his fainting voice, turning his back on Monkey.

But Monkey could not learn his lesson. He had to give and be spurned for giving; to give again and again be spurned. He couldn't help it. He loved Louis.

Louis, too, had come from the wild. Louis, in spite of the words he mimicked, remembered the speechless life of the forest. Louis, too, was far from home and a stranger in the world of men.

These, if Monkey could have reasoned, would have been his reasons for loving Louis. As it was, he had no reason. He simply knew, without thinking about it, that Louis was a kind of brother.

So—Monkey put out his friendly paw. And Louis, in his new phase, bit it.

Monkey rubbed his head against Louis, and Louis tried to pluck off his cap.

There was nothing Monkey could do to please him.

Daily he grew more cantankerous, swearing, singing, and swooning.

"That will *do*, Louis!" said Miss Brown-Potter. And Louis, instead of obeying her, merely mimicked her words.

"That will do, Louis! That will do, Louis!" he jeered at her and flapped his wings, as though he wanted to hurt her. "Whoa there, you! Gitt on! Gitt up!"

"That blasted bird!" said Uncle Trehunsey, for a moment forgetting that he was a guest.

The house was loud with vociferation. Its delicate echoes were lost in the noise. The din that Louis now constantly made was a challenge to Little Trehunsey. He owed it to himself, it seemed, to outroar everyone else.

And Victoria, with no ear for music, chose this inharmonious moment to try to play the piano. "God Save the Queen"—with wrong notes and the loud pedal—outdid even Trehunsey. The neighbours began to complain.

"Victoria, *please!*" begged Mrs. Linnet.

"Why me? It isn't fair, Mamma. Trehunsey makes as much noise as he likes!"

"Because you're the eldest," said Mrs. Linnet.

"Well, I never asked to be the eldest. I wanted to be an only child. If I get an alligator for Christmas, I will tell it to eat up Trehunsey."

Edward looked at her thoughtfully. "A hippopotamus would be better. Hippopotamuses don't bite. It would swallow him in one gulp."

"Children, how heartless—only a baby—alligators so dangerous and me with only—do go out—play in the garden —something—"

"I'm not going out with Victoria. The last time I did, she

trod on the dogs and said I'd be dead by tea-time." Edward's face gathered itself. It was getting ready to cry.

"Boys don't cry, but Edward does. And he *will* be dead, Miss Brown-Potter. He'll die before five—you'll see!"

"Oh, I don't think he will, Victoria. Nobody dies before tea."

"Are you sure?" asked Edward, tearfully.

"Very sure. It's a well-known fact. Especially when there are iced buns."

Iced buns were Miss Brown-Potter's failing. When she thought of them, her mouth watered. They were waiting now on a plate in the pantry. There was one, she remembered, with a sugared violet on the top. If no one else wanted it, she would take it for herself.

"Gitt on! Gitt up! That will do, Louis! Hold yer hoof up, can't yer?"

Louis, again, was on the warpath. He had been asleep on top of the bookcase. And Monkey, refusing to be refused, had leapt up to sit beside him.

"Hell's bells! Gitt up, you brute! Evil is with me day by day! My fan, dear! Give me my fan!"

Alternately shouting, singing, and fainting, Louis rushed at Monkey.

"Louis!" said Miss Brown-Potter, sternly.

Louis took no notice.

"That will do, Louis! That will do, Louis!" He danced on the shelf and jeered.

"I think, Mrs. Linnet," said Miss Brown-Potter, "we shall have to separate them. Suppose we *all* go into the garden. Louis can ride on Stanley's shoulder, and he, our friend—" She glanced at Monkey. "He can stay here and we'll shut the doors." She turned to Uncle Trehunsey.

"And what would you like to do, Mr. Truro? I'm sure you'll be glad to be free of us all and to take a little nap."

Uncle Trehunsey was stoney-faced.

To be free of them all, to have a good forty winks, was *exactly* what he wanted—a nice, quiet, lonely sleep with *The Times* over his face.

But now he determined that forty winks was exactly what he did *not* want. That woman had read his thoughts again! He'd be hanged if he'd take a nap!

"No intention of sleeping, thank you. Quite wide-awake. Will read the paper."

"Just as you like." She looked at Stanley.

And at once Stanley climbed the bookcase and offered his shoulder to Louis.

"Let us be off," said Miss Brown-Potter. And they went out, shutting the door behind them, leaving Monkey alone.

Alone—except for Uncle Trehunsey, who, once he was sure they were out of sight, opened *The Times* at the middle page and spread it over his face . . .

4

The house was still and very quiet—filled with the soundless sounds of silence; a petal dropping from a flower, the stir of a muslin curtain.

Upstairs, on the eiderdown, Badger was taking his siesta while Tinker slept on a nearby cushion.

Downstairs, in the drawing room, *The Times* gently rose and fell with Uncle Trehunsey's breathing.

From far away came the children's voices, like the echo of echoes of voices.

The house grew closer to itself. It drew in like the trees of the forest that crowd into a shade.

And Monkey was there in the midst of it, hunched up in the conservatory with his long arms wrapped about him.

He was alone for the first time. The first time—since when? Since what? Something was knocking at his mind, something that wanted to be remembered.

The crowding silence of the house brought back the jungle forest. He was in an airy world of branches, their dark leaves flickering about him. His nose wrinkled, sniffing the air. A hot, steamy earthy scent mingled with Miss Brown-Potter's flowers. Miss Brown-Potter's rubber trees, twined together to make a bed, creaked in a little breeze. And far away another bed—and he within it, warm and safe—was creaking among the treetops. Shadowy forms moved about him, hanging by tail and paw.

As he lay there in his leafy cradle, the wind rose, tossing the heads of the trees. He could hear the rain rustle and gather, feel it pelting upon his body and himself being pulled out of the nest. Somebody had him by the paw; a fostering tail wrapped itself about him.

Crouching there, warm and dry, in Miss Brown-Potter's conservatory, Monkey experienced the storm. He felt the swarming monkey shapes that seemed to want to protect and save him. Was it because he was young and dependent? Yes, but there was another reason, a reason he could not quite remember. Was it because they needed him? Was he, in some way, precious?

118

Then suddenly—a branch? an orange?—something crashed on the guiding paw and wrenched it away from him. The furry shapes scattered and fled, chattering as they went. He could hear the echo of frightened voices growing fainter in the distance.

Then towards morning, the wind fell. The rain ceased. The jungle was quiet—as quiet as Miss Brown-Potter's house that was crowding now about him. He listened for friendly monkey chatter. He watched for a furry head or a tail. But there was nothing, no sound, no sigh. They had gone away. They had left him behind. There was not a single monkey left.

He wrapped his arms more closely about him, not so much remembering as feeling in his whole body that he had been left alone.

And Miss Brown-Potter at the age of ten, mumpish in her white muslin, stepped down from her portrait frame and came and stood beside him.

For a long time or a short time—neither could have measured it—the two of them communed together, motionless as a painted child beside a painted monkey.

From the drawing-room came the sound of music. Somebody played. Somebody sang.

> *"Greensleeves was all my joy*
> *And, oh, Greensleeves was my delight,*
> *Greensleeves was my heart of gold,*
> *And who but my Lady Greensleeves?"*

And a face outside the conservatory peered in through the glassy panes.

It belonged to a tall, thin, scraggy man whose grey hair

waved in the breeze. He was beating time to the tune with a finger and gazing in at Monkey.

The music ended. The face disappeared. A handle rattled as somebody turned it. The door opened stealthily, and Professor McWhirter, in his long cloak and tartan kilt, tiptoed softly in.

He wore, as though it were a necklace, an adder looped about his throat. And a squirrel sat in his waistcoat pocket, nibbling at a walnut.

Step by step he crept to Monkey, folding his cloak tightly about him so as not to knock anything over. He reached out and touched an arm. And Monkey, waking from his dream, assumed the stranger was playing Tag—a game he had often played with Edward. He gave the kilt a friendly pull and leapt up into a rubber tree.

"At last, ma beastie!" a voice whispered. "Ah'll have ye noo, wi'oot a doot! They're all oot and awa'!"

"Who are all out?" asked a quiet voice.

Professor McWhirter swung about and a flower-pot crashed to the floor.

Miss Brown-Potter stood in the doorway. Stanley Fan was at her heels with Louis asleep on his shoulder. And behind him loomed a strange object—something that looked like an eiderdown with two large humps in the middle.

"Och, madam, ye startled me! Ye've made me break a cannister and mebbe a flower or two, as weel. They shouldna be left so nigh the edge. A body is apt to topple them." The Professor looked sternly at Miss Brown-Potter.

"They were not near the edge," said Miss Brown-Potter. "And there should not have been a body there."

"Ah see Ah must explain masel'. Ah was passin' by, taking

120

the air. And Ah paused for just a wee moment to listen to the singing yonder." He nodded towards the piano.

"Indeed?"

"Ay, Ah'm partial to the auld songs. And then I saw the beastie there. He was lookin'—well, forlorn, ye ken. In need of a friend, if Ah may so put it, like the young leddy beside him."

"What young lady?" asked Miss Brown-Potter.

Professor McWhirter glanced about him, and his eye fell on the portrait.

"That one." He gave a little nod. "A mopey young lass, just like the painting. She's likely slipped awa' the noo. But she was here a moment since, standin' beside the beastie."

"Then she's slipped away to her right place. I expect they were comforting each other. But you have not told me," said Miss Brown-Potter, "to whom I am indebted for this intrusion."

"Intrusion? Hee balou, madam! Wouldna any decent man intrude if he saw a beastie in need o' kindness?" The Professor's blue eye turned upon her, innocent as a baby's. If anyone was at fault, it suggested, it was not Professor McWhirter.

"Allow me, madam," he continued, as one conferring a favour. "Allow me to offer ye ma carrd."

And, with all the grace of a conjuror producing a hat from inside a rabbit, he reached down into a deep pocket and presented his piece of pasteboard.

Miss Brown-Potter, fastidiously, held it away from her as she read.

The One and Only
Professor McWhirter!

Animal Fancier and Collector.
Zoos, Circuses, and Pet Shops Catered For.
Suitable Situations Found
For Birds, Beasts, Fish, and Reptiles.
Highly Recommended.

"I see," she said. Her voice was stern. "So that accounts for—" She waved at the squirrel. It was running up and down the Professor as though he were an oak tree.

"Ay," he said, smoothly, his blue eye bright. "Ah had him from an auld pairson a-weary o'chasin' him roond the house."

"And the snake?"

Professor McWhirter fingered his necklace. "Ah, the snake is from a young laddie who was takin' him off to school in a box. Ah made a barrgain wi' him."

"I can well believe it," said Miss Brown-Potter. "And you'll sell them to zoos and pet shops!"

"Weel—" His brown eye gave a sly flicker. "Mony a mickle makes a muckle. And professors have to eat, ye ken."

"In your case, Professor—er—McWhirter, I do not see the necessity. There are far too many animal fanciers. I cannot help you, I'm afraid. We have nothing here for zoos—or pet shops."

"Not the wee beastie?" The Professor pleaded, looking around for Monkey.

But Monkey was not in the rubber tree. He was standing beside Stanley Fan, waiting for Louis to waken.

"Ah! That is not for me to say. He does not belong to me."

"Nay, Ah ken weel he belongs to Linnet. But Ah thought to masel'—since his house is burrnt—he'd mebbe like to be rid o' him."

122

"You misunderstand me, Professor McWhirter. He belongs to nobody but himself. Mr. Linnet is merely caring for him."

For a moment, something like admiration shone in the bicoloured eyes.

"Whur-uff! Whur-uff!" came two angry voices from somewhere behind Stanley Livingstone Fan.

The eiderdown had slipped sideways, disclosing its two black owners. They were barking and grunting at Professor McWhirter.

"A badger!" he cried, excitedly. "Ye'll surely no' be wantin' a badger! Ah'd be glad, ma'am, to take him off yer hands."

"His name is Tinker, Professor McWhirter. And I want him on my hands, thank you!"

"Weel, the doggie, mebbe. He'd have a good home."

"His name is Badger," said Miss Brown-Potter. "And he has a home already."

"Then what aboot the crested fowl?" The Professor looked longingly at Louis.

"Gitt on! Gitt out! Spit in yer eye!" Louis, waking from his sleep, rudely accosted the stranger.

"You have your answer," said Miss Brown-Potter. "Not the cockatoo, either."

"Then, ye'll give me the firrst refusal, ma'am—could Ah put it that way?"

"You could not put it any way," said Miss Brown-Potter, firmly.

Professor McWhirter heaved a sigh. "Well, madam, may Ah bid ye good day?"

"Nothing would give me greater pleasure." Miss Brown-

Potter bowed him to Stanley who bowed him politely to the door and down the steps to the gate.

Professor McWhirter strode away, with his head up and his eyes bright. The squirrel scampered along his arm, the adder swung from his neck. But, in spite of his recent experience, there was nothing in his gait or bearing to suggest that the animal fancier was in any way a beaten man . . .

5

"The audacity!" Mrs. Linnet exclaimed, as the family sat together that evening. "Sneaking in like a common thief—seeing ghosts, like my sister Alice—hearing music with nobody there—maybe take the spoons next—even Trehunsey—what shall I do—only one pair—it makes me anxious—"

"I wish he *would* take Trehunsey!"

"Victoria, that is most unkind—not nice in a little girl—how would you like it—your own brother—"

"Just for a day!" Edward amended. "It would give us a little rest."

"I wish he'd taken the blasted ape!" Uncle Trehunsey spoke to himself. He dared not say the words aloud, in case Miss Brown-Potter heard them.

Mr. Linnet tightened his arm round Monkey. The Professor was, indeed, audacious. And what was worse—unpredictable. You never knew where he would pounce next. How could he, Mr. Linnet, care for Monkey—away all day, working overtime—with animal fanciers, free as air, prowling about in the garden? He had no fears for his younger son. No one would ever snatch *him* away. But Monkey was another matter.

"Do not be anxious," said Miss Brown-Potter. "Tomorrow I shall get a locksmith who will put new locks on all the doors. Then we shall be quite safe."

Of course! Why hadn't he thought of that? But what if the animal fancier was also an expert picker of locks? Mr. Linnet put the thought aside. The locksmith and Miss Brown-Potter between them would see to everything.

He had a vision of them both, their forms doubled, even trebled, guarding the house from intruders. Miss Brown-Potter, like a goddess out of an old book, was dressed in long white falling robes with a helmet on her head. And the locksmith—the spit and image of himself—wore a city suit and a bowler.

There they stood, behind every door—Miss Brown-Potter with a gleaming shield, the locksmith carrying her spear—sternly defying anyone to pick a lock or turn a key.

Yes! Everything would be well tomorrow. And tonight, instead of in his hammock, Monkey would sleep with Mr. Linnet, safe at the foot of his bed . . .

6

But, alas, by the time tomorrow came, the locksmith had been forgotten. Everything, far from being well, was exactly the reverse.

Louis had been awake all night, moaning and groaning and singing hymns. No one had had a moment's rest.

"Blast the bird!" muttered Uncle Trehunsey. "Didn't get a wink of sleep. Wring his neck if I got the chance!"

Miss Brown-Potter came down the stairs.

"I must apologize, Mr. Truro. I'm afraid you have had a restless night. Louis is behaving so strangely. I am sure you must long to wring his neck."

Mr. Truro gave her a truculent glance. Reading his thoughts again, was she? Well, he hoped she knew that, along with the bird's, he would like to wring *her* neck, as well!

"Slept very well! Didn't hear a sound!" He took out his anger on *The Times,* slamming and slashing the pages.

"Hm," he said, as he spooned up his porridge. "I see it's Jubilee Day today. Twenty-second of June."

"I'd quite forgotten!" Mr. Linnet sprang up. "The crowds will be terrible. I must hurry."

"What does Jubilee mean, Papa?"

"*Diamond* Jubilee, Victoria. The Queen has reigned for sixty years—we named you after her, you know!—the whole nation is celebrating. I must be off!" He seized his hat.

> *"Time, like an ever-rolling stream*
> *Bears all its sons away—"*

sang Louis, gloomily. "My salts! Where are my smelling salts?" He looked enquiringly about him, and Stanley gave him a candle end.

Louis, with a loud sigh, flung the tidbit away.

"The night is dark and I am far from ho-ome," he sang, and began to circle on his perch, round and round, like a top.

126

Stanley brought him a sip of beer. Louis turned his back upon it.

"My fan, please! And a small cushion. Oh, dear, it's all too much for me!" Faintingly, he made his request, putting up a claw to his beak as though he were a delicate lady about to swoon away.

"I can't understand it," said Miss Brown-Potter. "First ferocious, then dejected. Louis, what can we do for you?"

> *"A few more toils,*
> *A few more tears—"*

croaked Louis, looking woebegone.

"Perhaps a drop of castor oil—always answers with Trehunsey—feel unable to give advice—been the mother of three children—but never of a cockatoo—" Mrs. Linnet was trying to be helpful.

"Oh, do be cross again, Louis! You're upsetting One and Two!" The dogs were Edward's barometer. You could always tell what he was feeling by the way One and Two behaved. If Edward was happy, so were they. If the dogs were upset, it was a sign that Edward, too, was troubled.

"Spit in your eye! Whoa, there!" Victoria stood by the perch and shouted.

"Victoria! That is not polite—little girls should be ladylike—"

"I was just encouraging him, Mamma. That's what he says himself."

Louis regarded her with displeasure and spread out his crest like a fan.

"Abide with me," he said, huskily, tugging at the metal band that was clamped about his ankle.

He plucked and pulled and sighed and panted. The band would not come off.

"We *are* abiding with you, Louis," Miss Brown-Potter assured him.

Monkey's eyes were fixed upon him. He knew there was something wrong with Louis. He had offered him, at arms' length, flowers, turnip, bits of string—all the things he himself liked—but Louis wanted none of them.

So Monkey took off his sailor cap, the only thing that was truly his own, and stretched it out to Louis.

The bird looked downwards into it, as though the cap were a well of sorrow. Then he sighed and turned away.

"Lead, kindly light," he croaked, and proceeded to pluck at his tail feathers with many moans and groans.

"That's a bad sign," said Miss Brown-Potter. "There's something really wrong, I'm afraid."

She stood there, watching helplessly, as Louis circled on his perch, whimpering and sighing.

Monkey moved. He could bear it no longer. He looked beseechingly at Louis and offered his paw, palm-downward.

Everyone drew a deep breath, waiting for Louis to bite it.

Instead, Louis examined it, cocking his head to right and left, cogitating, summing it up. Then graciously, as one granting a privilege, he put his wrinkled claw upon it and stepped onto Monkey's arm.

He lurched along it to the shoulder, hooked his claws into the fur, and, using Monkey as a ladder, made his way down to the floor.

The front door was open at its widest, letting in the day. Louis made for the square of light, waddling on ungainly feet, rocking from side to side.

"Louis!" Miss Brown-Potter called.

But Louis ignored the well-known voice. He stumped away deliberately, through the door and down the steps, falling from one to another.

"Louis!"

Again Louis took no notice. He was waddling now along the path, croaking as he went.

They listened. It was another hymn.

> "Onward, Christian soldiers,
> Marching as to war—"

The voice had a note of conviction in it. Louis, it seemed, had made up his mind. He knew where he was going.

At the gate, he tilted his head and sniffed. This way? That way? Where was the wind?

Ah, he had it! His crest stiffened. He opened his wings to their full width and took a lumbering run.

Whoosh! He was up! He was in the air! Uncertainly, floppily, he was flying—a wobbling blob of white and yellow—over the hedge and away.

"Onward, Christian soldiers," came floating back to the watchers.

"Extraordinary!" Miss Brown-Potter exclaimed. "I had no idea he could fly."

Something shadowy brushed past her. It was Monkey, like a furry arrow, darting after Louis. And Stanley, like another arrow, was darting after Monkey.

"Oh, no—please stop him—quiet, Trehunsey—always something going wrong—and me with only—Miss Brown-Potter—whatever will my husband say—?"

"It's no good worrying, Mrs. Linnet. There is nothing we

can do. I am sure Stanley will manage things. He's very dependable."

"But he can't hear, much less speak—and Professor McWhirter—no, Trehunsey—crouching behind every pillarbox—waiting to get his hands upon him—no good crying now, Edward—play with Victoria in the garden—"

"I won't, Mamma. She's unkind to the dogs."

"I'm not, am I, Miss Brown-Potter? You can't be unkind to what isn't there."

But Miss Brown-Potter did not reply. She was thinking only of Louis.

He was now flying more easily. His wings, idle for so long, were getting the hang of the thing.

Louis, however, was no chicken. Nobody knew how old he was. But, clearly—with such a vocabulary—he could hardly be in his first youth. The double effort of flying and singing would certainly make him short of breath. He was bound—so Miss Brown-Potter thought—to look for something firm to land on. And then Stanley would catch him.

And, indeed, several people later reported that a shaggy-looking cockatoo had been seen perching in a plane tree; or on a fence, even a clothesline. The same people also noticed that when the bird flew away, it was followed by something brown and furry which, in turn, was followed by something else—a blur of black and white and, yes—odd though it sounded—yellow breeches! They went through gardens and round corners, over roofs and under arches—so quickly that it was hard to name them. They were here and gone in the blink of an eye.

"Well, they're out of sight," said Miss Brown-Potter. "We will just have to wait and see what happens."

"And good riddance to bad rubbish!" said Uncle Trehunsey to *The Times*. Luckily, no one heard him.

"Should have tried treacle—good for the liver—and port wine sometimes very helpful—oh, my poor, poor Alfred—"

Mrs. Linnet wrung her hands, glad—for once—to have only one pair. The thought of wringing four hands was altogether too much . . .

7

Boom!

From away in Hyde Park came the sound of a cannon.

And, after a minute, Boom! again.

Each moment the crowd was growing thicker. Every pavement was packed with people, pushing, laughing, teasing each other. Some of them had been there all night, eating sausages, drinking beer, sleeping on the hard ground, aching in every limb. So today they were going to enjoy themselves, even if it killed them.

Boom!

The day was fine. The sun was a sunflower in the sky. Everyone wore his best clothes. The policemen, in new uniforms, joked with the crowd as they held it back. The sound of the cannon was almost drowned in the buzz of talk and laughter.

Boom!

Children were running everywhere, getting under peo-

ple's feet, trying to infiltrate themselves into the best posi-
tions. The bigger ones were pushed to the front; the little
ones sat on their fathers' shoulders.

"Listen! Can you hear the cannon? There it goes, George
—boom, boom! Sixty booms for sixty years. That's how long
the Queen has reigned. Here you are! Here's your Union
Jack! You'll be able to wave it in a minute. Not at the cannon, George—the Queen!"

Boom!

"Yes, 'Arry, she'll be comin' soon. Don't chew your flag-
stick, there's a good boy. She'll drive along in a grand procession. Let 'im past, will yer, mister. 'E's little and 'e wants to
see! All the way from Buckingham Palace (yes, 'Arry, she
lives in a palace) as far as St. Paul's Cathedral."

Boom!

"We shall see the Queen!" the children said. And they
thought of the queens in the storybooks with crowns and
sceptres, velvet robes, and long, fair, falling hair, beautiful
as stars.

Perhaps there would be kings, too, who would throw
them each a golden orange or a bag of sugar-candy! "How
wonderful!" the children said. "We shall be inside a fairy-
tale! Someone will wear the seven-leagued boots! There will
be giants! Dragons! Dwarfs! The Prince will kiss the Sleeping Beauty!"

A quiver ran through the waiting crowd. Its heads all
turned in one direction, a moving wave of faces.

"Back! Back! Don't clutter the street! You'll all see everything, don't worry!" The policemen linked their hands together. The crowd leant on the line of arms as though it
were a rope.

Boom!

From far away, music sounded—fifes, bugles, trumpets, drums.

"She's coming! Laura, mind my glasses! Papa can't see without his glasses. Yes, yes, she's coming now! Listen to the band, the marching feet. The procession has started. The Queen is coming!"

Boom!

"Here come the sailors, the men in blue. Hurrah, hurrah, sons of the sea! Have they seen mermaids? I suppose so. No, Delia, the Queen is not a mermaid. You wish she were? Don't be silly. Rule Britannia! Rumpty-tum!"

Boom!

"Ah! At last! The Infantry! Look, children! Soldiers with roses in their hats! Listen—here's another band! London is ringing—alive with music! No, Jane, it *isn't* unkind to roses. It's an old custom. Hurrah! Hurrah!"

Boom!

"And now the open carriages, all of them full of important people. Why are they wearing black top hats? That's what important people wear. Hurrah! Hurrah! Cheer, Bertie! Who's that? The Sultan of Morocco. No, of course he hasn't a magic carpet. Why? I'll tell you another time. Don't kick that poor policeman, Roger. He's only doing his job. Hurrah!"

Boom!

"The Household Cavalry—scarlet and gold! Riders in their shining breastplates! Golden helmets! Silver stirrups! Galahad! Lancelot! St. George! No, Emily, there is no Dragon. You're quite safe, dear. Hurrah, hurrah! Oh, you *wanted* a dragon? Never mind! Look, Emily! The Queen is coming. Well, you needn't look if you don't want to. And it's no good nagging at me for dragons. You will have to wait

133

till you get home. Ah, here she is! Hurrah, hurrah! Sixty years a queen! Hurrah!"

Boom!

"Back! Back! Keep in your places!" The policemen leaned against the crowd.

Boom!

"Let 'im through, mister. Give 'im a chance. 'E's not tryin' to pick yer pocket. 'E wants to see the Queen!"

Boom!

"The ponies, the beautiful cream ponies, pulling the Queen in her carriage! Here she comes, William. Take off your hat! Why don't you want to take it off? Not a queen? Of course she is. Well, queens get old, like everyone else. Hurrah, hurrah, good old girl! Now, William, if you don't behave—"

Boom!

"Victoria! Our hearts are with you! Yours isn't—did you say, Sarah? You hadn't wanted this kind of queen? You wish she had long hair and a crown? Well, she's wearing a hat with a black pom-pom. What more do you want?"

Boom!

"No, Alfie, no! Stop arguing! The Queen just hasn't *got* a king. And she's not going to give out tangerines. You'll get one another time—be patient!"

Boom!

"Hurrah! She's almost in front of us! The Queen—God bless her! Wave your flag! *Wave your flag,* I said, Robert! And of course you can't go home now. We brought you here to see the Queen and, by Jehoshaphat, you'll see her, if I have to— What is this? She's stopping! The Queen's carriage has come to a standstill! What has happened? Can you see? What did you say—a *cockatoo?* A cockatoo walking across

134

the street? Singing a hymn? You can't mean it! Didn't know cockatoos could sing. No, Belinda, you *can't* have it! If it really is a cockatoo, the police will have to deal with it. What! Rather a cockatoo than the Queen? Belinda, I'm ashamed of you!"

Boom!

"Look, look! There it goes! It was a cockatoo, after all. A white one with a yellow crest. It's flying over the heads of the crowd, over the trees into Green Park. There! You can see it! Look, Flora!"

Boom!

"Here, stop shoving, none of that! What's going on? He stood on my foot! Somebody pushing through the crowd! Went so quickly, I couldn't see. A monkey? Don't be silly, Ernest. Monkeys are in the zoo."

Boom!

"Two of them! I distinctly saw them! Must have been a couple of boys. Dreadful! Shouldn't be allowed! Holding up the Queen like this! There goes a copper after them! Freddy, what are you cheering for? You like this better than the procession? Not a word when the Queen goes by—and you cheer a couple of ragamuffins!"

Boom!

"There! The horses are moving on. The trouble's over. Hurrah, hurrah! Those boys, whoever they were, have gone. Nancy! You stay here with me. You can't go running after strangers. What a ridiculous thing to say—a couple of boys compared to the Queen! There she passes! Hurrah, hurrah! Mother of Empire! Good old Vicky! Nancy, I am warning you—!"

Boom!

The Queen had passed. The eight cream horses had carried her off, away to St. Paul's Cathedral. The marching drums grew faint in the distance. The procession went rolling on its way.

Boom!

The cannon continued its salutations. It still had many booms to go.

The crowd, which had cheered from a single throat, broke up into many voices. There was a flatness in the air, soda water without the bubbles, quiet after the shouting.

But the Jubilee was not yet over. The city would ring all day with music. Coloured balloons would fill the sky. At dusk there would be a blaze of lights. Bonfires would glow on every hill. People would dance in streets and parks, and all the children would stay up late to watch the fireworks working.

So the crowd parted, knowing that it would meet again, dragging its offspring by the hand, going this way and that.

One of the crowd scuttled away, peering eagerly about as though searching for something.

This was a tall, scraggy man with hair that waved in the breeze. A long cloak was wrapped about him, and under the cloak he wore a kilt. In his hand he carried a wooden box with one side made of glass, and anyone looking through this window would have seen a couple of piebald mice running round a wheel. A frog peeped over the edge of his pocket, and a string bag with a hedgehog in it swung from his waistcoat button.

As he hurried away through Green Park, the man was muttering to himself and glancing up every now and again as though what he was looking for might possibly be in a tree.

"They came this way," he told himself. "Or Ah'll eat ma

136

good auld tartan. They were after the crested fowl, belike. And where it goes, they, too, will go. And where they go"—he smiled slyly—"Professor Alexander McWhirter will no' be far behind."

Off he went, peering round each tree, looking under park benches and into litter baskets.

In Hyde Park the cannon was still at work. Boom! Boom! One boom a minute—all the way up to sixty . . .

8

Louis, on top of the Nelson Column, was taking a little rest.

Down below him, the streets were crowded. People came flocking from everywhere, like pigeons after breadcrumbs.

Louis sighed. His heart was going boom! like the cannon. It was not as young as it once had been. But a short flight, then a rest—that was the way to do it!

Very well, then. Here goes! "Onward, Christian soldiers!"

Louis gathered himself together, waddled to the end of Nelson's nose, and tumbled into the air.

His next landing would be the street. He needed to exercise his legs.

But what were all these people doing? Why were they crowding and pushing? There wasn't a single patch of pavement where a bird could make a landfall. Oh, well! It would have to be the gutter!

He planed down on to a chosen spot, looked with disgust at the orange peel, glanced at the sea of gaping faces, and prepared to cross the road.

Then there was shouting all about him—people exclaiming, tut-tutting, protesting. "Whoa there, can't you!" somebody said. To Louis it was a familiar phrase. Horses were hurriedly reined in. Behind them a carriage came to a standstill. A black lace parasol fell sideways as though whoever was holding it had suffered a nasty jolt.

Louis continued on his way. Whatever the difficulty was, it was no affair of his.

But then a man in uniform darted towards him with a stick.

Louis, from old experience, disliked both sticks and uniforms. He made a quick decision.

With a great effort, still singing, he heaved himself up vertically and lurched across the upturned faces. He staggered, rather than flew through the air, up and down, like a seesaw. The Green Park fell away behind him, and street after street of murky buildings. Then he spied a small round patch of flowers—daisies, roses, arum lilies—and decided to land upon it. He rested contentedly for a moment, panting for breath and croaking. Then up again and away again, onward, ever onward.

And an elegant lady, gazing in at a shop window, was surprised to find that a cockatoo had been sitting on her hat.

Did Louis know, as he sped through the sky, that Monkey, sniffing the air for him, was following below? That Stanley, also sniffing the air, was following after Monkey? And that somebody else in a long cloak, eagerly peering right and left, was after all three of them?

If he did, he gave no sign. He had other things to think of.

He was over Regent's Park now, weary, breathless, but still determined—a typical Christian soldier.

He steadied his wings as he planed down, and a large jumble of low buildings, surrounded by a protective fence, came looming up beneath them.

A zebra gave a high whinny. A tiger answered with a roar. Macaws screamed. Seals barked. A gorilla growled despondently.

Louis' singing missed a note. These were the sounds he had longed to hear! Down he came, tumbling through the air and over the iron railings. He plunged along between the cages, knocking off someone's cap with his wing, and flew through an open gateway.

> *"Onward, then, ye pe-eople,*
> *Join our happy throng!"*

Louis sang triumphantly as he landed on a perch in the birdcage. And someone already sitting there seemed to be glad to see him . . .

9

"Good evening to you, Professor McWhirter!"

The man in the green cloak gave a start. His kilt swung sideways. So did the hedgehog.

139

"Hoots, Inspector! Ye made me jump! Ah wasna' expectin' to see ye!"

"Well, I didn't expect to see *you*, Professor—it being a holiday and all. We're closing the Zoo early tonight. Everyone wants to celebrate. Were you looking for some of your old friends?"

"Well, ye might call it that." The Professor was guarded. He was not going to let the Inspector know that the friend he was looking for was Monkey. For Monkey was not—as yet—a friend.

"Ah was just keepin' in touch, ye ken."

"I do know, Professor. You're so good with the animals. And they always like to see their pals. It makes up to them for being in cages."

"Animals?" The Professor was vague. His eyes were searching everywhere. His mind was on one animal, and, as far as he knew, it was not in a cage. "Och, ay, the animals, of course!"

"You understand them so well, Professor. Just look at Toby! He's scented you. See—he's almost dancing."

Inspector Higget, of the London Zoo, pointed to a sad-looking lion that was running its tail along the bars, trying to catch the Professor's eye.

"Ah, Toby, ma lad! Hoo are ye the noo? But where's Jenny, Inspector Higget? Should she no' be here with her mate?"

"But haven't you heard?" the Inspector exclaimed. "Jenny has just had six cubs! No other lioness in the Zoo has ever had a litter of six. We're rather pleased with ourselves."

From the look on the Inspector's face you might have thought that he himself was the father of the litter.

140

"Six! Ye stagger me, Inspector. Ma heartiest congratulations! So Jenny's within, all tucked away, and lookin' after the weans. Hum. Ha." The Professor's eyes had a thoughtful look—thoughtful, and rather greedy.

"Well, they're too young yet to be shown to the public. Down, Toby, there's a good boy! You'll see Professor McWhirter again. It's closing time now, you know. Good heavens, look at that open padlock!"

He pointed to a lock on the cage that was insecurely fastened.

"That's awful dangerous, Inspector. And verra, verra careless!"

"Careless it is!" The Inspector agreed. He leaned over the outer rail and closed the lock with a snap. "It's that young keeper, Tom Locket. This is the second time he's done it. I'll have to warn him again."

"Ye should, indeed," said Professor McWhirter. "Ye never can tell wi' open locks. A pairson might be gettin' in."

The Inspector laughed indulgently. "I don't think anyone would try it. No Daniels in this lion's den! He's far too wild and tricky."

"And, as well, a pairson might get oot!" The Professor's smile was roguish.

"Ha, ha! You will have your little joke! Not much chance of that, I think. There's no place safer than the London Zoo! Well, I'll walk with you to the exit gate. Good evening, Bunce! Off for the night?" The Inspector turned to a passing keeper.

"Professor McWhirter, this is Bunce. He's working with the Tropical Birds. All well in your department, Bunce?"

"It was, sir, till this afternoon. But then—well, I'm a bit worried. Good evening, Professor McWhirter, sir. I've seen

141

you around quite a bit today. You seemed to be looking for something."

"Lookin'? Och, ay! Ah've been aboot. Ah'm partial to animals, ye ken."

The Professor, with his back to the birdcage, was continuing his search. Something was moving. Was it—? No! Only a branch in the breeze.

"What's wrong, then, Bunce? Is it serious?"

"Well—odd, sir. Odd is what I'd call it. I was going me rounds at three o'clock, and when I opened this here gate, something flew in and knocked off me cap. And when I looked up, there it was. A Carpentarian Cockatoo!"

"A Carpentarian, you say? Haven't we one already?"

"Yes, sir. And we're looking for a mate. But we don't want any common bird. No hoi polloi, if you understand me. But I thought I'd better leave it be, until I got instructions."

"Where is it? Ah, yes, there it is. Up there on the topmost perch. Can you see, Professor?"

"What? Och, ay! Ah'm no' blind yet. Ah saw it floppetin' over the rails round aboot three o'clock."

Professor McWhirter, having tracked the crested fowl to the Zoo, had no further interest in it. It wasn't birds he was after.

"Well, they seem to be quite comfortable, Bunce. I'd call them even sentimental. Let them be—just for tonight. You'll want to get off and see the sights. We'll sort it all out tomorrow. Good night to you. Coming, Professor?"

The white shapes crouching feather to feather were like a single bird. The two yellow crests mingled as each bird preened the other's breast. Up and down went the busy heads —eyes closed, lost to the world—in their mutual act of kind-

142

ness. Sentimental was indeed the word for Louis and his companion.

"Er—I don't want to hurry you, Professor!" The Zoo official made it clear that that was exactly what he did want. "But I know you'll be anxious to see the fireworks—"

"Fireworks? Nay, Ah canna stand them!" The Professor had something else to think of. There! What was that at the end of the bench? A rustle of paper? A body moving?

"It's a great day, isn't it, Professor? Sixty years a queen— God bless her!" Inspector Higget went babbling on.

"Well, it's no' a great day for me!" The animal fancier was testy. He was being bundled out of the Zoo, and he hadn't laid eyes on Monkey. Ah! A shadow flitting behind the kiosk! He darted eagerly towards it, but Inspector Higget grabbed his arm.

"Well, here we are at the exit gate. I'll see you off the premises—that's my job, you know—ha, ha! Good night, Professor. Glad to have met you!"

The gate of the Zoo gave a loud click, and Professor McWhirter, clutching his cape, found himself out in the street.

He stood there, peering through the bars, his brown eye watchful and wary. He was daunted—true!—but still hopeful. At least he knew where the fowl was. And on that fact he could build his plans.

The hedgehog gave a little grunt. The striped mice squeaked in their wooden box. The frog settled closer into the pocket.

"Ay, beasties, Ah'm no forgettin' ye! Ah'll get ye to suitable situations and then Ah'll come back here!"

Professor McWhirter moved away, muttering to himself.

143

Safely off the premises! Drat that pliskie Zoo Inspector! He needed to be on, not off! For there, on those very premises, Monkey—he had no doubt of it—was somewhere to be found.

So—Inspector Higget had been glad to see him!

Well, he had not been at all glad to see Inspector Higget!

10

London was ablaze. Not burning, but ablaze with light—bonfires, floodlights, Chinese Lanterns. Rockets went hissing through the air, popped, and broke into showers of stars, many-coloured, resplendent. Orion, by comparison, was like something on a bargain counter.

There were Catherine Wheels the size of cartwheels; iridescent Waterfalls; Roman Candles; Golden Fountains; Flower Pots; Fizzers; Bangers.

In Hyde Park, there were six brass bands. And a huge balloon, as big as a room, soared up through the teeming stars and vanished in the darkness. The grownups knew it was just a firework. But the children did not believe that. They were certain that, within the balloon, the Queen, perched on a golden throne, was mounting up to Heaven.

The city was like an enormous fairground. People danced in the shining streets and flung themselves into fountains. Some of them even jumped into lakes, fully dressed and hatted.

At the far end of Regent's Park, beyond the fireworks and

the clamour, the Zoo lay dark and quiet. Occasionally a lion roared, telling the world of his homesickness, begging it to take note that a cage is no place for a lion—or any other animal.

The world, however, took no notice. It was too busy enjoying itself. And, anyway, it had never learned the language of beast or bird.

Yes, the Zoo was quiet. But the wire of a cage, every now and then, would give a sudden thrum, as though somebody creeping past had mistakenly brushed against it. There was also a little picking sound, as of someone cutting a thread of wire in order to make a hole. Pick, pick! Thrum! Pick!

And away in Putney, Mr. Linnet, as though he, too, were a caged lion, was pacing up and down.

The older children were out in the garden exclaiming at the rockets.

Mrs. Linnet was doing two things at once—trying to keep Trehunsey quiet and comfort her troubled husband.

"Please don't worry—no, Trehunsey!—people often disappear—my grandmother, seventy-one—found in Spitalfields in her nightgown—lost her memory—rock-a-bye—discovered by my cousin Cedric—my grandmother, not her memory—there, there, go to sleep—grandmother not a monkey, of course—well, we only have to hope and pray—wear yourself out walking. Alfred—also your shoes—another cup—?"

Mr. Linnet shook his head. He had swallowed several cups of tea, and none of them had taken away the ache he felt inside him. What was Monkey doing now? Was he lost? Stolen? Strayed? Had he been found by Professor McWhirter? His imagination presented him with the direst kind of picture—Monkey in a pet-shop window, waiting for

145

someone to buy him. Monkey in a box marked *Fragile* going by train to a distant zoo. Monkey performing in a circus while the vulgar crowd applauded.

Hark, what was that? For the hundredth time he ran to the door. But once again, it was nothing, no one. Only a rocket going pop and raining down its stars.

He looked across at Miss Brown-Potter. There she sat, in a pool of lamplight, sewing a handkerchief for Stanley.

Mr. Linnet was struck with remorse. His thoughts had been entirely of Monkey. But Miss Brown-Potter, he realised, must be wondering where the others were.

She put down her work and smiled at him.

"I have every confidence in Stanley. I am sure he will bring them home."

Suddenly Mr. Linnet felt better. Another cup of tea, after all, was exactly what he needed. Mrs. Linnet dashed to the teapot.

Away in his corner, Uncle Trehunsey was smiling in horrid glee. *He* had no confidence in Stanley. What, confidence in a brat of twelve who was also deaf and dumb? Absurd! He could now look forward, he was sure, to freedom from apes and birds. And from Stanley Fan, for all he cared. He only wished that Professor McWhirter would steal away Miss Brown-Potter, too. Life would then be worth living and he head of the house again.

The night wore on. Mr. Linnet paced. The rockets popped. The bands played.

Across London, in Regent's Park—the far end that was dark and quiet—the picking sounds continued. Pick, pick! Thrum! Pick!

Someone, under cover of darkness, was working away industriously to make a hole in the wire . . .

11

London woke up with a large yawn, looking—and feeling —squeamish. No one ever really enjoys the morning after a party.

The city had to be put in order—streets swept, fountains cleaned, the grass in the parks mown and watered.

It was just the same with private gardens. Lawns and flower beds, even hedges, needed careful attention. Indeed, some hedges, it was said, had been ruined overnight. Gaps and holes had appeared in them, and no one knew whom to blame. Was it, perhaps, the work of children? Inquiries were put to the neighbours.

But not one neighbour owned up. The grownups had no interest in hedges, and the children declared indignantly that whoever made the gaps and holes, it certainly wasn't them.

The day was a cranky sort of day. Jubilees, it was widely felt, were all very well for queens. They could lie on comfortable feather beds with flunkeys to wait upon them. But for everyone else—the Queen's subjects—a Jubilee was exhausting.

But at last the day, as days do, came to its twilit end. Fathers came home and put their feet up. Children went eagerly to bed. The stars shone modestly in the sky, not grudging the rockets their giddy moment, content with their own eternity. The Diamond Jubilee was over.

But in one household it left behind a series of repercussions. For Mr. Linnet's lucky stars were still at work upon him.

He had put in extra time at the office; and now he was leaping down from the bus and tearing along the lamplit street to Miss Brown-Potter's house.

"What news?" he demanded, breathlessly, as he burst in at the door.

Nobody answered. There was no news.

"Professor McWhirter—has he been here?"

No one had seen Professor McWhirter.

"All right! I will go to the police."

Miss Brown-Potter looked up. "Do you really think that wise, Mr. Linnet? Might you not be doing more harm than good? I have no great faith in the police. I would rather leave it to Stanley."

"No great faith in the police—the best police force in the world! Who does the woman think she is?" Uncle Trehunsey blew his nose and muttered the words to his handkerchief.

"You mean—there's nothing to do but wait?"

"That is exactly what I mean." Miss Brown-Potter threaded her needle and bent again to her sewing.

"But policemen often very kind—helping children across the road—found my sister's purse once—three shillings and a penny stamp—and very good-looking, some of them—perhaps if I heated a bowl of soup—" Mrs. Linnet was doing her best to ease the situation.

Edward came in, leading the dogs. He had been busy in the garden, planting his tombstones on the lawn.

"Shall we play Ludo?" Victoria asked, her voice, for once, quite gentle.

"Yes," he agreed, equally kind.

They played together quietly. Neither wanted arguments. Neither even wanted to win. The loss of Monkey, Louis, and Stanley was heavy upon them both.

Up and down. Up and down. Mr. Linnet paced and waited.

He took a bowl of soup and waited.

He began to pace again and waited.

"Children!—should really go to bed—never get up in time in the morning—missing your beauty sleep like this—"

"Please, Mamma!" They both pleaded. Mrs. Linnet had not the heart to insist.

The room was silent—except for the rattle of Ludo dice and Mr. Linnet's pacing.

Miss Brown-Potter's grandfather's clock gathered itself together. It groaned and rumbled and struck ten. And as it sounded the last note, something went thump at the front door.

Mr. Linnet and Miss Brown-Potter sprang to open it.

And Monkey, Stanley Fan, and Louis, wrapped together as one bundle, fell into the waiting arms.

"At last!" Mr. Linnet's voice was shaky. The children patted the formless mass of flesh and fur and feather. Mrs. Linnet hovered and clucked. Little Trehunsey bellowed.

The bundle sorted itself out and became three battered, bedraggled shapes, every one of them speechless. The Linnets could exclaim and enquire, but none of the truants, naturally—Louis being already asleep—was able to speak a word. Only by the look in their eyes could you know that Monkey and Stanley Fan were happy to be home.

"I knew he would manage," said Miss Brown-Potter, as Stanley with a weary smile handed Louis into her keeping and collapsed upon the floor.

"Has he fainted away?" asked Victoria, enthralled at this piece of drama.

"It is just exhaustion," said Miss Brown-Potter, as she steadied Louis on his perch. Then she knelt down at Stanley's side. She felt his forehead. It was cool—and grimy. She felt his feet. They were grimy—and warm. She put a cushion under his head and tucked a rug about him.

And Monkey, seizing the tablecloth, wrapped it about the rug.

"Oh, he's limping!" Miss Brown-Potter cried. "See—there's a gash on his leg." She ran her hands over the furry limbs. "It looks as though he had crawled through wire. We must doctor it."

"Water—ointment—disinfectant—" Mrs. Linnet ran to the medicine chest.

Monkey watched the procedure with interest as Mr. Linnet salved the wound and tied his handkerchief about it. He was grateful. He had received a present. He looked about him eagerly for something to give in return. But his eyes were closing. He was almost asleep.

"They are all worn out," said Miss Brown-Potter. "What they need is rest."

Mr. Linnet took his friend by the paw and led him to his hammock.

Monkey eyed it with satisfaction but not, apparently, for himself. It was just the thing—it seemed to him—for Mr. Linnet to sleep in. So he tugged and pushed and hauled at him in an effort to lift him up.

"No, no, it's *yours*," said Mr. Linnet. "I'm much too big for it. TOO BIG!" he repeated at the top of his voice, as though, if he magnified the sound, Monkey would get the meaning.

The words were gibberish to Monkey, but somehow he understood.

Even so, he was not content. There still was something he could do.

So he stooped and unknotted the handkerchief and tied it round Mr. Linnet's leg. Then he leapt into bed.

"Where have they been? What were they doing? Why are they so dirty?"

Victoria's questions, for once, were apt. But nobody knew how to answer them. Perhaps they would never be answered.

What did it matter, thought Mr. Linnet. Monkey was safely home again. That was enough for him. He made up his mind that, until the locksmith repaired the locks, he would sleep at Monkey's side. And if that wretch, Professor McWhirter, so much as put a nose round the door, he would find someone waiting for him!

The household was happy, the wanderers home. But if that was enough for Mr. Linnet, it was far too much for Uncle Trehunsey. The ape, the bird, and the boy were back. His dream of a peaceful life was shattered . . .

12

"Good morning, Louis!" said Miss Brown-Potter.

"Polly wants a cracker!" Louis replied.

Miss Brown-Potter raised her eyebrows. She had never heard him say that before. The phrase was more suited to a parrot and a rather common parrot, at that. Where could he have learned it?

Stanley brought him his candle end. Louis gave it a finicky sniff and turned his head away.

"Millet seed, Georgie! Polly's Georgie! Millet seed and chickweed!"

This was said in a mincing voice, quite unlike Louis' usual croak. And when they brought him millet seed, he hungrily wolfed it down.

"Extraordinary!" said Miss Brown-Potter. "He seems to have changed his habits."

"Pretty Boy! Where's my Pretty Boy!" Louis, speaking in coaxing accents, thrust out his head at Monkey.

Monkey hastily backed away. Such a gesture, two days ago, would have filled him with grateful joy. But now it seemed to disturb him.

"Georgie scratch Polly!" said Louis, sweetly, as he sidled along the perch.

Monkey leapt to the top of the piano.

"All right, Louis! I'll do it." Victoria ran to the perch.

"Do take care, Victoria—always bad-tempered—nasty bite —might take one of your fingers off—and fingers irreplaceable—"

"No, he won't, Mamma. He likes it."

It was true. Louis, who had never cared to be fondled, was now cooing blissfully as Victoria ruffled his crest.

His habits had indeed changed—also, it seemed, his character.

Where he had once been taciturn, except for his sudden bouts of shouting, he now chattered incessantly in the sentimental, garrulous way of a lady addicted to gossip.

He stood on the table by Miss Brown-Potter telling her

confidentially—as though she had never heard it before—the story of Little Bo-Peep.

And to Uncle Trehunsey, whom hitherto he had always hated, he confided the distressing fact that Johnny was long at the fair.

> *"He promised to buy me a bunch of blue ribbons*
> *To tie up my bonnie brown hair."*

"Grrrr out!" said Uncle Trehunsey rudely, swatting at him with the *Morning Post*.

Louis was hurt but not offended. No matter what anyone did, it seemed, he would forgive and forget. He was full of affection for them all, and none of them felt the better for it.

"Why can't he be like he used to be?" Victoria complained.

"The dogs don't like him now," said Edward. "They think he's rather silly."

"What is he saying?" asked Miss Brown-Potter, as Louis flew to Mrs. Linnet and whispered into her ear.

"Can't hear exactly—it tickles me—sounds like a line of 'God Save the Queen'—and he lives at Twenty-two Stubbs Lane."

"Well, really, I almost wish he did. I can't think what has come over him. He was *never* sentimental."

Miss Brown-Potter's voice was troubled. How could anyone change so quickly? She could not fathom it.

Neither, it appeared, could Monkey.

He would take his stand beside the perch, gazing up at the noble crest with a question in his eyes. Where was his haughty, unfriendly friend? Where was the fierce glint of the eye? Where was his forest brother?

153

And Louis would preen and lean towards him—familiar, saucy, and flirtatious—winningly trying to charm him. "Curly Locks, Curly Locks! Where's my Pretty Boy!"

And Pretty Boy Monkey would leap away with a kind of fear in his eyes.

"He's uneasy," said Miss Brown-Potter, watching. "There's something he doesn't understand."

What could it be, they all wondered. Monkey had, clearly, loved Louis, and Louis had turned his back upon him. And now, it seemed, Louis loved Monkey, and Monkey, far from being glad, was troubled by so much affection.

"It may, of course, be just a phase. His jaunt to—well, wherever he went, Twenty-two Stubbs Lane, perhaps—has unsettled him for the moment."

"Or old age—" Mrs. Linnet suggested. "Senile, perhaps— like my father's mother—no memory—just sweet and simple—very annoying—nobody liked her—"

"Well, no one is going to like Louis if he keeps up his hysterical nonsense."

But whether anyone liked him or not, Louis continued to keep it up and even became more talkative. It seemed as though he could not stop.

He addressed Mr. Linnet as "Daisy, Daisy" and begged him to give him his answer, do. Stanley was asked, "Where and oh, where has my little dog gone?" and of course could give no answer. The repertoire seemed to be endless.

But three days after his adventure—wherever it had taken him—the situation changed. Louis appeared to be out of sorts. Calling anxiously for "Georgie," he began to pluck at his feathers.

"This is too much!" said Miss Brown-Potter. "Do be sen-

sible, Louis, please. You have so much strength of character."

But this appeal to his better nature had no effect on
Louis.

"Twenty-two Stubbs Lanc! Georgie!" As he spoke, he
clambered down from his perch and sat himself on the edge
of his food tray, bending his beak to his breast.

"Polly wants Georgie! Where's Georgie!" It sounded like
a cry for help.

"I think he's in pain," said Miss Brown-Potter, as the
family crowded round the perch. "He's panting and groaning. What is it, Louis?"

"Oh, dear! Poor Polly!" said Louis, faintly. His body
rocked from side to side. He moaned. He sighed. His eyes
turned upward.

Monkey leapt down from the top of the bookcase and
came to stand by the perch. Something was wrong. He
seemed to know it.

"Pretty Boy," said Louis. "Oh, poor Pol—" His voice
failed him. His body heaved.

Then, suddenly, there was a plop. Something fell into the
tray.

"He's laid an egg!" Victoria cried. And Louis, with a sigh,
fell backwards, with his feet turned up in the air.

"So that was it!" said Miss Brown-Potter. "Poor Louis!
And I never guessed. It has all been too much for him—or
her!"

"Is he dead?" asked Edward, anxiously. "If he is, the dogs
won't like it. They might be dead themselves one day, and
they don't want to think about it."

"I'm afraid, Edward—" said Miss Brown-Potter. But she
never finished the sentence.

155

Stanley Fan, hearing no sound, but easily catching the vibration, had hurried from the room.

Someone, very insistently, was ringing the bell of the front door . . .

13

"Excuse me, madam, my name is Bunce—Mr. Bunce of the London Zoo. Your servant boy let me in, but he didn't seem to hear what I said."

A young man, in a uniform rather too big for him, was standing in the doorway. In one hand he held his peaked cap. The other carried a large birdcage, covered with a blanket.

"He is not my servant. He is my friend." Miss Brown-Potter smiled at Stanley.

"Beg pardon. No offence, I'm sure. Perhaps I'd better explain myself."

"I think it would be a good idea," said Miss Brown-Potter, kindly.

"Well, I've come to ask—not intruding, of course—whether you happen to have about you a—well, to put it in a word, madam—a yellow-crested cockatoo?"

Mr. Bunce was uncomfortable. It is not a normal thing to do, to ring a perfect stranger's doorbell and ask, for no apparent reason, if they have a cockatoo.

"I did have one," said Miss Brown-Potter. "But I'm sorry to say that he is dead—or perhaps I should say 'she.' "

Mr. Bunce turned as pale as a lily.

"Dead?" he said, in a hollow voice.

"Yes, alas! Three minutes ago. After laying an egg."

"Dead? An egg?" Mr. Bunce repeated, looking like one who had just been told of the loss of a dear relation.

"Well, he—or she—must have been quite old. And his—her—time had probably come." Miss Brown-Potter sounded tranquil. "Death comes to everyone at last. No good comes of repining."

"Er—could I, madam, view the—?"

"The body? Certainly. There it is."

All that now remained of Louis lay stiff and silent in the food tray, eyes closed, legs in air.

Mr. Bunce knelt down by the tray. He examined Louis' upturned feet and burst into bitter sobbing.

"It is! I was afraid it was. Oh, Nellie, my own dear Nellie!"

Nellie! They all looked at each other. Had Mr. Bunce gone mad?

"The name—" Miss Brown-Potter was very gentle. "The name, Mr. Bunce, is Louis."

"It is not, madam. See for yourself!" Mr. Bunce gathered up the corpse and thrust Louis' claws towards her.

Miss Brown-Potter bent to look. The printing on the metal anklet was clearly legible.

"Nellie," she read out. "Nellie Bunce. Property of the London Zoo."

"So it wasn't Louis, after all!" Victoria broke the shocked silence.

"And we never knew—birds exactly alike—my aunt had twins—couldn't tell them apart—pity!—but natural mistake—" Mrs. Linnet put in a distracted word.

157

How had it happened, they all wondered. They had seen Louis fly away. And after much anxiety, they had seen him brought back on Stanley's shoulder. And now it appeared that Louis was Nellie. What a transformation!

"One of us knew," said Miss Brown-Potter, nodding her head at Monkey. "That was why he was so uneasy. He knew —and he had no way to tell us."

"Oh, Nellie, Nellie!" cried Mr. Bunce, rocking the body in his arms. "She was like a family to me, madam, me being but an orphan."

Miss Brown-Potter was sympathetic. She knew what it was to be left alone.

"Such a beautiful talker, she was! So quick at songs and nursery rhymes. And her character—so ladylike, loving to everyone, and sweet—sweet as a bowl of syrup!"

"It was, indeed!" agreed Miss Brown-Potter, speaking no less than the truth.

"Oh, Nellie, if you could only speak!" The cry came from Mr. Bunce's heart. And then the miracle happened.

"Pretty Boy?" murmured a fainting voice.

The keeper gave a start of surprise.

"She's not dead—after all!" he cried. "Quick—some brandy! Here we are!" He plucked a small bottle from his pocket. "Just a drop of this, Nellie. There, that's better, isn't it?"

Nellie gave a ladylike cough. "Georgie?" she murmured, anxiously. "Twenty-two Stubbs Lane?"

Mr. Bunce smiled at Miss Brown-Potter. "My name and address!" he said, proudly. "Yes, it's your Georgie, Nellie dear!—come to take you home. It must have been the egg, madam. She's never laid an egg before, and the effort made her swoon away."

Nellie eased herself up. "Where's my Pretty Boy?" she enquired, rolling her eye at Monkey.

Monkey leapt to the end of the room.

"No, no! That's not Pretty Boy!" Mr. Bunce was reproachful.

"Daisy, Daisy!" murmured Nellie, clawing her way to the uniformed shoulder and whispering into her friend's ear.

Mr. Bunce laughed delightedly. "She half crazy, she says, madam, all for the love of me!"

"Yes, well— We're all glad, Mr. Bunce, that you have your own bird again. But you haven't told us—"

"How it happened? Well, of course, you'd want to know that, madam. It stands to reason, doesn't it? But, seeing Nellie dead, so to speak—well, it knocked me down with a feather."

"I quite understand," said Miss Brown-Potter, settling herself to listen. She knew how to be patient.

"Well, the other night I was going off duty—yes, Nellie, Georgie's here!—when all of a sudden a white cockatoo flew into the Tropical Birds. That's me, madam, the Tropical Birds. Then it took one look at Nellie here and landed on the perch beside her. Well, it gave me a turn. I didn't like it. But Inspector Higget said leave it be, it being the Jubilee and all, and we'd deal with it tomorrow."

Miss Brown-Potter, all attention, nodded.

"Well, next day, when I unlocked the cage, there was only one bird there. The other had been stolen, madam. Someone had made a hole in the wire, big enough for a man—or a boy. Inspector Higget didn't half slay me. Might have lost the whole Tropical Section and then what would we do, he said. Yes, Nellie, she's lost her sheep, but they'll come home wagging their tails."

"You were saying?" Miss Brown-Potter prompted. What she wanted to hear about was not Nellie but Louis.

"Well, then we mended it, of course—the hole, I mean, not the bird. But I felt in my bones there was something wrong. Nellie didn't say good morning! She flies to meet me every day—yes, you do, don't you, Nellie? But this time, madam, she turned her back. That's enough of Bo-Peep, Nellie. Sing Little Boy Blue."

Miss Brown-Potter serenely waited. The story was evidently a long one and Nellie and her repertoire an intimate part of it.

" 'She's off her food!' I thought to myself," Mr. Bunce continued. "So up I climbed to see what was wrong. And, oh, madam, I was shocked! You should have heard the things she said. To think of Nellie, so refined, using such language —it broke my heart."

"I am sorry for that," said Miss Brown-Potter. "A broken heart is a painful thing."

"It was. It was like a knife in my bosom. And then I looked at Nellie's name-tag and it wasn't her at all!"

"Who was it?" Miss Brown-Potter asked. She knew they were now at the heart of the matter.

"I'm coming to that," said Mr. Bunce. "But I have to take my time. Well, then I told Inspector Higget. And he said, 'They've got the wrong bird, Bunce. Taken Nellie and left their own!' He's as clever as a book, the Inspector. As soon as he read the tag, he knew. 'Twenty-seven Belvedere Gardens. That's the place to look, Bunce. You just hop along there,' he said, 'and I'll deal with the rest.' "

"The rest?" said Miss Brown-Potter, quickly. "What do you mean by the rest?"

"Well, we have to find the culprit, madam. But that will

be for Inspector Higget. All I know is, he's got a witness, even more than one, perhaps. And he's taking the matter to the police. It'll have to go to court, he says."

"I see," said Miss Brown-Potter, gravely. The thought of the culprit—whoever he was— having to go to a court of law was not a happy prospect.

"Well, it stands to reason, doesn't it? You can't have people climbing in, making holes in the Zoo!"

"But—since you have your own bird back, I would have thought the matter could drop. Why carry it further?"

"Ah, but you've got to right the wrong! Somebody made a hole in the Zoo. Somebody took my Nellie away and left another bird in her place—a bird with your address on its leg. You can't get around that, can you?"

Mr. Bunce knew the order of things. An eye had to be paid for an eye. After all, it stood to reason.

"But, Miss Brown-Potter—" Victoria cried, doubtless embarking upon a question. The question, however, remained unspoken, extinguished by a loud cry from the throat of Mr. Bunce.

"Brown-Potter! Did you say *Brown-Potter?* Can it be, madam, begging your pardon, that you are *the* Miss Brown-Potter?"

"I am *a* Miss Brown-Potter," said Miss Brown-Potter.

"Female explorer? Friend of Stanley and Livingstone? Discoverer of the Uncommon, Screechless, Blue-Breasted Owl in Equatorial Africa? Presented a pair to the London Zoo? Mated—the pair of owls, I mean—and now sitting on a clutch of eggs? Is that who you are?" cried Mr. Bunce. He was breathless with excitement.

"Well, yes, I am," said Miss Brown-Potter, calmly accepting her moment of fame.

161

"Miss Brown-Potter!" said Mr. Bunce, apparently struck with wonder. "And your Christian name, if I may ask?"

"Sophia," Miss Brown-Potter answered.

"Sophia!" Mr. Bunce was enchanted. He tested the syllables on his tongue. "If one of the eggs is a female, madam, I shall name it after you. Think of it! A clutch of Brown-Potterianas and one of them to be called Sophia! Inspector Higget will be delighted. I must go right back and tell him. Yes, Nellie, you're going home! I'll just put you into your nice cage— Good gracious, I had quite forgotten—!"

Mr. Bunce's face clouded. He looked with displeasure at the birdcage. Then, with the air of someone compelled to perform an unpleasant but necessary duty, he swept the blanket from it.

A scream of anger split the air.

"Hell's bells! Whoa, there! Hold yer hoof up, can't yer?" Louis emerged and flew to his perch.

"Really, madam, I'm ashamed! To have to bring back such a dreadful bird! And to you—of all people, Miss Brown-Potter! To think you should have to hear such language!"

Mr. Bunce shook his head at Miss Brown-Potter's unhappy fate.

"I am used to it." Miss Brown-Potter smiled. "And I'm fond of him, Mr. Bunce."

Fond of him? Mr. Bunce knew better. It was just her nobility of heart, the heart of a great female explorer. No one on earth could be fond of Louis!

"Spit in yer eye! Gitt on! Gitt out!" said Louis, in his trooper's voice.

Mr. Bunce turned his back in disgust and escorted Nellie to the cage as though she were a duchess.

"There you are! Sit on the perch like a little lady! We'll

soon be home and you'll get a cracker! I wonder, madam—"
He hesitated. He was about to beg a favour and knew it
was a lot to ask.

"I wonder if I could have the egg? It's Nellie's first, and
I'd like to keep it, just as sort of a memento—"

"Of course you would! I will get it for you."

But the egg was nowhere to be found. It was not in the
tray. Not on a chair. Not on the piano. Not on a shelf. It had
disappeared as if by magic.

"Extraordinary!" they all said.

"Did you take it, Victoria?" Mrs. Linnet was anxious.

"Mamma, you're always blaming me! I never even
touched it."

"I wouldn't want it," said Edward, quickly. "The dogs
never cared for Nellie."

Not care for Nellie! The keeper stared. The little fellow
must be joking. *Everybody* cared for Nellie. And there
wasn't a dog to be seen.

"It's a pity it's lost," he said, sadly. "It must have been a
lovely egg. But you can't have everything, I suppose. And
after all—" His face brightened. "I've got my Nellie back
again, and I daresay, in the course of time, she'll lay another
one. So, thank you, madam, Miss Brown-Potter. It's been a
pleasure, so to say, you and Nellie between you. Well, I must
get back to the Tropical Birds. You'll be hearing from the
Zoo, of course. Or else the police. One or the other."

Mr. Bunce, still bent on righting the wrong, regretfully
took his leave.

Miss Brown-Potter stood on the doorstep watching him
walk away, a young man in a uniform that seemed to be
made for a larger man; a young man carrying in a birdcage
all that he had of family back to the London Zoo.

So that was where Louis had been! He had spent the night in the Tropical Section. And someone had made a hole in the wire and stolen him away. Or rather, someone had abstracted Nellie, mistaking her for Louis. The first part of the problem was solved, Miss Brown-Potter reflected. And Fate, as she knew from experience, would reveal the rest in its own good time. It was just a matter of waiting.

The drawing-room, when she returned to it, had an air of quiet contentment. Uncle Trehunsey was still asleep. Mrs. Linnet and the two children were chatting together like three children. Louis was eating a candle end. Stanley was standing at his side offering beer in a teaspoon.

And Monkey, peaceful and contented, was sitting on the floor by the perch unwinding all the reels of thread in Miss Brown-Potter's sewing basket.

Miss Brown-Potter made no protest. It was Monkey's way, she well knew, of doing something helpful . . .

14

The days passed.

Family life went on as usual, up and down, like a switch-back.

The locksmith came and did his work in order to foil Professor McWhirter. But Mr. Linnet, just to be sure, slept at night on the drawing-room sofa to be within reach of Monkey.

Louis, after his night out, seemed to have settled down. He still shouted, complained, and sang. But his moment of passion and rage had passed, and a quiet word from Miss Brown-Potter had all its old power to restrain him.

And, of course, with Louis himself again, Monkey again proffered his friendship. And again Louis turned his back. He needed help from nobody, not even his forest brother.

The daily problems came and went, and somehow everyone survived them, except that Uncle Trehunsey's temper seemed to grow steadily worse.

This was because of the morning paper.

On the morning after the Jubilee he had woken up feeling fresh and cheerful. Stanley, Monkey, and Louis were gone—forever, as he hoped. And at any moment his nephew Alfred would bring him the morning's *Times*. He was looking forward to reading the news and seeing photographs of the Queen.

But things had turned out differently.

It was Miss Brown-Potter who brought the paper. "You'll want to read all about the Queen," she told him, with a smile.

There she was, at it again, telling him what he wanted! He had snatched the paper from her hand and flung it across the room.

"Never read daily papers, thank you! They're nothing but tommyrot and twaddle!"

And what had Miss Brown-Potter done? She had agreed with him.

"How right you always are, Mr. Truro! Just what I would have said myself. I will tell the newsboy not to call."

And the woman—blast her impudence!—the woman had kept her word. The newsboy's visits were discontinued, and

Uncle Trehunsey was left to simmer in the stew he himself had made.

He fumed and fretted continually. What was going on in the world? Who was alive and who was dead? What about wars and tidal waves and burglars caught with the swag, red-handed? None of the household seemed to know, none of them seemed to care. And to make matters worse, the ape, the bird, and the boy had come back and were welcomed as though they were long-lost princes instead of a trio of riff-raff.

Like a desert camel thirsting for rain, Uncle Trehunsey thirsted for news and longed to be anywhere else in the world but the house in Belvedere Gardens.

Both wishes were granted, as we shall see, though in a roundabout, backhanded way, very far from his expectations. The danger in making any wish is the chance that it may come true. And Fate has a way of doing things that is often quite unscrupulous . . .

15

News came in the form of Mr. Linnet. He rushed up the steps one Friday evening and burst in at the front door, panting with excitement.

"I've done it! I've made the Twenty Pounds. Count it, please, Uncle Trehunsey! And I'm not to go to work on Monday. They've given me a holiday!"

He waved a letter in the air as his family crowded about him.

"What is in it? Read it, Papa!"

"It's from the General Manager. This is what it says: 'Our Mr. Perks will call on Monday to discuss with you certain serious matters. Will you, therefore, kindly remain at home and thus be at his disposal?' There, now! What do you think of that? They probably mean to raise my wages!"

Mr. Linnet's eyes were bright. He knew that he was a good worker—careful, punctual, and tidy. Moreover, he truly loved his work. It gave him pleasure to do it well. And now they were going to reward him. He would buy a present for everyone. A pretty summer dress for his wife—the old one was getting very shabby. And for Miss Brown-Potter? His thoughts stumbled. What could he ever give Miss Brown-Potter? All he could do was die for her, and that she didn't need.

"Or perhaps a little presentation—!" Mrs. Linnet rejoiced at the news. "Silver sugar-tongs or a cruet—my grandfather given a gold watch—been with his firm for fifty years—never kept good time, however—very proud of you, Alfred—"

Uncle Trehunsey counted his money. The fact that it was all there, twenty hard-earned golden sovereigns, gave him a feeling of frustration. There was one thing less to grumble at.

"Fight the good fight with all thy might!" Louis added a line from the hymn book to the general celebration.

"Police! Police!" Victoria shouted. She had seen Stanley staring through the window and had rushed away to join him. "There's one of them coming up the path. What do you think he wants, Mamma?"

Uncle Trehunsey craned his head, watching the solid navy-blue figure striding toward the door.

The door-knocker banged and shook the house. The door-bell gave a commanding peal.

Miss Brown-Potter turned to Stanley. But Stanley clasped his hands together and gave her a look of entreaty. Something was wrong. For a reason yet to be made clear, Stanley, who answered to every need, was anxious not to answer the door. Silently she reassured him, nodding her head and smiling.

Another knock. Another peal.

"Would *you* go, Mr. Linnet, please?" Miss Brown-Potter inclined her head.

Mr. Linnet ran to the door, closely followed by Mrs. Linnet, with Little Trehunsey in her arms and the children at her heels.

And presently the Policeman entered, standing majestically in the doorway, a symbol of the law.

Uncle Trehunsey turned from the window and eyed him with satisfaction. Somebody—or so he hoped—was about to get their deserts. But where was the ape? Where was the boy? They seemed to have disappeared.

"Excuse me, madam." The Policeman coughed. "But am I addressing Miss Black-Potter?"

"Brown-Potter," answered Miss Brown-Potter, standing there as if made of marble, her long cloak falling about her.

"Black or brown, they're much the same." The Policeman dismissed his mistake as a trifle. "Well, I've come about the illegal entry—the one in the London Zoo."

"Hold your hoof up! Whoa, there!" shrieked Louis from his perch.

"Louis!" said Miss Brown-Potter, gently. And Louis, rolling a baleful eye, reduced his voice to a mutter.

"The dogs don't like policemen. Their feet are too big!" wailed Edward.

"He's a cry-baby, isn't he, Mamma?"

"Now, Edward. Now, Victoria—"

"Don't you worry, young feller-me-lad. Joe Boskin never hurt a dog. And it isn't dogs he's after." The Policeman glanced about the room. Where were the dogs? He couldn't see them. Shut up in kennels, he supposed.

"An illegal entry, you were saying—" Miss Brown-Potter reminded him. "But why should you come to me about it?"

"Well, who else would we come to, madam? The clues all lead to this address. It was printed on the bird's anklet. I'd have thought you'd be expecting a visit. Surely you read the papers?"

"NO, WE DO NOT!"

Uncle Trehunsey, stung to the quick, gave violent vent to his feelings.

Not read the papers! The words appeared to stun the Policeman. How could you ever know anything, unless you read the papers?

"Mr. Truro decided—and I agreed—that there's never any news in them. They're nothing but tommyrot and twaddle," said Miss Brown-Potter, calmly. She smiled across at Uncle Trehunsey who looked as though he would like to strike her.

"Well, I don't know what you call this—" The Policeman rummaged in a pocket and produced a newspaper cutting.

There was the Queen sitting up in her carriage. There was the cloudy mass of faces, all with their mouths wide open. And there was Louis crossing the road, the hooves of horses rearing above him, his beak agape as though he were singing.

"If that isn't news, I'm an Eskimo!" The Policeman's words were a reprimand. "Why, it's been a scandal for three weeks—a parakeet holding up the Queen and two boys charging after it."

"I see no boys," said Miss Brown-Potter, as she handed the cutting to Mr. Linnet.

"They may not be in the picture, madam. But several people have testified that they pushed through the crowd and disturbed the peace. One was wearing yellow breeches, and the other was in a fur coat with a sailor cap on his head."

"But what has this to do with the Zoo?"

"That, madam, is where the police come in. We tracked them there through witnesses. The whole story is in my notebook." The Policeman coughed and began to read.

" 'On the morning of the Jubilee,' says a lady called Mrs. de Quincey Belmore, 'I was looking in at a shop in Bond Street when a bird alighted on my hat, making horrible noises. It was followed, when it flew away, by two boys—one in yellow trousers, the other in a fur coat.' The same two boys, you see, madam." The Policeman smiled a superior smile. "And the next thing we know they're in Portland Place, a stone's throw from the Zoo. A woman, by the name of Muckett, says: 'I was a-scrubbin' of the doorstep when a parrot lights on the edge of me bucket and two lads nearly knocks me down—one in yellow what-you-may-call-its and the other wearin' a fur jacket.' "

"You fool! You jackass!" cried Uncle Trehunsey. "That wasn't a boy in a fur jacket. Anyone with half an eye—"

"IF YOU PLEASE!" The Policeman held up a lordly hand. "I'll thank you, sir, to be polite. No one insults this uniform, not with Joe Boskin in it. And Mrs. Muckett, like anyone else, knows a fur coat when she sees one. Now, where had I got to? Ah, yes!" He consulted his notes again.

"Well, the bird is now *within* the Zoo. Testified to by Inspector Higget and a keeper by the name of Bunce. It's dark. It's just about closing time. The boys are hovering about—"

"You saw them?" asked Miss Brown-Potter, quickly. Mr. Linnet's back stiffened.

"Not with my own two eyes, no. But a Mr. Hodge from Cheapside saw them. He'd jumped in the lake and lost his boots and was drying himself at a bonfire. 'I see a couple of lads,' he says, 'fiddling with the wire. One had yellow bows at the knee and the other was wrapped in a kind of hearthrug. But being as I was with a lady, the incident ran out of me head, like water out of a bottle.' "

"I see. And did it run in again?"

"It did, madam, a little later. I was on duty in Regent's Park, and he came and told me, as was proper. So of course I went in search."

"And you found them?" Miss Brown-Potter enquired. She and all the Linnet family had become, as it were, a single ear, as they listened to the story.

"No, they'd gone, I'm sorry to say." The Policeman's voice was disapproving. "There was nothing but a gaping hole. And a queer old fellow in a kilt, peering among the bushes."

Mr. Linnet stifled a groan. That fellow in a kilt again! Would he never be free of Professor McWhirter?

"So I stopped and asked him if he'd seen them, and he went off pop like a rocket. 'That's no' a laddie!' he says to

171

me—I'd described the way they looked, of course. 'The one in a fur coat is a monkey, ye great gawky galoot!' Well! That was no way to speak to the law. And I told him so, as you may suppose."

Miss Brown-Potter and Mr. Linnet did, indeed, suppose it.

"And then—just think!—he tried to bribe me. Five pounds, if I found the monkey for him. A valuable specimen, he said, that he wanted for his collection. So then I realised he was mad. No one goes round collecting boys. Mad as a March Rabbit he was, with guinea pigs poking about in his pockets and a white rat running round his hat-brim!"

"But it *was* a monkey, you idiot!" Uncle Trehunsey pounded the floor. He had depended on law and order, the kind of law and the kind of order that would put things right for Trehunsey Truro. And here was a servant of law and order throwing everything into confusion.

"I'll thank you, sir, to mind your language." The Policeman held up his hand again. "Boys may be boys, but they're still human. No need to call them nasty names."

"But he's *not* a boy, I keep telling you! He's an ape, a monkey, a baboon. You're an ape yourself, if you don't believe me!"

Uncle Trehunsey waved his stick, and the Policeman, flushing angrily, was just about to seize upon it when Miss Brown-Potter intervened.

"Mr. Truro, I am sorry to say, is badly afflicted with gout."

"Gout!" The Policeman's face cleared. The old chap was not insulting him. He was simply driven wild by pain and didn't know what he was saying.

"That's what my old grand-dad had. Stark raving with it, he was. Threw a cricket ball at me once and nearly put out my eye. And curse! My goodness, you should have heard him! Why, you're an angel, Mr. Truro, compared to my old grand-dad."

An angel! A silly feathered thing in a halo! Uncle Trehunsey was affronted. He was a match, any day, for anyone's old grand-dad. He wished that he had a cannonball to throw at old grand-dad's grandson.

"So there we were—" Having disposed of Uncle Trehunsey, the Policeman resumed his story. "The two boys had stolen the bird—the wrong one, as it turned out—and were bringing it, the police assume, back to this address. You will not deny, I suppose, madam, that Nellie did arrive here?"

"Oh, dear, no!" answered Miss Brown-Potter. "No one would think of denying that. Her visit was unforgettable."

"Well, if she arrived, then someone brought her. And the evidence points to these two boys. It shows them heading south for Putney and always described in the same way. Constable Cobb, in Hyde Park, saw them. 'The one in the sailor cap,' he says, 'offered to shake my hand. Cheeky, I thought it, and went in pursuit, but he climbed up a tree and vanished.' "

The thought of Monkey presenting his paw and Constable Cobb rejecting it was repugnant to Mr. Linnet. Had he been a terrier, he would have nipped the Policeman's leg.

"And now where are we?" the Policeman enquired. The question was merely a matter of form, for he alone knew the answer. "No less a place than Belgrave Square! Lady Mary Muffett states: 'Saw them hail a hansom cab that was waiting to take my two children to the Swans' party in Cheyne

173

Walk. The cabby drove away with them, leaving my children behind.' A hansom cab—whatever next?" The Policeman was indignant.

"I have no idea," answered Miss Brown-Potter. "The story is yours, not mine."

"Well, believe it or not, they went to the party. 'Two hooligans,' says Mr. Swan, 'presented themselves in fancy dress —one disguised as a sort of monkey, the other as a page boy. I sent a footman to deal with them, but they ran off down the street.' You see, madam, we're getting hotter. Cheyne Walk is along the river, and from there it's a step to the Battersea Bridge where they're seen by a Mr. Thrummer. 'One boy,' he says, 'was in yellow breeks. The other was in his underwear—a pair of brownish combinations—and hanging by his tail from a lamp-post.' "

"What did I tell you?" bawled Uncle Trehunsey. "Hanging by his tail, you said. Well, what hangs by its tail but a monkey?"

"Now, sir, you leave all this to me. You've enough to do, taking care of that foot." The Policeman's voice was indulgent. "We believe that to be a slip of the tongue. What Mr. Thrummer meant was leg. Most boys like to hang by their legs."

"I don't," said Edward. "It makes me giddy."

The Policeman dismissed the remark as un-boyish.

"And where does that bring us?" asked Miss Brown-Potter, pursuing the thread of the story. Fate, in the person of the law, was revealing, as she had known it would, all that Stanley, Louis, and Monkey had not been able to tell.

"Almost home." The Policeman was cheerful. He was nearing the moment, he was sure, when he could make an arrest.

174

"We've come to Theodora Buildings, two or three streets away from here, where a Mrs. Mildred Twistle says, 'I'm bringing home a bag of washing, and a lad in a hair-shirt tries to help me. Insists on carrying it, he does, and spills it all on the pavement. A fat lot of help, I don't think!' "

"Well, at least he tried," said Miss Brown-Potter, who had many such memories of Monkey.

"And lastly, there is Mr. Tarpitt of Kingsley Drive, just around the corner. 'Two boys,' he says, 'crashed through my hedge, making a nasty hole. It was dark, but I'll swear in a witness box that the one wearing the fur coat ate three of my best begonias.' "

The Policeman's notebook closed with a snap. He had come to the end of his shameful tale and was ready to pounce on the villains.

"Well, there is the evidence, Miss Brown-Potter. It brings us practically to your door. So—what have you to say?"

"Very little, I'm afraid. No great crime has been committed. Both birds are safely home again. And that should be the end of it."

"But, madam, don't you understand? It's the principle of the thing. We can't have boys making holes in the Zoo, riding about in hansom cabs, eating people's begonias—and let them off scot free! It wouldn't be right. They have to be punished. Have you no respect for the law?"

"Not a great deal," said Miss Brown-Potter. "It is often so very stupid."

Stupid! The law? The Policeman was shocked. Could it be that Miss Brown-Potter, too, was driven mad by gout? And therefore not responsible for anything she said? He gave her the benefit of the doubt.

"Well, whatever you think of the law, madam, my duty is

to find those boys." He sniffed the air like an eager bloodhound, peering under chairs and tables, cocking his head at the grand piano with its huge wide-open lid.

"Well, they're not in this room, evidently. But they could be elsewhere in the house. With your permission I will search it."

"Pray do so." Miss Brown-Potter smiled. "You will find no doors or cupboards locked. The cellar is a little damp. I hope you will not catch cold."

"Ha, ha! The damp won't worry me. I've never had a cold in my life!" Shrewdly making up his mind to search the cellar with special care, the Policeman strode away. Ladies, he thought, never realised that by trying to warn you off the scent they were probably giving the game away.

"But—Miss Brown-Potter—" cried Victoria. She was clearly determined to ask a question.

"Victoria!" said Miss Brown-Potter, in the voice she used for Louis. And Victoria found herself, like Louis, reduced to uneasy silence.

The Policeman's footsteps shook the house. They could hear him scrabbling in cupboards, clumsily crawling under beds, trying to silence Tinker and Badger as he rummaged about in the eiderdown.

Uncle Trehunsey's thoughts were cheerful. The ape and the boy, apparently, had hidden themselves in some murky corner while he had been looking out of the window. Well, they couldn't hope to escape the law, no matter how artful they were. Despite the increasing pain in his ankle—it seemed to be bound about with rope—he permitted himself a smile. He pictured the two of them in prison, or away in some colony, perhaps, hauling rocks up a hill. The pictures filled him with pleasure.

Mr. Linnet's imagination presented him with similar scenes, and they filled him with consternation. He sent Miss Brown-Potter a questioning glance, hoping for a sign. Where were Monkey and Stanley hidden? Why had she let the house be searched?

But Miss Brown-Potter made no move. She stood there, straight as a poplar tree, tranquil and unconcerned.

She was waiting. They were all waiting—silent, watchful, expectant.

The Policeman was now coming up from the cellar, his feet thump-thump on the kitchen stairs. And somewhere a pair of voices sang—

> *"O believe me, if all those endearing young charms*
> *That I gaze on so fondly today*
> *Were to change by tomorrow and fleet in my arms*
> *Like fairy gifts fading away—"*

Light footsteps were running up and down. Taffeta skirts rustled and fled. Somebody laughed and hurried away. Then again there was silence.

Atishoo!

The sound of a sneeze made everyone jump. And there at the door the Policeman stood, a changed and sorry sight.

His rosy face was black with coal dust. His helmet, with a dent in the crown, sat sideways on his head. And the uniform with Joe Boskin in it had shrunk at least six inches.

Atishoo! The Policeman sneezed again. He had caught the first cold of his life!

"There's two feet of water id your cellar, badab, and the coal shed leaves buch to be desired." He trumpeted into his handkerchief.

177

"Indeed it does," Miss Brown-Potter agreed. "I have sent for the carpenter many times, but he never seems to come. I am sorry you had to get so wet. Did you find what you were looking for?"

"I did dot, badab. The only persons perceived by be were the gentlemad ad the young lady—visitors, I daresay—cavorting on the stairs. I asked them about the two boys, but they only laughed and ran away. I can't say they were helpful."

"Not visitors," said Miss Brown-Potter. "You were speaking to my parents."

"Your parents?" The Policeman stared. The old girl's barmy! he told himself. Those people on the stairs were young, and she must be easily—

"Fifty-four," said Miss Brown-Potter, as though she had read his thoughts.

Fifty-four! Then what he had seen had been—oh, no! The Policeman shuddered at the thought. It was he who had disappeared, not they. They had run right through him and never seen him. For them, he was nothing but space and air.

"I am glad you saw them," said Miss Brown-Potter. "I like to know they are there."

"*You* bay like it, but I do dot. I wasn't sent to look for ghosts, just a couple of lads. I'b satisfied they're dot in the house. But that doesn't say they won't be—sobeday."

"Someday?" Miss Brown-Potter echoed.

"Well, chickens and troubles cobe hobe to roost. And you don't know that the boys won't, do you? So, badab, I will take my leave. Always remembering, of course, that it may be au revoir—atishoo!"

The Policeman, amid a cloud of sneezes, stumbled towards the front door. Mr. Linnet rushed to let him out, waved him hurriedly away, and dashed back with his question.

But he found that he did not need to ask it.

Miss Brown-Potter's eyes were shining. She had folded back the wing of her cloak, and Stanley Fan, amid exclamations, was stepping out from beneath it.

"He was there all the time and nobody knew!" Victoria clapped her hands.

"Gracious me—would never have guessed—almost faint with anxiety—remember when we lost my sister—six weeks old, found in a drawer—mother rather absentminded—however, no bones broken—" Mrs. Linnet fussed and clucked.

Uncle Trehunsey's disappointment was clear upon his face. He had hoped that Stanley was well on his way, if not to Australia, at least to jail. And here he was being petted and patted like any Shah of Persia.

But where was the ape? He looked about him. And the band on his ankle seemed to move.

"Oh—ouch—murder—ooh!" He let out a roar of pain.

Stanley Fan sprang to his aid, but somebody else was already there. Someone, indeed, who had been there for quite a little time.

A tail uncurled itself from the ankle; the rug rose up as if bewitched, disclosing a slim brown shape.

Uncle Trehunsey's mouth opened, but no word could he say. The realisation that he himself, and he alone, had sheltered the culprit from the law, left him—for once—quite speechless.

"We are not divi-ided, All one body we!" Louis broke into his hymn again, as Monkey went round the family circle hugging each in turn.

"Hark! What was that?" said Miss Brown-Potter. "Louis, do be quiet!"

Something—or somebody—was tapping. A wren at the window? A child at the door?

Tap, tap. Tap, tap. The sound was urgent.

"It's coming from inside his cap!" Edward pointed at Monkey. And Monkey, at the same moment, put up his paw to his head.

Tap, tap. Tap, tap. What could it be?

Slowly Monkey took off his cap and held it out before him.

Within the cap lay a white egg. And within the egg there was something moving, making a crack in the surface.

Tap, tap. The watching family held its breath as a beak came thrusting through the shell and a small, wet shapeless shape fell into Monkey's paw.

"Mamma, it must be Nellie's egg! He hid it in his cap!" Victoria had to put into words what everyone else understood without them.

"He hatched it out himself," said Edward. "The dogs are very pleased."

"Bread and milk!" Mrs. Linnet cried. "Or cod-liver oil—and a little sugar—" She hurried away to the kitchen.

"On then, Christian soldiers, On to victory!" Louis, not to be deterred, burst into song again.

"Cheep-croak!" came an echo from Monkey's paw.

Miss Brown-Potter bent down and stroked the clumsy, naked thing.

"Hallelujah!" she said to Mr. Linnet. "Our friend will have a friend!"

"Hallelujah, indeed!" echoed Mr. Linnet, looking from Monkey's friend to Monkey.

"What does Hallelujah mean?" Victoria demanded.

"I think," said Edward, thoughtfully, "it has something to do with praise."

With a snort, their great-uncle found his voice.

"Hallelujah, fiddlesticks! It's just another blasted bird . . ."

PART III

Friend Monkey's Kingdom

1

Mr. Perks was an important person. He was the Chief Clerk of the London Shipping Company, who knew every detail of every ship as well as he knew his own face, which was one that kept itself to itself and gave nothing away.

Mr. Perks could tell, without referring to a list, the exact moment when the *London Trader* was expected in Bombay; where the *London Belle* would be on the fifteenth of September; how many patches had to be sewn on the sails of the *London Explorer;* why the *London Adventurer* carried two anchors instead of one.

The seas of the world, and all their ports and anchorages, flowed through the mind of Mr. Perks, with dolphins, whales and treasure-trove, mermaids, messages in bottles, penguins, polar bears. But Mr. Perks never noticed them. For him they were merely words and phrases, to be written down in a ledger.

Today was Monday. And Mr. Perks, long and flat as an account book, was walking along Belvedere Gardens with a message for one of his underlings—a checking-clerk whose name was filed under the letter L.

Mr. Linnet, as requested by the head of the firm, had obediently stayed at home. What had the letter said? "To discuss certain serious matters." He permitted himself a little smile. General Managers, he thought, had a curious way of expressing themselves. Serious matters! And yet, when he came to think of it, what could be more serious, in the very best sense of the word, than the recognition of faithful service?

"This way, sir," he said, cheerfully, as he opened the door for Mr. Perks and led the way to Miss Brown-Potter's father's study.

He waited shyly while Mr. Perks, carefully examining the room, chose the most imposing chair and placed his case on the desk. The dispatch case, Mr. Linnet noted, was thin and flat and without a bulge. It did not appear to contain a cruet, or even a pair of sugar-tongs. So the serious matter could only refer to a rise in his weekly salary!

"How very kind!" thought Mr. Linnet. It was something he had never expected, and he hoped to do his best to deserve it.

"Well!" Mr. Perks said, windily—one of his front teeth was missing, and his breath, as he spoke, whistled through the gap. "You certainly do yourself proud—a megogonny desk, or whatever you call it, and all those picture paintings!" He glanced at Miss Brown-Potter's ancestors who stared from the walls in their gilded frames.

"Oh, I don't live here," Mr. Linnet protested, quickly disclaiming the grandeur. And Miss Brown-Potter's ancestors seemed to turn their heads to look at him.

"Not live here?" whistled Mr. Perks.

"Oh, no! This is Miss Brown-Potter's house. I'm just a sort of guest, you know. I don't really live anywhere—at any rate, not for the moment. Well, I do and I don't, if you get my meaning."

Mr. Linnet's happy excitement was making him quite

confused. Besides, his present situation was difficult to explain.

"My own home," he tried again. "Though it isn't really mine, of course, is being repaired, Mr. Perks. We—I—*it* —well, it caught on fire."

"What do you mean—you do and you don't? Try to be more precise, Linnet. Everyone lives somewhere, you know. And you gave us this address for the files."

Mr. Perks seemed displeased, as though Mr. Linnet were a shipping item that had willfully got into the wrong column.

"Oh, they do, sir, I know, and so do I. As a rule, I live next door, with my uncle. Or rather, I mean my wife's uncle. Well, mine or hers, we're never quite sure. Not that it really matters."

"Not matter? Your own uncle and he doesn't matter?" Mr. Perks' disapproving words came piping through the gap.

Mr. Linnet sighed. How could he possibly explain that whomever Uncle Trehunsey belonged to, the effect was just the same.

"I'm afraid you have an untidy mind. It always pays to be accurate, Linnet. Well, I daresay you know what I've come about." Mr. Perks raised an enquiring eyebrow as he slipped some papers out of the case.

Mr. Linnet looked modestly down. To answer, he felt, would not be becoming.

"No? I'm surprised!" Mr. Perks studied his clip of papers. "Well, of course, it's about your two children—"

"Three!" interrupted Mr. Linnet, whipping a photograph out of his pocket. He handed it across the desk, glancing proudly at what, to him, were a very pretty little girl, a thoughtful and poetic boy, and a bonny, bouncing baby.

Mr. Perks studied the photograph. He saw three children

187

grouped together, a simpering, self-conscious girl, a rather dejected little boy, and a naked infant on a sheepskin rug, scowling into the camera.

It is strange that two people can look at the same picture and see such different things.

"Hm." Mr. Perks seemed unimpressed. "This must have been taken some time ago."

"Oh, no, quite lately, Mr. Perks. A month or two at the most!"

"A month or two! I can hardly believe it! To have started off on the downward path at such an early age! So young to be making such a commotion! Really, most deplorable!"

"Commotion? Off on the downward path?" Mr. Linnet stared.

"Yes, yes, the commotion. The breach of the peace. Caused by two children from this address. Come, Linnet! You look as though you had lost your wits. You will not ask me to believe, I hope, that Miss Brown-Butter has any children!"

"Potter, sir," said Mr. Linnet.

"Potter? What potter? Who said anything about a potter? Please stick to the point!"

"The name of the lady, Mr. Perks."

"Oh! Well, Potter or Butter, what does it matter? Miss Potter has no children, I take it?"

"*Brown*-Potter," said Mr. Linnet. "No, sir." Stanley Livingstone Fan, he reflected, was Miss Brown-Potter's friend. He could not, in truth, be called her child.

"Then it all comes back to you, Linnet. Well, don't just sit there shaking your head. You must know what I've come about. Surely you read the papers?"

"No, sir. At least, not recently. I've been saving every

188

penny, you see, to pay back the sum of—er—twenty pounds."

"In debt to the bank? This is most improper. Especially for anyone employed by the famous London Shipping Line." Mr. Perks looked round for his hat as though, at the name of his company, he would have liked to raise it. But the hat had been left in the front hall.

"Not to the bank, sir. To my—our—uncle." Mr. Linnet thought of the golden sovereigns and all the work he had done to get them.

"Really, I am quite shocked! I have always thought you a model worker—methodical, punctual, and precise. And, above all, honest. But now I find you are just the reverse. You pretend you don't know where you live. You fob off your uncle on to your wife, and then borrow money from the poor old man! No wonder your children have gone astray. You have not been a proper example."

"Mr. Perks, there must be some mistake!" Mr. Linnet took the photograph and stowed it, safe and warm, in his pocket. "My children are quiet and good-mannered. They haven't done anyone any harm. There's a misunderstanding, somehow, somewhere—"

Suddenly he was all confusion. His happy excitement had fled away. Wherever this conversation was leading, it was not leading, he realised, to a rise in his weekly wage.

"Ah, Linnet, Linnet," sighed Mr. Perks, sorrowful rather than angry. "This attitude is ill-advised. There is no mistake at all, I assure you. The police are not given to making mistakes. Nor, I venture to say, are we—we of the London Shipping Line." Mr. Perks looked again for his hat, and again the hat was missing.

"And, anyway, it is all in the papers—which, of course, is

my reason for coming to see you. Perhaps you would like me to repeat the story."

Mr. Linnet was silent. The word "police" had a chilly sound. Not given to making mistakes, indeed! Well, if Joe Boskin was anything to go by, they were given to making nothing else!

Mr. Perks' hand slipped into the case and produced a newspaper cutting.

"It is now thought," he read aloud—and Miss Brown-Potter's ancestors seemed to lean from their frames to listen—"that the breach of the peace during the Jubilee procession—"

Mr. Linnet gave a groan and turned it into a cough. The Jubilee procession again! Was he never to hear the end, he wondered, of fur coats and yellow breeches?

"That the breach of the peace," Mr. Perks repeated, "was the work of two scrapegrace children. They belong, the police are now convinced, to a checking-clerk employed by the London Shipping Line, who lives in Belvedere Gardens."

"To me, Mr. Perks?" Mr. Linnet was startled.

"May I go on?" enquired Mr. Perks, and did not stay for an answer.

"This pair of hooligans," he continued, "pushed their way to the front of the crowd and there took advantage of a poor dumb creature by forcing an old white cockatoo to cross the road in front of the Queen, thus bringing the march to a standstill. Because of this unforeseen delay, the Queen arrived at St. Paul's Cathedral two and half minutes late.

"The incident has caused a widespread feeling of repugnance. Several people have expressed the opinion that the London Shipping Company should send an apology to

190

Buckingham Palace. Others have shown their disapproval by deciding never again to travel on any ship of the London line. Still more have been heard to comment on the general lack of discipline in modern family life. 'Are we British people,' one writer asks, 'or a nation of Hottentots?' ''

Shaking his head at the last sentence, Mr. Perks folded the cutting. He looked across at Mr. Linnet as a judge might look at a pickpocket.

"You can't alter the facts, Linnet. Well, what have you to say?"

The words were a mere formality. It was clear that Mr. Perks believed there was nothing to be said.

Widespread repugnance! Apology! Children belonging to a checking-clerk! The phrases repeated themselves in his head till Mr. Linnet was dizzy.

"But it wasn't like that at all," he faltered, feverishly hunting for suitable words. His heart expanded with fatherly protest. It was anguish to hear his children blamed. Hottentots, indeed! But how could he unravel the story; how explain to Mr. Perks that his so-called facts were wrong? That Louis, far from being dumb, was a garrulous bully of a bird and the cause of all the trouble; that the only peace Edward ever disturbed was the peace of his own fanciful mind; that Victoria, at the very utmost, would have asked the Queen a question; and, moreover, that neither of his children had been within miles of the procession?

And even supposing he could explain—would Mr. Perks believe him? Indeed, if by chance such a thing did happen, would matters not go from bad to worse? Mr. Perks, with his sense of rectitude, would be bound to tell the police the truth and notify the papers. And then, Mr. Linnet realised, the fat would be in the fire.

191

He knew enough of the law to be sure that his own children were far too young to come within its reach. But what of Stanley, who was older? If the true facts were made known, Joe Boskin would certainly come and take him, and Miss Brown-Potter would grieve. The thought was distressing to Mr. Linnet.

And what of Monkey? They would shut him up for disturbing the peace, shoot him, perhaps, like a mad dog.

This thought, too, was unthinkable.

On the other hand, there was Rose, his wife. If he failed to let the truth be told, she would suffer at having her children libelled.

Once again, Mr. Linnet's thoughts were altogether too much. His heart was like a battlefield, with all its conflicting loves. Where were the lost days of his life when all was calm and humdrum; when right was right and wrong was wrong and he, a simple working-man, could recognise which was which; the days before the fateful day when he had first met Monkey?

He felt himself thrust into a corner, unable to turn to right or left, and glanced about the room for help.

If only Miss Brown-Potter's relations, who surely knew the facts of the case, could give him some advice!

But their faces stared from the gilded frames, serene and unconcerned.

"We, too," they all seemed to be saying, "have had our human problems. We, too, have had to face them alone. You must do the same."

And Mr. Linnet, looking at them, suddenly made up his mind.

He would leave things exactly as they were. Edward and Victoria would not be troubled by a newspaper lie. Their parents would bear the slander for them. That was what parents were for.

But the truth would hurt Stanley Livingstone Fan.

The truth would also hurt Miss Brown-Potter.

And the truth would be the end of Monkey. He would go with Joe Boskin willingly, never for a moment doubting that Boskin was a friend. In his mind's eye Mr. Linnet saw them, the blue serge back and the furry brown one walking away forever. Was such a thing to be endured?

No! The soundless answer spoke within him, and his right hand closed on the hilt of a sword. He was now a Crusader, with his back to the wall, fighting a rabble of Infidels. They fell before him right and left. He could hear their piteous cries for mercy—

"I said—'Have you anything to say?'" Mr. Perks was impatient.

The last of the Infidels fell dead. The Crusader stepped across the bodies to Miss Brown-Potter's father's desk.

"Nothing," he said, and shook his head, well knowing that the word "nothing" was full of everything.

"The only possible answer, Linnet." Mr. Perks was complacent. "I am glad to find you so sensible and ready to face the facts. Well, all that remains for me to do is to give you this—er—package."

"What package?" asked Mr. Linnet, faintly. He was limp from his recent exertions.

"Oh, just the usual thing, you know. A month's salary in cash and a letter to say that you are dismissed."

"Dismissed!" He had never thought of that. The sword fell from his nerveless hand and clattered to the floor.

Mr. Perks did not seem to hear it. He was merely surprised, apparently, at Mr. Linnet's surprise. "Well, what else did you expect, Linnet? You can't behave as you have done—"

"But *what* have I done?" cried Mr. Linnet.

"Do I have to explain?" Mr. Perks was testy. "You have been the cause, through your two children, of bringing the London Shipping Line into serious disrepute. We have been slandered in the papers, forced to apologise to the Queen, and on top of that we have lost money, through the cancellation of tickets. After all this, you could hardly expect the Company to keep on an unreliable servant."

Unreliable! The word was a wound. Was this where his great decision had led him? He, the most accurate of workers, to be sent away from the work he loved! Never again to see the ships, swimming like swans to their moorings; and wait, sniffing the tarry air, while men, still salty from the sea, unloaded their seaborne freight!

"But the cargo, what about the cargo? Who will there be to check it?"

Mr. Perks smiled disdainfully. "Do you think you are the only man who can check a cargo, Linnet?"

Mr. Linnet was silent. That was exactly what he did think. There were those who could count and tick off lists. But a cargo required not merely checking. It needed, Mr. Linnet was sure, the presence of Mr. Linnet.

"Well, I think we've covered everything. So I'll be getting along." Mr. Perks rose to his feet wearing a smile of satisfaction at the thought of a job well done.

The one-time checking-clerk opened the door, hoping that the hall would be empty. He needed to be alone.

But the hope was not to be realised.

Edward, Victoria, Stanley, and Monkey were sitting together on the floor, playing a game of Old Maid. Or rather, the children were trying to play while Monkey, accepting each card as a gift, immediately presented it to anyone who would have it.

"Papa!" Victoria leapt to her feet. "Papa, may we see the gold watch?"

"Not now, Victoria, not now."

Edward glanced at Mr. Perks and backed away on his knees.

"Beware of the dogs! They bite," he said. It was clear that neither he nor the dogs thought much of Mr. Perks.

"So these are the two young reprobates! Shocking, shocking!" said Mr. Perks, glancing from Edward and Victoria to Stanley Livingstone Fan.

Behind him Mr. Linnet trembled. Now would come the dreadful moment when the yellow breeches and the brown fur coat—not to mention the famous sailor cap—would hit Mr. Perks in the eye. And that would be the end of it. The cat, at last, would be out of the bag. And his own choice, so painfully made, would prove to have been in vain.

But people, for the most part, see only what they expect to see. The truth was there for Mr. Perks, staring him in the face. But no understanding dawned in his eyes. He merely looked at Stanley Fan and gave a disgusted sniff.

"That boy is only half-clothed, Linnet. You should get him a decent pair of trousers."

He turned to find Monkey bowing to him and took the bowler hat he offered.

"A monkey! Good heavens! I'd have thought you had enough to do providing for your children. And there's something wrong with his head, Linnet. It's moving under his cap!" Little Louis was stirring in his cosy nest. "You should have him looked at by a vet, or better still, send him to the

195

Zoo. They'll take good care of him there, I assure you. It is not a kindly thing to do to keep wild animals as pets. But, of course, that's your concern."

Mr. Perks shrugged his shoulders, dismissing forever from his mind Mr. Linnet and his affairs. And clapping the bowler hat on his head, he gave the group a chilly nod and hurried off down the steps.

Mr. Linnet gave a long sigh, a sigh in which relief and distress were very closely mingled. His decision had not been in vain, after all. It had bought freedom for Stanley and Monkey. But the price—the cloud of this silver lining—had been his own dismissal.

He watched Mr. Perks go down the path, wondering why the bowler hat looked so like a pea on a pumpkin. He was later to discover the reason. Monkey, to whom all hats were the same, had mistakenly given the wrong one away. And from now on, since he could not afford another, Mr. Linnet would be forced to wear Mr. Perks' hat, which was far too big for him.

But just now none of that mattered. He gazed after the retreating figure till it and the day seemed to tremble slightly, like sunlight reflected in water. His usual jauntiness had left him. His shoulders sagged as though under a weight.

Behind him, the watchers were uneasy. Children are troubled when their loved grown-ups retire into troubles of their own.

Edward came and hugged his arm. "The dogs love you, Papa," he said.

Stanley Fan stroked his sleeve. It was a silent message.

Victoria put her arms round his waist and kissed the back of his jacket.

And Monkey, presenting the King of Hearts, took a handkerchief from Mr. Linnet's pocket and pressed it to Mr. Linnet's nose.

It was then Mr. Linnet realised that the trembling of the sunny day was because he himself was weeping.

He blew his nose and smiled at them, grateful for their affection.

2

"Unreliable?"

The word that had so stung Mr. Linnet had the same effect on his wife.

"Really cannot believe my ears—such a hard worker, so good at sums—just like my brother in Islington—arithmetic prize at the age of eight—and Victoria growing out of her coat—Edward needing new boots—will work my fingers to the bone—but, of course, with only one pair of hands—"

Mrs. Linnet clucked at her husband as though she were an anxious hen that had suddenly seen a fox.

"Of course he's unreliable!" Uncle Trehunsey, apparently, agreed with Mr. Perks. "Once that ape was in the house, he became a different man! Didn't he lose my twenty pounds?"

"It was all paid back, Uncle Trehunsey!" Mr. Linnet, still smarting from his wound, for once defended himself.

"And bring my beautiful home to ruins?"

"Only the beds and chairs and sofas!" Mr. Linnet protested.

"Well, you've nobody else to blame, Alfred!" Uncle Tre-hunsey's voice was cheerful. He was feeling better every minute, for now he was cock of the walk again and Mr. Linnet in his old position of poor, dependent relation. "You've made your bed and must lie upon it!" he declared with horrid glee.

Mr. Linnet felt bound to agree with him. He had indeed made his bed and was tossing upon it uneasily. From the moment when, at the top of the gangway, he had taken Monkey into his arms, his life had been full of uncertainty, no one day like another. And now, because of that chancy moment, he had brought disaster upon himself—worse still, on his wife and children.

Heavy of heart, he glanced at Monkey. And Monkey, sensing that something was wrong, offered him his paw. It was warm and slightly wrinkled, like a kid glove left too long in the sun, and Mr. Linnet clasped it firmly. Ruefully, he realised that if the moment came again, chancy though it well might be, he would do the same thing again.

"So don't rely on me to support you. I've quite enough to do without that!" Uncle Trehunsey went booming on.

"Indeed you have!" agreed Miss Brown-Potter. "You have to look after that foot, Mr. Truro, and pay those dreadful doctor's bills. No one could ask you to do more."

She smiled at him, serene as ever, and Uncle Trehunsey, a pricked balloon, subsided into his old position—a guest in a house that was not his own. He wished that the floor of the house would open and swallow its smiling owner.

"Of course they couldn't," said Mr. Linnet. "I shall have another job in no time."

He spoke more bravely than he felt. Mr. Perks, very noticeably, had refrained from giving him a reference. And without some word to recommend him, would any other shipping line agree to take him on—especially after reading the papers? He did not feel very hopeful.

"I wonder, Mr. Linnet—" said Miss Brown-Potter, breaking the chain of his thought. "Would you not think it a good idea for us all to emigrate?"

"Emigrate?" He stared at her. Leave home, leave England, the world he knew? What a terrible thought! Could it really be Miss Brown-Potter, so sensible, so—as he thought —like a kind of goddess, who was making this suggestion?

"Why not? Equatorial Africa would be an excellent place. We could go to my old home at Umtota."

"Umtota?" said Mr. Linnet, faintly. The very name appalled him. "You mean—you really have a house there?"

"Well, not a house. It's a kind of hut. The Fan tribe— Stanley's tribe, you know—build them of grass and green branches and plaster them with mud. Of course, during the monsoon, the mud tends to melt a little, but at other seasons of the year such homes can be very pleasant."

Monsoon! For years Mr. Linnet had been in love with the beautiful, echoing word. Monsoon, monsoon—how his ear enjoyed it!

But—experiencing what the word stood for might be a different matter. Forty days and nights of rain and his mud house melting away around him—what would he think of the monsoon then?

"And living is so very cheap. You can get all the things you need for nothing—figs, wild grapes, cocoanut milk, birds' eggs, nuts, bananas. Occasionally, when the Fans go hunting, they will bring one a haunch of wild pig. And as for clothes—though mine, of course, never wore out—one can easily find something to trade for a strip of flowered cotton."

Flowered cotton! Mr. Linnet recoiled, his thoughts going head over heels.

Ever since he had been a child he had dreamed of far-off places. Their names had rung in him, like bells, colouring his daily round, filling him with a homesickness that itself was a kind of joy.

But now, when faced with a far-off place, offered it as experience, he felt nothing but dismay. The thought of himself in flowered cotton, sitting under a wild fig tree, chewing a haunch of wild pig, gave him no pleasure whatever.

"But think of cannibals, Miss Brown-Potter—eating everyone in sight—missionaries, their own mothers—Trehunsey a very tempting morsel—man-eating tigers, too, of course —Edward so liable to colds—and Victoria never liked bananas—" Mrs. Linnet gasped for breath.

"If the cannibals didn't eat Trehunsey, perhaps a crocodile would, Mamma!" Victoria sounded hopeful.

"Oh, no, it wouldn't!" Edward assured her. "Miss Brown-Potter would rescue him, the way she rescued Stanley."

"Now, Edward! Now, Victoria!"

"Umtota!" snorted Uncle Trehunsey, expressing extreme disgust.

"Totumpta! Pumpota!" echoed Louis, as he tried to make the word his own.

And a small sound came from Monkey's cap, something between a wheeze and a croak. Little Louis was beginning to talk.

"Oh, there wouldn't be cannibals, Mrs. Linnet. I don't believe they exist anymore. And man-eating tigers are very

200

rare. Leopards, yes, occasionally, but you only have to give them a poke and tell them to get along—and they go."

It was evident that Miss Brown-Potter was speaking from experience. But Mrs. Linnet was not convinced that any leopard *she* might meet would get along if she poked it.

"And think of the voyage!" she protested. "Seasickness, whales, tornadoes, rocks—my aunt Amelia went to New Zealand and wrote and told us Never Again—"

"It's all right, Rose!" Mr. Linnet broke in. "We don't need to emigrate, I'm sure. I'm bound to get a job."

He smiled at his wife to reassure her and flung a glance at Miss Brown-Potter.

"I would do anything," said the glance. "Anything you could ever ask, except—forgive me!—this. I'm a simple man, not adventurous—except in my own imagination. I never asked for my dreams to come true; I like them as they are. All I want is a quiet life, stuffy and warm as a worn coat. I cannot go to Umtota!"

He stood there, feeling that he had betrayed her, one hand holding the King of Hearts and Monkey swinging from the other—a small man to whom too many things had happened all at once. Silently, in that long glance, he pleaded for understanding.

But Miss Brown-Potter was unperturbed. She simply exchanged a look with Stanley who smiled and ran to the kitchen. They could hear him filling the kettle with water.

"It was only a suggestion," she said. "Let us all have a cup of tea . . ."

3

It was astonishing, Mr. Linnet thought, as he trudged home wearily every evening, how many people in the shipping world seemed not to need his services.

"What?" they all said. "Sacked from the *London* without a reference? There's something fishy about that." And then the light would dawn.

"Oh, you're the chap with the *two children!* Yellow trousers and brown fur coats. Shocking piece of impudence. Sorry! No, we've nothing!"

Mr. Linnet sighed. Reluctantly, he gave up hope of ever checking cargoes again. He would try for another sort of job.

Bookkeeping? Yes, he was good at sums and also at making lists. But nobody wanted a list made, especially by a checking-clerk who couldn't produce a reference.

"No! No! No!" everyone said. He could hear the Noes echo behind him as each evening—with Mr. Perks' hat at a jaunty angle—he climbed the steps of Belvedere Gardens and opened the front door.

But his jauntiness deceived no one. Each of them knew, at the first glance, that once again he was coming home with no news worth the telling.

Monkey would rush to take the hat and hang it in some impossible place for Stanley Fan to rescue.

Victoria plied him with endless questions—when, how, where, and why.

Little Trehunsey, though that was really nothing new, received him with noisy protests.

Uncle Trehunsey smiled with pleasure. "I told you so!" was clearly written on every line of his face.

And Mrs. Linnet hovered and fussed, as she brought him his favourite dishes. "Just another spoonful—Alfred—have to keep up your strength—"

Edward was the only one who could not disguise his feelings. He would sit on the stairs, hugging the dogs, anxiously watching the scene. What, he wondered, happened to children whose fathers failed to find work? Would he, Victoria, and Trehunsey be sent away to an orphanage? The dogs would certainly not like that. The dogs might even die.

Mr. Linnet took it all in. He knew exactly what they were feeling—the children, in their own way, anxious, and their mother doing her best to pretend there was nothing at all to be anxious about. It would have been easier, he felt, had they called him names and blamed him.

As for Miss Brown-Potter, she merely smiled at him each evening, neither pretending nor worrying. Her constant calm was a reassurance.

But the person who helped Mr. Linnet most, oddly enough, was Louis.

All day long he sat on his perch, playing with his new word as a cat plays with a mouse.

Tumtato? No! Totatum? Wrong! Pumpomta! Wrong again!

He worried the word, he stormed at it. He would get it if it killed him.

And Mr. Linnet, watching him, would find a kind of comfort. If Louis refused to be defeated, he could do the same.

So every morning he set off again, determining not to be outdone by a grumpy old bundle of feathers.

He was down now to the menial jobs, the ones that did not need a mind that was good at making lists.

"Plenty of breath and a sweep of the arm—that's what you need!" said *Brighter Windows,* who had advertised for an extra man.

Mr. Linnet was equipped with both. And mentioned, hoping to clinch the bargain, that he had a family to support. Also an animal—a monkey.

"A monkey!" The manager gave a startled cry and put the space of the office between them.

"You keep away from me, you hear? Monkeys are full of fleas and shifty. Sweet as caramel one moment and the next they stab you in the back. Why, you might come to work with your hand bit off! Besides, you've got no reference. How do I know you're who you are? You might even be a burglar!"

It was no good. In spite of Mr. Linnet's avowal that he was not, had never been, and never would be a burglar; that Monkey hadn't a flea to his name and would rather be stabbed in the back than stab, the manager was adamant. Window cleaners who lived with monkeys wouldn't do for *Brighter Windows.*

And Mr. Linnet, who had liked the thought of looking in on various lives—members of the government, with their feet upon the desks before them, lazily passing laws; ladies sipping tea together from delicate china cups; children riding on rocking horses away to the end of the world—had to go to the Public Library and peruse the *Times* once again for Situations Vacant.

Then he took a bus to Waterloo Station where Honest, Sturdy Men as Porters were Urgently Required.

This time, Mr. Linnet decided, he would mention neither his family nor the fact that he lived with a monkey.

Fortunately, as it turned out, he did not need to do so. Nor did the Station Master, it seemed, require a reference.

"I take a man as I find him," he said. "I'm afraid, though, after what you've been getting, you won't think much of a porter's wages."

And Mr. Linnet, on hearing what the wages were, felt sorry for railway porters.

"But perhaps I could work my way up and become a Ticket Collector!" In his mind's eye, he was already there, in brass buttons and braid on his cap.

"Tickets, please! Thank you, madam. No, sir, we do not go to Dover. The Restaurant Car is in the rear. Dinner is now being served."

"Well, that would take about ten years," the Station Master was saying.

"*Ten years!*" The brass buttons vanished away. The tickets dropped from his hand.

"Don't decide now," said the Station Master. "Come and see me tomorrow." He ushered Mr. Linnet out past a line of Honest, Sturdy Men all waiting to be taken on as Urgently Needed Porters.

"Where did you get the 'at, mate?" The prospective porters laughed and whistled.

Mr. Linnet hurried past them. These were the men he would have to work with, men too insensitive to see that Mr. Perks' ill-fitting bowler was not a joke but a tragedy—at least for the man who had to wear it.

Never mind! A job was a job. He would not earn much as a railway porter, but it might be possible, he thought, to get an evening job as well—perhaps in the Lost Luggage Department. He could check the portmanteaus and Gladstone bags as once he had checked the shipping lists. The Station Master was a kindly man. He would listen, perhaps, to this suggestion. And a railway station was, after all, another kind of harbour. Trains came panting into it, as ships came sailing to London River, bringing back news of the world.

Mr. Linnet felt his heart lifting. The prospect, if not exactly bright, was not without possibilities. He would see the Station Master tomorrow. Tomorrow something would be decided.

Tomorrow—what a beautiful word—as full of echoes as the song of the cuckoo. Tomorrow, tomorrow! Cuckoo, cuckoo!

The extravagant thought delighted him, and for the first time in many days, Mr. Linnet, as he ran up the steps, was smiling to himself . . .

4

An awful silence greeted him.

There they were, all bunched together, staring at him without a word, as though afraid to speak.

Were they, at last, beginning to blame him, weary of seeing him, night after night, come home with nothing to tell?

Had the camel's back at last broken? And what had been the straw?

Mr. Linnet took off the bowler hat and waited for Monkey to take it. But Stanley Fan, instead, stepped forward, mutely shaking his head.

And Mr. Linnet knew.

Among the anxious, wordless faces, Monkey's face was missing.

"He's gone!" The words were a statement, not a question. For Monkey, had he been there, would have leapt across the room to greet him.

"It wasn't our fault!" Victoria cried.

"Don't cry, Papa! Think of the dogs!" The thought that his father might burst into tears was terrible to Edward. The world was dangerous enough. If his father were to break down now, everything would collapse.

"Nobody's fault—" Mrs. Linnet insisted. "Children and Stanley—and Stanley only a child himself—making toffee in the kitchen—Miss Brown-Potter away shopping—I giving Trehunsey his bath and Uncle Trehunsey sound asleep—runs in the family, of course—my father always a good sleeper—"

"And even if I wasn't asleep—" Uncle Trehunsey snapped, from his corner. "I don't intend to spend my life looking after a pack of baboons!"

"But you might, perhaps, have seen him go! Did you notice the time? Was he by himself?" Mr. Linnet was urgent.

"I saw nothing, I heard nothing, and I'll say nothing. What an ape does is not my business." Whatever he knew, if anything, was locked in Uncle Trehunsey's breast.

"It could only have been Professor McWhirter! His card!

207

What did I do with his card?" Mr. Linnet rushed through his pockets.

Not in this one, not in that! Then, suddenly, he remembered. The Professor had given him a card, and he, with a gesture of contempt, had flung it on to the wharf.

"Well, they'll have his address down at the docks. Somebody there is sure to tell me." He darted for his hat.

"Mr. Linnet!" said Miss Brown-Potter, gently.

He stood in his tracks, with his back towards her, chafing to be off.

"Is it wise to be so precipitate? He would never leave you willingly. And if anyone has taken him, he will surely try to escape. Give the situation time. Wait—and let it ripen."

Wait? How could he? In his heart he was already away, dashing towards the docks. And as for time—well, time might ripen pears and plums, but if he left events to time, they might be ripened to such an extent that Monkey, along with Professor McWhirter, might even now be heading for Hamburg, or Constantinople, or Vladivostok.

"But, Miss Brown-Potter, don't you see—?" He turned to her imploringly, and the words went dead on his tongue. Confronted with her untroubled presence, Mr. Linnet was silent. He knew that she knew what he was feeling. He remembered the day of the Jubilee, and how she had waited for Stanley Fan to bring home Monkey and Louis. And now, he knew, she was trusting him to wait as she had done.

With an effort, he turned away from the door and held out the bowler to Stanley. And as he did so, another hand —or was it, perhaps, a wrinkled paw?—stole around from behind his back, tumbled something into the hat, and seized it by the brim.

Mr. Linnet spun about.

There stood Monkey in the doorway, with Little Louis, newly fledged, riding upon his shoulder.

Everyone gave a cry of joy—except the two Trehunseys. And, of course, Stanley Livingstone Fan, who nevertheless gave vent to his feelings by hopping about on one leg and beaming like a seraph.

"Papa! He put something in the hat. Look, it's full of jewelry! If there's a bracelet, can I have it?" Victoria danced with excitement.

"Oh, Alfred, not in your best trousers—of course you can't, Victoria—those things don't belong to us—they'll have to be pressed again tomorrow—trousers no good without a crease—especially when hunting for a job—"

For Mr. Linnet was down on the floor, kneeling eye to eye with Monkey and marvelling at the curious fact that as soon as he had agreed to wait, the situation had ripened. For here was Monkey, home and safe, eagerly pressing upon his friend a glittering diamond necklace.

"Do you think he stole them?" Edward asked, shocked at the mere idea.

"Stop, thief! Stop, thief!" cried Uncle Trehunsey, as though he were running through the streets, hot on the heels of a robber.

"I'm afraid so, Edward," said Mr. Linnet. "He must have sensed that I was in trouble, and he chose this way to help me."

He looked at Monkey with gratitude that was mixed with exasperation. One problem had indeed ripened, but with Monkey every ripened problem seemed to give birth to another. Would he never learn that enough was enough—even, perhaps, too much?

"But where did you get them?" He flung out his hands. If

only Monkey, who knew so much, also knew how to speak! Who was the owner of the jewels? Where did he—or she—live? And had the police—God forbid!—already been informed?

"Tell me!" he cried in desperation, seizing Monkey by the shoulders, as though to shake an answer from him.

But what were answers to Monkey? Nothing! He only knew that his friend was troubled. So, he dipped his paw into the hat and eagerly pressed on Mr. Linnet a diamond-studded earring.

"That's mine!" cried a breathless voice from the garden.

Quick, light feet ran up the steps, followed by other, heavier footfalls.

Someone, with someone looming behind her, paused in the open doorway.

A slender finger pointed at Monkey.

"There he is!" the voice panted. "And there are all my jewels!"

5

Mr. Linnet sprang to his feet, staring, with his mouth open, at the vision in the doorway.

She was more like a sweetmeat than a person, in her long pink lacy gown, her small pink slippers on naked feet, and her hair like a waterfall of gold.

The sudden appearance of this vision, out of nowhere, as it seemed, and into Miss Brown-Potter's hall, with its battered old chest and mahogany hat-rack, seemed to strike everyone dumb.

Uncle Trehunsey, stung to unwonted courtesy by the sight of so much beauty, tried to struggle to his feet and had to be picked up by Stanley. Little Trehunsey, checked in mid-cry by the same vision, held out eager hands towards it, as though it were a fruit-drop.

"Mamma!" Victoria broke the silence. "Why is she running about in her nightgown? You never let me do that!"

"It is not a nightgown," the vision declared. "It is what is called a negligee."

"The ladies on chocolate boxes wear them," Edward remarked, reflectively. "The dogs," he informed the room at large, "do not care for chocolate boxes."

"Edward!" His father was indignant, shocked that any son of his could be blind to so much beauty.

"Now, Edward, now, Victoria!—don't know what children are coming to—saying exactly what they think!" Mrs. Linnet apologised. "Never had negligee myself—though my great-aunt Kate, who went on the stage—most unfortunate, of course—tea-gowns, flowers, Turkish Delight—but children hardly to be blamed—none of us knowing your name, you see—"

"But *everybody* knows that, surely! My picture is always in the papers. The beautiful Mrs. de Quincey Belmore at the opera; the beautiful Mrs. de Quincey Belmore at a garden party. Or at the races. Or on the river. Really, I get quite tired of it. Photographers always pestering me. So boring, don't you think?"

She put the question engagingly. But since none of her audience had ever been pestered by photographers, none of them replied.

211

"Well, there you are. That's who I am. And this—" She nodded at the black-garbed shape that loomed like a cloud behind her. "This is Williams—my butler, you know. And those—" She pointed to the bowler hat. "Those are my diamonds!"

"This is a great relief to us." Miss Brown-Potter held out her hand. "We were so distressed about the jewels, wondering where they could have come from. Now we can give them back to you."

Mr. Linnet gathered up the treasures. He would pour them into those flowery hands, their owner would give him a grateful smile, and the whole unfortunate incident would be brought to a happy conclusion.

But the beautiful Mrs. de Quincey Belmore completely ignored the gesture. She was staring hard at Miss Brown-Potter, with a pretty puzzled frown.

"Haven't we met before?" she asked. "I seem to know your face. Oh! You were the one—or rather, *he* was—" She waved a dainty hand at Monkey. "Who offered me a pound of butter. Butter—to *me!* What a droll idea! He was wearing that same blue sailor cap. You remember, Williams!"

Williams, a large, bald, gloomy man, more like a bishop than a butler, emerged from behind his mistress.

"Now that you mention it, madam, yes!" he said, sepulchrally.

"What a coincidence, isn't it! Gives me butter and steals my jewels. And, oh, dear, what a shock he gave me. There was I, dressing for dinner, wondering what to wear tonight, when in he leapt through my bedroom window, grabbed up a fistful of diamonds, and darted out again. I gave a shriek, didn't I, Williams?"

Williams allowed himself a nod.

" 'There's a wild beast stealing my jewels,' I cried. But by the time Williams arrived—he's such a slowcoach of a man, one foot plomping after the other, exactly like a tortoise—"

"One foot after the other, madam, is the usual method of propulsion. I do not care for hurrying. I have my dignity."

"Well, *I* hurried, I assure you. There he was—the beast, not Williams—streaking off across the lawn with the diamonds dangling from his paw. And there was I after him, forgetting I wasn't properly dressed. And Williams, of course, was after me, plodding along like a snail. Oh, dear, what a race we had—all along Kingsley Drive, with everybody staring."

"Who could help it?" thought Mr. Linnet. Meeting a goddess in Kingsley Drive was enough to make anyone stare.

"He went like the wind," the goddess continued, nodding her head at Monkey. "Hopping over walls and hedges. Well, naturally, I couldn't do that—"

"God forbid!" Mr. Linnet breathed.

"And Williams, the clumsy creature, *wouldn't,* so we had to take the long way round. Then suddenly I saw his cap and that white parroty thing on his shoulder. He was hurtling over somebody's gate. So I dashed through it after him. And here we are, though Heaven knows where—"

"Twenty-seven Belvedere Gardens," said Miss Brown-Potter, smiling. "So all is well that ends well. And your jewels are safe, as you see."

Again Mr. Linnet held out the jewels, hoping for a rewarding smile.

"Oh, give them to Williams. He's got pockets." Their owner airily waved him away.

The jewels passed from hand to hand, and Williams, as

though they were sacred relics, stowed them away on his person.

"And now, Williams, you must take me home and then go and tell the police."

Police! Such a word, upon such a tongue, was shocking to Mr. Linnet. Had all not ended well, after all?

"But is that necessary, do you think?" Miss Brown-Potter stepped into the breach. "The police are so very incompetent."

"Oh, do you think so? How very strange! I find them all so helpful and clever. So good at getting one hansom cabs."

Mr. Linnet's heart beat faster. The thought of finding a hansom cab for the beautiful Mrs. de Quincey Belmore tempted him, for a dizzy moment, to look for a job as a policeman.

"And he didn't realise he was stealing," Miss Brown-Potter continued. "One can't expect an animal to behave as you or I would do. I'm sure you don't wish to do him harm—"

"But he did *me* harm! He took my jewels!"

"And now you have your jewels back. So, you see, it was just a storm in a tea-cup. I'm afraid, if you do inform the police, they will never give you a moment's peace. Courtrooms instead of garden parties, no time for operas or the races—such a trouble for you!" Miss Brown-Potter was all concern for Mrs. de Quincey Belmore.

"No garden parties? I couldn't bear it! The diamonds aren't as important as *that*. My husband—he's a diamond merchant—simply loads me with them. And unfortunately I prefer pearls. But he never listens to what I say."

Really! Mr. Linnet thought. To persist in the role of diamond merchant instead of learning to dive for pearls—the man must be a scoundrel!

"And sitting in court-rooms—how horrible! Oh, no, I will not inform the police. Neither will Williams—will you, Williams?"

Williams, stately and disapproving, portentously shook his head.

"I cannot be certain of that, madam. I should have to consult my conscience."

"Oh, bother your conscience! Don't think about it! What beautiful gloxinias!" Mrs. de Quincey Belmore tinkled. "But how do you get them to grow so large? The ones my wretched gardener brings me are hardly the size of a shrimp."

The great rosy trumpet flowers glowed in the middle of the table, looking as though at any moment they might burst into martial music.

"It's quite simple," said Miss Brown-Potter. "The only thing a plant needs is for someone to make a fuss about it. Sometimes I give them a pinch of pepper—or sugar, vanilla, curry powder—it doesn't really matter. These I brought up on olive oil, with just a suspicion of nutmeg." She picked up the silver nutmeg-grater that lay beside the flowers.

"Indeed?" said Mrs. de Quincey Belmore, with a mixture of envy and irritation. "I'll dismiss my gardener at once. It's not my fault that he has six children. I *must* have gloxinias like these!"

Mr. Linnet's eyes widened. What? Sack a gardener with six children and jobs so hard to get? No, no! He would not believe it of her.

"And look how they blend with my negligee! Pink is the colour that suits me best. Everybody says so!"

215

"Then, won't you take them?" said Miss Brown-Potter, lifting the blushing mass from the table.

"Oh, really, I couldn't. It's *too* kind." Mrs. de Quincey Belmore protested, while firmly grasping the flower-pot. "You see! Pink really does become me." She glanced at herself in a nearby glass. "Olive oil, did you say, and—curry?"

"Nutmeg!" amended Miss Brown-Potter. "And perhaps you would like the grater, too."

"Oh, *no*, Miss Brown-Potter," Victoria wailed. "It's the one your Aunt Matilda gave you!" She had loved the silver grater herself. She could not bear to part with it.

"I think Aunt Matilda would understand," said Miss Brown-Potter, quietly.

"Oh, I couldn't think of taking it!" But even as she spoke the words, Mrs. de Quincey Belmore's fingers were wrapped about the treasure. "Look at my nutmeg-grater, Williams! Did you ever see anything so sweet?"

Williams appeared to be unimpressed.

"Sweet it may indeed be, madam. It is also bribery and corruption."

"Bribery?"

"If I might explain the word, madam—"

"Nonsense, I know what bribery means. Would you say that you were bribing me?" Mrs. de Quincey Belmore demanded.

"Indeed, no," said Miss Brown-Potter, sincerely. "I would rather say I was thanking you. The flowers, and the grater—are a present."

"There, Williams, she's thanking me—though for what, I can't remember. My husband says I've a head like a sieve. But I always remember, eventually. Good heavens, how late

it is! Williams, what are you dawdling for? Take the flowers
—carefully, now!—and I will carry the nutmeg-grater."

She turned about in her frothing laces and stumbled
against the tin tray.

"Pumpomta! Totoota! Gitt on! Gitt out!" screamed Louis
from his perch.

"Gracious!" cried Mrs. de Quincey Belmore, dropping a
slipper and staggering backwards. "That's the creature that
sat on my hat! In Bond Street, it was—on Jubilee Day. Two
boys were running after him. One was in yellow—just like
him!" She nodded across the room at Stanley. "Their picture was printed in all the papers. And the other boy wore—
what *was* it, Williams?"

She put up a lily-white hand to her brow, and Mr. Linnet
and Miss Brown-Potter exchanged an agonised glance. Was
the visitor about to remember that the other boy had been
clad in fur and also a sailor cap?

"Oh, dear, it was on the tip of my mind and now it has
gone again. What's this?"

Monkey, making his humble bow, was presenting Mrs. de
Quincey Belmore with her own pink satin slipper.

"You clever thing!" she cried in delight, as she ran her
fingers along his arm. "And aren't you soft and warm, and
cosy! You'd make the most beautiful fur cape."

Fur cape! Mr. Linnet froze.

"Oh, you must let me have him. I'd adore it! I'll pay you
anything you like. And the bird on his shoulder, too, of
course. I've always wanted a stuffed bird!" Mrs. de Quincey
Belmore beamed and clapped her hands in anticipation. "I
may have them, mayn't I?" she chirruped, as certain as any
spoiled child that she would get what she asked for.

The question met with a chilly reception. Mr. Linnet, speechless with rage, gave her a stony stare. However could he have thought her pretty? It shamed him to remember it.

"I'm afraid," said Miss Brown-Potter, firmly, "that neither is for sale."

"Oh, but they must be, I really want them." Mrs. de Quincey Belmore pouted. "I shall send my husband. He'll persuade you—no matter what the price. So, au revoir, my beautiful cape!" She kissed her hand to Monkey. "Home, Williams! Do stir your stumps and try to be less of a tortoise."

With a quick flutter of silk and lace she swept towards the door. Away she floated down the steps, laughing, commanding, contradicting, with Williams, like a reproachful bishop, plodding along behind her.

"Woof, woof!" barked Edward after them. The dogs were seeing the visitors off.

"She didn't say 'Thank you' or 'Good-bye.' That wasn't good manners, was it, Mamma? And she took Aunt Matilda's nutmeg-grater." Victoria was weeping.

And Trehunsey, robbed of the large pink fruit-drop, gave vent to his displeasure.

"Now, Edward, Victoria, Trehunsey!" said Mrs. Linnet, mechanically. She was looking with anxious eyes at her husband who was looking at Miss Brown-Potter.

"I'm afraid," said Miss Brown-Potter, slowly, "that our friend, Mrs. de Quincey Belmore, will not always have a head like a sieve. She will remember, eventually. Williams will see to that. And then—"

"I know, I know," said Mr. Linnet. He was squirming and twisting inside himself, like a worm caught on a hook. Whichever way he moved, it hurt.

218

In spite of the flowers and the nutmeg-grater, it was clear that Williams, because of his conscience, or his mistress, because of her lack of hers, would go to the police. That—or the husband would come and bargain, a rich man brandishing a chequebook. And either way—whether they had him put in jail or slaughtered to make a fur cape—they meant no good to Monkey.

Fate, Mr. Linnet realised, was playing chess with him. And since Fate was by far the better player, he had only one move left.

He would never, now, be a railway porter, still less a ticket collector. All such plans would have to be scrapped, if he made that one last move.

He looked at his wife and his three children. And then he looked at Monkey. Between them his heart was torn in two. Nevertheless, his mind was made up. And, knowing that she knew this was so, he turned to Miss Brown-Potter.

"There is only one thing to do," he said. "We shall have to go to Umtota."

Mrs. Linnet, swooning at the thought, subsided on to a sofa. A loud groan broke from Uncle Trehunsey. And from somewhere in Monkey's vicinity, a new voice, hoarse and sweet and young, declared itself for the first time.

"Hallelujah!" it said.

Everybody turned and stared. Little Louis, having found his tongue, was so overcome with embarrassment that he hid his face behind Monkey's ear. And as he did so, Louis himself gave a jubilant clap of his wings.

"Umtota!" he shouted, triumphantly. "Umtota! Gitt on! Umtota!"

Each of them, father and son, had suddenly found a word . . .

6

"I can't see why we have to bring *this!*"

Mr. Linnet peered round from behind the blackboard that was propped upon his knee. He had just squeezed into the four-wheeler that had driven up to the gate.

It was a tight fit. There was Uncle Trehunsey's foot to be thought of, and Mrs. Linnet had brought not only all her own possessions but those of everyone else as well.

"Must think of children's education—don't want them like my Uncle Cyril—never learned to read and write— ended up as mayor of Brixton—schools may not be good in Umtota—taking every precaution—"

Mr. Linnet sighed. He felt it wiser not to remark that far from their being no good school in Umtota, there probably wasn't a school at all.

"And where might Umtota be?" asked the cabman, as he tossed the doll's house to the roof of the cab.

"The other side of nowhere, that's where!" Uncle Trehunsey exploded. "Tomfoolery, all this gadding about, and all because of an ape!"

"Well, there's still time to change your mind. You could stay here, Uncle Trehunsey."

"What—cook my own meals, make my own bed, care for my gout myself—no, thank you!" Uncle Trehunsey, apparently, by deciding to travel with the Linnets, had chosen between two evils. "Oh! Ouch! Get away, you brute! Can't you hold him, Alfred?"

For the tenth time in two minutes, Mr. Linnet had to prevent Monkey from sitting on Uncle Trehunsey's foot.

"Mamma, I haven't any room!" Victoria was fractious.

"Trehunsey's kicking me," said Edward. He was hunched in a corner beside his father, with one arm round the two dogs, the other hugging a string bag filled with sugar clocks and tombstones.

"Now, Edward, now, Victoria!"

"In Africa?" enquired the cabman, as he heaved up a shabby leather trunk.

"Yes," said Mr. Linnet briefly. He knew no more than the cabman did where Umtota really was.

"It's just about there," Miss Brown-Potter had said, putting her finger on the map. "If we take a ship to Sierra Leone, we can make our way by slow stages—trekking, canoeing—we'll manage somehow."

Trekking? Canoeing? With trunks and a doll's house! Had he sufficient strength for that, Mr. Linnet had wondered.

He steadied the blackboard on his knee, thinking of the journey before him and already feeling homesick. He longed to be aboard the ship, secure from the terrible tempting thought that he still could change his mind.

He felt for the tickets in his pocket. What a job he had had to get passages! Shipping clerk after shipping clerk had turned him away at the mention of Monkey. What did he think ships were, they asked him—travelling circuses?

And then, as a last, lucky chance, he had heard of a man who knew a man whose cousin was Captain of the *Southern Pearl,* a sailing ship going to Sierra Leone—even to countries far beyond it—with a cargo of pins and needles. Natives anywhere, it was said, would do anything for a pin or a needle.

But would the Captain of the *Southern Pearl* take passengers as well as cargo? He would, it turned out, on one condition—that the passengers helped with the work of the ship. And what did the Captain feel about livestock—a dog, a badger, a bird or two, and, well, a monkey, perhaps?

And the Captain hadn't flickered an eyelash. He not only didn't object to livestock. He was used to them, he said.

The relief Mr. Linnet then had felt now flooded him again. As the last trunk soared to its place on the roof, his spirits rose up with it.

"At last!" he thought, as the cabman leapt up on to the box and whistled to his horse. "We're away! We cannot turn back now!"

He glanced out through the rear window and saw that Miss Brown-Potter and Stanley were already locking the front door. In a moment or two, Mr. Linnet knew, the hansom cab that awaited them would be cloppetting after his own four-wheeler on its way to the *Southern Pearl.*

He smiled encouragingly at the children and took a firmer grip on Monkey . . .

Miss Brown-Potter and Stanley Fan walked down the path together. Each of them carried a small bag. Except for Louis' metal perch they had no other luggage.

Louis waddled along behind them, climbed up by the wheel of the cab, murmured "Spit in your eye!" to the cabman, and settled himself on the seat.

"Tinker! Badger! Come on! We're waiting!" Miss Brown-Potter called and coaxed, but Tinker and Badger, at the top of the steps, were creatures turned to stone.

222

"What can be wrong?" murmured Miss Brown-Potter. "Of course! We've forgotten the eiderdown!"

But Stanley had thought of it already. He hurried back, unlocked the door, and returned with the treasure under his arm.

Tinker and Badger sprang to their feet and galloped after it.

There they all were, inside the hansom, and Twenty-seven Belvedere Gardens was now a deserted house.

"Where to, ma'am?" The cabby whirled his whip.

"The London docks. Ah, but wait one minute!"

Miss Brown-Potter leaned forward and listened.

From the drawing room came the sound of music. Someone was playing. Someone was singing.

> *"You'll take the high road*
> *And I'll take the low road*
> *And I'll be in Scotland before you,*
> *For I and my true love*
> *Will never meet again*
> *On the bonnie, bonnie banks of Loch Lomond."*

Miss Brown-Potter smiled to herself. The house, she knew, would never miss her. It had its happy ghosts.

"Drive on!" she said to the cabman . . .

7

"And so," said Captain Twice to his assembled passengers, as the *Southern Pearl* was being readied to move away from the wharf. "We shall all, as you see, be kept busy."

He was reading out the names from a list and assigning everyone his duties.

"You, Mr. Linnet—"

There was no reply. Mr. Linnet was leaning over the ship's side, intently watching the cluster of people that had gathered to see it depart. Was there among them a cloaked figure, with long grey hair that waved in the breeze and a swinging tartan kilt?

There was! Professor McWhirter, with a ferret wrapped about his neck, was darting in and out of the crowd with a bagful of furry creatures. Bought from some sailor, Mr. Linnet assumed, as he ducked his own head cautiously and dragged the one in the sailor cap hurriedly down beside it. Even at the last minute, the animal fancier, if he saw them, might try to get at Monkey.

The rattle of the anchor and the sound of the gangplank being withdrawn was music to his ears. The ship was putting off from the wharf. Already a sizable stretch of water lay between it and the land. So, unless the Professor swam after them—with the ferret and all of the other creatures—Monkey was safe at last.

"*Mr. Linnet!*" Captain Twice repeated.

"Ay, ay, sir!" answered Mr. Linnet, in what he hoped was a nautical manner.

"You, Mr. Linnet, will be jack-of-all-trades, help with the anchor, set the sails, man the pumps, run up the rigging—"

"*Run up the rigging?*" Mr. Linnet blanched. He hadn't bargained for that!

"And Tom Locket will be here to help you, Mr. Locket of the London Zoo, who has made this trip many times before —though not on this ship, of course." The Captain nodded at the tall young man who was standing at his elbow.

"The London Zoo?" Mr. Linnet faltered. Had he broken every link with home and turned his face towards Umtota, only to be confronted now with a person from a zoo? So— Tom Locket had made the trip before! Now, why would such a man do that? The answer was not far to seek. To look for specimens, of course! Well, thought Mr. Linnet, grimly, there was one specimen that the man from the Zoo would never bring back to London!

His hand went out automatically, but it fell upon empty air. Quick as ever to make a friend, Monkey was holding out his paw, and Tom Locket, apparently pleased, was taking it in his hand. Mr. Linnet mentally vowed to keep his eye not only on Monkey but on Mr. Locket as well.

"And next comes—ah, yes!—Mrs. Linnet. Could you help from time to time in the galley? I'm sure you're an excellent cook."

"Only too glad to be of service—once had an aunt who went to New York—terrible journey, nearly died—but, of course, a mother's duties, Captain—and unfortunately only one pair of hands."

"Then you're no exception, Mrs. Linnet. The help of one

225

pair will be quite sufficient." The Captain glanced again at his list. "And now we come to Mr.—er—Truro."

Uncle Trehunsey, spread out over three deck chairs, looked furious and unfortunate.

"Oh, no, Captain Twice—afflicted with gout—left big toe the size of a sausage—very feeble—needs to rest—couldn't possibly work, I assure you—" Mrs. Linnet protested.

Uncle Trehunsey, she well knew, was as strong as an ox, or stronger. But she dreaded the scene that would surely follow if Captain Twice was foolhardy enough to suggest that he make himself useful.

"Left big toe? Why, that's nothing! He still has the use of his hands, Mrs. Linnet. So—Mr. Truro will peel the potatoes, and when he has some spare time, he will learn how to splice a rope."

The two Linnets closed their eyes and waited for the storm. But no sound came from the deck chairs. Captain Twice and Uncle Trehunsey, like two wolves locked in deadly combat, were staring at each other. And at last, after a long minute, Uncle Trehunsey turned his head and looked in the other direction. He had gone down, like a toy ninepin, before the stronger will.

"And now for you, Miss Brown-Putter—" The Captain calmly returned to his list.

"Potter, Captain," said Miss Brown-Potter.

"Potter? Oh, I beg your pardon. Well, could you, please, Miss Putter-Potter, along with—er—Stanley Livingstone Fan—" The Captain eyed Stanley's yellow breeches as though he thought them unsuitable. "Could you undertake to swab the decks?"

"Certainly," said Miss Brown-Potter. Stanley nodded and smiled.

"Well, that leaves—let me see—ah, yes! General and Mrs. Post."

General Post was a large man with rather indefinite outlines. This haziness was due to the fact that everything he wore was knitted. His trousers were knitted, his jacket was knitted, his shirt and tie were both knitted, and the white thing peeping out of his pocket looked like a knitted handkerchief.

"I thought, General—" the Captain began.

"So did I, Captain," the General broke in. "And thinking's not an easy thing—bad for the mind—but, still, I did it. And this is what I decided. I shall be your look-out man. I've brought my field-glasses, as you see." The General pointed to a knitted bag that hung from his knitted belt.

"But, General—" Captain Twice protested. "I made it clear, when you asked for a passage, that everyone would have to work—"

"And so I shall, my dear fellow. It won't be too much for me, I assure you. I'll just lie back in my deck chair and report to you whatever I see—except when I'm taking a nap, of course. And Mrs. Post—"

"Will knit," said Mrs. Post, firmly. "I will knit you a pair of bedsocks, Captain."

"Er—thank you. You are very kind." The Captain had no need of bedsocks, and he already had a look-out man. But there was something about the Posts, a formidable simplicity, that knocked him down, like another ninepin.

"Well, what about your servant?" he said, determined not to be utterly routed. "What's his name—Bhima?" He looked at his list. "Now, I suggest that he, General—"

"Should look after me? But, of course, Captain. That is what I brought him for. Not that he really does much. These

227

Hindus—they're so feather-brained. Worship cows. Kiss their hands to the moon. Ah, there you are, Bhima, you foolish fellow, hiding behind my back, as usual."

Everyone stared as the foolish fellow, clad in a long white knitted garment—a cross between a shirt and a shroud—crept from behind General Post and stared, in his turn, at Monkey. His dark eyes glowed in his dark face as they took in the furry shape and the tail and the friendly outstretched paw. Then Bhima uttered a loud cry, stretched himself prone on the deck, and put his forehead to Monkey's foot.

"You see, Captain? He's full of whimsies. Bowing and scraping to a monkey! Do get up, Bhima, you silly lad. You'll ruin Mrs. Post's handiwork."

"Bowing to a beastly ape!" Uncle Trehunsey was indignant.

"Oh, I wouldn't call him that, you know. Must be polite to the dumb creatures. Seems a decent little chap. Helpful, too, I shouldn't wonder."

The General had stated a simple fact. Monkey was indeed helping.

Having assumed, apparently, that Bhima had had a fainting fit, he was tugging and pushing with all his might to get him to stand upright; and, further to fortify his admirer, was offering him a piece of carrot which he took from under his cap. This so affected the sensitive Bhima that he had to be forcibly prevented from prostrating himself again.

"Now, now, that's quite enough!" Captain Twice seized the thin brown arm. "This is a sailing ship, not a playhouse!" He flung Bhima away from Monkey and turned to Victoria and Edward.

"You children, too, can make yourselves useful. Work

with Sam—he's the cabin-boy." He waved his hand at a gnarled little man, who was sitting on a pile of rope, reading a paper pamphlet.

"Why is he called a cabin-boy? He's got a beard and he's quite bald." Victoria tugged at her mother's arm.

"Now, Victoria—things not always what they seem—my grandfather at ninety-two, just like a man of eight-nine—"

"He's sixty-three," said the Captain, tersely, and proffered no other explanation. "Well, ladies and gentlemen, that is all—except for one important thing. You are free to go anywhere in the ship, except such places as are marked Private. These, since they have to do with the cargo, are expressly forbidden to passengers. I hope you will make a note of this."

"Splendid man!" thought Mr. Linnet. The Captain, by some miracle, had triumphed over Uncle Trehunsey, sensibly dealt with Mrs. Linnet in the matter of her missing hands, and now he was further proving himself by taking such care of his cargo. Though why he thought the passengers would tamper with crates of pins and needles, Mr. Linnet could not imagine.

"And so, I wish you a pleasant voyage," Captain Twice was saying. "We shall have calm seas and an easy passage. Of that I can assure you."

"Can't see how he can know that—weather is Nature's affair, not his—red sky at night, shepherd's delight—but my father always took an umbrella—often glad of it, I'm sure—and even captains can make mistakes—" Mrs. Linnet was whispering to her husband.

"Hush! He may hear you!" said Mr. Linnet.

But the Captain had other things to think of. He was busy

229

dragging Monkey away from an entrance in the stern of the ship. Above it, in unmistakable letters, was printed the one word, PRIVATE.

"Mr. Linnet," said the Captain, sternly. "You must keep this creature out of mischief!"

"Ay, ay, sir," answered Mr. Linnet, keenly aware, from experience, of the difficult task before him . . .

8

Mrs. Linnet lay awake in her berth, being rocked by the Bay of Biscay. She was thinking what a pity it was that the sea had so much water in it. You never knew where you were with the ocean. Dry land, any piece of land—even Umtota, thought Mrs. Linnet—was infinitely preferable.

Hark! There it was again—and again!—the sound that had woken her up.

"Alfred! There's a goat bleating!"

"Rubbish!" Mr. Linnet yawned. "It's just the creak of the ship's timbers."

"Mamma!"

"Now you've done it," groaned Mr. Linnet.

Edward abruptly sat up in his bunk. "Where is God?" he demanded.

"Here, Edward," Mrs. Linnet replied.

"But you said he was here when we lived in Putney!"

"So he was—I mean, is. God is everywhere, that's why."

"But he can't be here and in England, too. It's such a long way away." Edward was manifestly anxious.

"It's a mystery," said Mr. Linnet. "Nobody really understands it. You have to take it on trust, Edward. Now, go to sleep, the two of you. I can't have my nights disturbed like this when I have to get up so early."

A mystery? What a relief! It was things that were not mysterious that Edward always worried about. But a mystery could take care of itself. He fell asleep at once.

Mr. Linnet turned over in his berth. He put out his hand to the heavy something that lay across his feet. Its warm furriness reassured him.

"All is well," he thought to himself, as he let the waters of the Bay of Biscay rock him, too, to sleep.

Indeed, Mr. Linnet needed rest, for jack-of-all-trades on a sailing ship was not an easy job. He found himself running all day long, ordered here, ordered there, doing the work of at least three men. Tom Locket was usually at his side and, therefore, inevitably, at Monkey's, to help him to learn his trade.

He was an apt pupil. In no time he could set a sail, lay aloft, beat to windward. He learned to take soundings and heave the lead, fall to leeward and square away and other nautical procedures.

Indeed, Mr. Linnet sometimes felt that he, Tom Locket, and the Captain were the only sailors on the ship. The other seamen worked hard enough, but somehow their hearts did not seem to be in it. They appeared, no matter what they did, to be thinking of something else.

Moreover, they did not behave like sailors. They called the Captain by his Christian name and addressed each other

231

formally as Herbert, Winthrop, Percival, Chidwick, Throgmorton, Neville, or Bertram. And they wore such extraordinary clothes—Norfolk jackets, deer-stalker caps, knickerbockers, velvet waistcoats—quite unlike the natty garments of the men of the *London* line.

Mr. Linnet was disappointed. In all his years as a checking-clerk he had dreamed of the joys of life at sea—the mateyness, the frivolity, the rollicking swagger of it all.

But Herbert, Chidwick, and the rest had nothing rollicking about them. They never sat on upturned barrels, waving cannikins of rum and shouting, "Yo, ho, ho!" Not one of them, Mr. Linnet was certain, kept a wife in every port.

Still, they seemed to be earnest and devoted, and studious into the bargain. For each of them kept a book in his pocket and read it in his spare moments.

More than once he had come upon Throgmorton, standing with one hand on the helm and holding in the other a book called *Forty Effective Cures for Snakebite.*

The reading matter of the other seamen seemed equally uninviting. *The South American Llama and Its Habits* peeped out of Percival's pocket. Chidwick's constant interest lay in *A Hundred Ways with Wire Netting.* And bound volumes of *The Locksmith's Gazette* were always in demand. These were kept in the saloon alongside *Equatorial Birds, Iron—Does it Bend or Break?, How to Make a Wooden Crate,* and *Caribbean Holiday.*

Mr. Linnet, in a rare spare moment, had opened the last-mentioned book in the hope of finding some light reading, only to discover that its subtitle was *A Month with the Great Sea Turtle.*

"Four weeks with a turtle—good heavens!" he said, as he

put the book back on the shelf. It was not the kind of holiday that *he* would ever have chosen . . .

9

The *Southern Pearl* had seen better days. She wheezed and muttered like an old crone as she lumbered towards the South Atlantic.

The Captain's prediction had proved correct. The seas were calm, the passage easy. Even Mrs. Linnet, who had confidently expected disaster, was able to leave Little Trehunsey, safely ensconced in a coil of rope, and scramble eggs in the galley.

Victoria contented herself—and tortured everybody else —by asking continual questions. And Edward, because of a mutual interest in dogs, struck up an acquaintance with General Post.

"I call mine One and Two," he said. "And they're sitting on my knee." He did not have to see a dog to know that it was there.

The General stared, with some surprise, at Edward's empty lap. The little chap had made a mistake. Common-enough thing to happen. He even made mistakes himself.

"How many battles have you been in?" Edward wanted to know.

"Not one. I never cared for fighting."

It was now Edward's turn to look surprised.

"Then—how did you get to be a general?"

"Well, that's a very curious thing. I began as a second lieutenant, of course, and always behind the lines. Nothing much to do, you know—card games, dances, a little golf. And then I just went up and up—lieutenant, major, colonel, general. Never quite knew why it was, except that they could rely on me. Dependable chap, they probably said. I expect I'll be a field marshal next."

"I'm sure you will," said Mrs. Post, clicking her needles beside him.

"I shall like the hat," said General Post. "I believe it has feathers in it." He turned to salute Uncle Trehunsey who was hobbling to his chair. "And how are you today, Mr. Truro?"

Uncle Trehunsey sighed like a martyr and swore at his bag of potatoes.

"Poor chap, poor chap!" said General Post. "Once had gout myself, you know. But Flora—that's my wife—cured it. Put me into knitted garments and, of course, it did the trick. You should get married, Mr. Truro. What about that Miss Brown-Batter? Seems a sensible sort of woman. She anything of a knitter?"

Uncle Trehunsey closed his eyes. He didn't know how much of a knitter Miss Brown-Potter was. And as for marrying the woman—a wife who smiled and agreed with him!—he would just as soon be dead.

"No!" he said, with a loud groan, which was echoed by Louis from his perch.

"A few more years shall roll," he croaked. "Gitt on! Gitt out!" he shrieked at his son, who had paused for a moment upon the perch.

234

Louis did not care for life at sea. Still less did he care for Little Louis. He had no paternal feelings.

Little Louis, on the other hand, was constantly rejoicing. From one end of the ship to the other his strengthening voice repeatedly shouted its sole triumphant cry, the first word he had ever heard. Wherever Monkey happened to be, there, too, was Little Louis. He seldom left his friend's shoulder except at the rare tempting moments when Mrs. Post, by chance, let fall a ball of knitting wool.

This was something he could not resist. He would seize upon the thread with his beak and fly round the General and his wife, wrapping them both in a woolly net.

Then Bhima would come on silent feet and carefully unwind them, pausing—if Monkey were anywhere near—to put his hands together and bow. This he did continually, though nobody knew why.

And Monkey, who bowed to everyone, inevitably bowed to Bhima. And so it went on, again and again, as though the two of them were dancing an old-fashioned minuet.

But Monkey, to Mr. Linnet's cost, was never easy to find. He was always in and out of things, helping one or another.

He took an onion from Mrs. Linnet, who needed it for a soup, and presented it to Captain Twice, who really did not want it. He removed Trehunsey from the coil of rope and carried him up aloft to the crow's nest. And Little Trehunsey's horrified father had to smuggle him down to safety again, stuffing the child under his jacket, in case Mrs. Linnet should see him.

Whenever Monkey was anywhere near, the seamen would sigh resignedly, well knowing that at any moment Monkey would hinder them by helping.

He sat beside Sam, the cabin-boy, gazing at his open book with what appeared to be deep respect.

"Do you think he's learning the alphabet?" Victoria enquired.

No. Monkey was merely biding his time till Sam looked away for a moment. Then, like a flash, he snatched out a page, tore it into two halves, and, handing one to Mr. Linnet, daintily nibbled his own half as though it were a sandwich.

And the cabin-boy merely shrugged and sighed. "There will always be a gap, now, in my knowledge of the Tufted Mongoose."

But after that, whenever Monkey was about, he was careful to read with the book half-closed, not taking any risks.

"Sam," said Captain Twice one day—he sounded apologetic. "Shouldn't you sometimes sweep the cabins? We can't let dust accumulate. Last night I found a large cockroach walking over my pillow."

Sam took his glasses from his nose. "My dear Sidney," he said, severely. "I can't do everything, you know—answer this young woman's questions, study a most important book (Mr. Linnet noted the title, *Gorillas, Wild and Captive*), and *also* do the cabins. Dust has never hurt anyone. I will see to the cockroach tomorrow."

"Thank you, Sam. You are very kind." The Captain appeared to be grateful.

"He's *the* authority on gorillas!" Tom Locket whispered to Mr. Linnet, gazing admiringly at Sam.

But Mr. Linnet hardly heard him. He was hoping his wife had been out of earshot when the Captain made his disclosure.

"*I* will sweep the cabins, Captain!" he cried, in eager haste.

236

And, seizing a broom, he charged through the companion-way as though he were a kind of St. George and the cockroach a kind of Dragon. He had no intention, he told himself, of being woken by his wife and told she had heard a cockroach hissing.

Last night it had been a wolf howling.

"Just wind in the sails. Now, go to sleep."

Another time a bear had grunted.

"The cargo shifting a little, perhaps."

And then it was a lion roaring.

"A sea lion, probably. Another name for walrus." I suppose she'll hear an elephant next, he thought, as he fell asleep.

And, sure enough, Mrs. Linnet heard one.

"Alfred! An elephant trumpeting!—listen, there it goes again!—know a trumpet when I hear one—my cousin Harold played the cornet—Alfred, have you gone to sleep—?"

"Yes, I have!" Mr. Linnet had said, escaping from the dilemma.

And now, tired of broken nights, he was hunting for a cockroach. Ah, at last! Here it was—making a nest in the Captain's sponge.

"I've disposed of the—er—thing," he said, consigning the cockroach to the ocean as Mrs. Linnet came out of the galley to take a breath of air.

The cabin-boy looked up from his book. "Well, if you've nothing else to do—" Nothing to do? thought Mr. Linnet, who was working from dawn to midnight. "You might give Miss Brown-Potter a hand. I don't like to see such a splendid woman—first person ever known to climb to the top of Kilimanjaro—swabbing the deck like a navvy."

"Kilimanjaro!" Mr. Linnet was startled. The highest peak

in Africa, all snow and cloud and eternal mist, and Miss Brown-Potter going up it! Would there ever be an end, he wondered, to the things he did not know about her?

"Ask any man on the ship—he'll tell you. Wearing only a bonnet and shawl and elastic-sided boots. Native bearers falling behind and she ploughing on alone. Tremendous feat! Take my seat, dear madam!"

As Miss Brown-Potter came swabbing past, Sam rose up from his coil of rope and gallantly bowed her to it.

"Just discussing your great climb," he said, as she sat down.

"Oh, that!" Miss Brown-Potter waved it aside.

"And is it true—as the *Times* said—that you once were very nearly eaten by one of the cannibal tribes?"

"Oh, Miss Brown-Potter, you promised me—no cannibals in Umtota—!" Mrs. Linnet let out a reproachful wail.

"No, of course not. And there *are* no cannibals in Umtota. It was just mistaken identity and in quite another district. They mistook me—it was dark, you see—for a rather well-known witch. Don't worry, Mrs. Linnet, I beg you. It's perfectly safe in Umtota."

"Where *is* this Umtota?" Sam enquired. "I never heard of the place."

"Well, when we disembark at Freetown, we will travel southwards through Sierra Leone until we get to—"

"Sierre Leone! But, my dear Miss Brown-Potter, we're not going *there!* And certainly not to—"

"Sam!" The Captain's voice, as he joined the group, seemed to hold a note of warning.

The cabin-boy caught the Captain's eye and clapped his hand to his mouth. For a moment he looked like a guilty child. And then he recovered himself.

"Oh, *Sierra Leone,* you said? Of course! My mind was wandering for a moment. And Freetown—hum—a very nice port. Wonderful country, I dare say—" The cabin-boy's voice trailed vaguely away. He now seemed, inexplicably, to have lost all interest in Umtota.

"And what about him?" He nodded at Monkey, who was busily preventing Stanley from properly swabbing the deck.

"He, too, is travelling to Umtota!" said Mr. Linnet, firmly. Sam's behaviour, he was thinking, was really very odd. Surely every sailing man, even a simple cabin-boy, should know where his ship was going!

"Is he indeed?" Sam looked appraisingly at Monkey. "Interesting markings, those—the patches of white on forehead and neck. Unique in my experience, and I've met a lot of monkeys. I wonder now—" His eyes were shrewd. "Would you ever think of parting with him? I'd give you—hum—an excellent price."

"He is not for sale," said Mr. Linnet. "Excuse me, I have to get on with my work."

Inwardly fuming, he seized on Monkey and tried to hustle him away, out of the reach of Sam.

But Monkey did not want to be hustled. He was trying to wrest the mop from Stanley in an effort to swab the deck himself.

"Quick-tempered sort of chap, aren't you? It was only a suggestion, you know!" Sam remonstrated, mildly.

"Not at all—extremely patient!" Mrs. Linnet, like an avenging angel, flew to her husband's defence. "Always putting up with things—leaving comfortable home for distant, unknown lands—and last night, when the hyena laughed— just the wind, he said, squeaking—probably said it to ease

239

my mind—very kind man and most forbearing—and me with only—oh, my pie—!"

She made a frantic dash for the galley, from which came the smell of burning pastry.

Mr. Linnet was mortified. He hardly knew where to look. He decided to speak to his wife very plainly when he got her alone in the cabin.

"Well," he said, sheepishly, to the Captain. "It does sound like a squeak, you know, when it rushes through a loop of rope. And it couldn't, of course, have been a hyena—a hyena in mid-Atlantic!"

"Of course not. I thought your description very proper. What did you think, Sam?"

"I agree with you, Sidney—very proper! The wind can do anything, you know, anything at all."

"Well, I must be—er—laying aloft!" Mr. Linnet escaped from the scene, leaving Monkey to Stanley.

Up there, alone with the sea and the sky, he considered the conversation. Were there any other ships, he wondered, where the captain consulted the cabin-boy in all important matters? And where cabin-boys read books all day and refused to dust the cabins?

Few, if any, he decided. And the thought made him feel uneasy.

Never mind! It could not be very long now before they disembarked at Freetown. Day by day the running sea was bringing him nearer to Umtota.

He would let that be enough, he thought. He would let it be all that mattered . . .

10

The night was hot and humid, for the ship was now breasting the Tropics. In the family cabin, the sleeping breaths rhythmically rose and fell.

Mr. Linnet lay between sleeping and waking, rocked in the lap of the sea. He had not, as he had promised himself, spoken plainly to his wife. For who was he, he asked of his pillow, to protest against family loyalty, however unfortunate or misplaced?

Far away a hyena laughed, and he knew that he was dreaming.

"Wind in a knot of rope," he muttered, and floated away on the dream.

A moment later, or so it seemed, he was woken by somebody knocking. He leapt out of bed and into his clothes.

"Thank you, Chidwick! I'll be there in a moment." It was Chidwick's kindly morning habit to waken Mr. Linnet.

Knock! Knock!

Mr. Linnet rubbed his sleep-filled eyes. The cabin door was wide open. But Chidwick was nowhere to be seen. And from somewhere deep inside the ship the knocking that had woken him was still continuing.

He clamped on Mr. Perks' hat and put out a hand to his rumpled berth. But no answering paw met it. Monkey was not there.

"Up already, my dear fellow?" Chidwick hailed him as he reached the deck.

Mr. Linnet looked about him. Monkey was nowhere to be seen. But something else caught his eye.

Along the horizon lay a faint blue smudge, darker than cloud, darker than sea. His heart leapt up. Was this their landfall? Was this the country where the Sphinx lay couched, the land of mountains, jungles, deserts? And tribes of dark ancient men who had known the world when it was new?

"Is it Africa?" He waved at the smudge.

"*Africa?* Good heavens, no!" Chidwick scoffed at the mere idea.

Mr. Linnet was disappointed. Freetown, clearly, was still far off. So, apparently, was Monkey. He was not on the deck, not in the crow's nest, not asleep in the bunted sails, not hiding behind the hatches.

Very well, then, he would try the cabins.

"Certainly not," said a female voice, as he timidly knocked at the General's door. "How could he be here? I'm dressing!"

Shocked at having made the suggestion, Mr. Linnet sped away.

Miss Brown-Potter, cloaked, booted, and bonneted, had not seen Monkey since the night before. Neither had Stanley Fan.

Uncle Trehunsey, knocked at and questioned, replied with a few well-chosen words. Monkey, clearly, was not with him.

The seamen, all of whom seemed preoccupied, had nothing to report. But of course Mr. Linnet could search their cabins if he thought it would be of use.

So, taking a lantern, he went below, swinging his light into each dark cuddy. There was nowhere any sign of Monkey, but he noticed at the foot of each berth a neatly rolled-up bundle of clothing, tied with a piece of rope. Was that how sailors kept their belongings, as though ready at any moment for an unexpected departure?

Knock! Knock!

The sound vibrated beneath his feet accompanied by a murmur of voices. Was Monkey there? In the ship's hold? Terrified that this might be so, he darted towards a shadowy doorway over which a printed notice said:

ENTRY FORBIDDEN TO PASSENGERS

Mr. Linnet was by nature a law-abiding man. Under other circumstances the word FORBIDDEN would have stayed him. But now he hardly gave it a thought. His foot sought and found a ladder, and he felt his way down, rung by rung, till he reached a solid floor.

He swung his lantern cautiously. He would have to go carefully, he knew, so as not to stub a toe on the cargo.

The little swinging pool of light disclosed a large barrel of beef, green branches in a tub of water, an enormous roll of wire netting, and a bundle of wooden slats. And around these, as if walling them in—or walling away the rest of the hold—were sandbags neatly stacked.

But where was the cargo? He held up the lantern for a better view, and his old experience as a checking-clerk brought home the truth in a flash. There was no cargo—or nothing that he knew as cargo. There wasn't a pin or a needle in sight, far less a crate of either. The ship was in ballast, her keel steadied, not by any cargo at all but by endless walls of sandbags.

Mr. Linnet stood and stared, his mind a jumble of questions. Who had been knocking? What were the green

243

branches for? Why had the Captain been so concerned for a cargo that didn't exist? And above all, where was Monkey?

He listened, hoping for a sound. But all around him, as though it were waiting for him to leave, lay a watchful, breathing silence.

Knock!

The sound was very close to him. It came from behind the nearest sandbags.

"Do you think that's enough?" The voice was Tom Locket's.

"For the moment. We don't want to hurry things." Sam's accent was unmistakable.

Mr. Linnet looked round for a way of escape. But events were moving too quickly for him. Tom Locket came out from behind the sandbags, a crowbar swinging from his hand and on his shoulder—Monkey!

He looked with dismay at Mr. Linnet. Then his face broke into a friendly grin.

"I expect you were anxious!" He gestured at Monkey. "He followed me when I came down here. I tried to persuade him to go back. But—you know what he is!" He grinned again.

"Did you think we had stolen your pet?" asked Sam, greeting Mr. Linnet blandly, as though they had met in Piccadilly instead of in the hold of a ship in highly suspicious circumstances. "All right, young fellow, don't knock me down!"

The last words were spoken to Monkey who, at the sight of his old friend, had given one of his great leaps and landed in his arms.

Mr. Linnet held him tightly. If only, he thought—as

others, indeed, had done before him—if only Monkey understood English and could be taught, or in some way warned, not to consort with strangers!

From above came the sound of heavy footsteps.

"You all right, Sam and Tom? You ought to be about finished now." The Captain, swinging a lantern before him, peered down into the darkness.

"What are you doing there, Mr. Linnet?" His face and voice were both stern. "Passengers are expressly forbidden to go beyond this point. Bring that animal up at once and let me have no more nonsense. I won't have him disturbing my ship."

"Ay, ay, sir," murmured Mr. Linnet. The Captain seemed such an upright man. It was hard to connect him with anything fishy. Maybe he did not even know that his cargo was nothing but sandbags. Even the knocking and whispering might have an innocent motive.

Nevertheless, as he and Monkey and the lantern came lurching up the ladder, Mr. Linnet was quite determined that, from now until the end of the voyage, he and his friend would be bound together by something other than affection.

So, looping a rope round Monkey's waist and tying the other about his own, he proceeded to his work.

It was not easy. Monkey accepted the thing as a game. When Mr. Linnet went aloft, Monkey swung from the crosstrees above the sea as though from a jungle branch. Down on the deck it was just the same. When Monkey bowed to the bowing Bhima, Mr. Linnet, perforce, had also to bow. Only the Captain's proximity prevented this stately comedy from going on forever.

Today the Captain was everywhere. So was the cabin-boy. It was strange to see Sam without a book, intently talking to each of the seamen as though he were giving instructions.

What was happening? Had the ship arrived at some special point—of latitude or longitude—that required the serious attention of every one of the crew?

But which point? And what was the smudge on the horizon that seemed, to Mr. Linnet's fancy, hourly to grow nearer?

"Can't see a thing!" said General Post, putting his field-glasses to his eye. "Must be imagining it, old chap!"

"Always imagining something or other. Drat this potato!" snapped Uncle Trehunsey, who could not see the smudge, either.

But Mr. Linnet saw it plainly. "Is it an island?" he asked Throgmorton, who all day long was heaving the lead and calling the number of fathoms.

"Possibly." Throgmorton was vague. No one was willing to explain.

And the Captain, as if deliberately, hurried him from one job to another without a moment's pause. By nightfall Mr. Linnet was spent. He had never felt so exhausted.

He stretched himself out on one of the hatches, where his wife and Miss Brown-Potter were sitting, flanked by the General and Mrs. Post and the snoring Uncle Trehunsey. The constellations were large and close, and the Southern Cross, like a golden signpost, stood up in the southern sky.

Mr. Linnet dozed. He dreamed. He dreamed that he was telling the Captain, man to man, that there was no cargo.

"What? No pins and needles?" the Captain was saying, when somebody tugged at his sleeve.

246

"Ay, ay, sir," muttered Mr. Linnet, scrambling up from the hatch.

But it wasn't the Captain. It was Edward.

"Edward!" Mrs. Linnet exclaimed. "Only your nightgown and bare feet—probably catch your death of cold—"

"It was hot, so I took the dogs for a walk. And then I saw him, Papa. He was talking to Sam and Tom Locket, and he went away through the door marked Private."

"Saw whom?" said Mr. Linnet, yawning.

"Professor McWhirter, Papa!"

Mr. Linnet sat up with a start. His son was fanciful, he knew. But he was not untruthful.

"Thank you, Edward." His voice was quiet. "Will you go back to bed, now? Your mother will tuck you in."

Mr. Linnet watched them go, hand in hand, but at arm's length, so the dogs should not be stepped on.

Professor McWhirter on the *Southern Pearl?* Instinctively, he reached for Monkey. But how had the fellow got on board? Run up the gangway at the last minute when Mr. Linnet had ducked his head? Or was he, perhaps, a stowaway? No! A stowaway would remain in hiding. He wouldn't be up on the main deck chatting with Sam and Tom Locket.

Tom Locket and Sam! Suddenly, in a lightning flash, the truth dawned on Mr. Linnet. Why had he been so blind, so dense? Why had some sixth sense made him uneasy and yet not shown him the facts? The Professor, Sam, and Tom Locket were *all* animal fanciers. So were the other studious seamen—zoologists, probably, to a man!

Helter-skelter into his mind came the pieces of the jigsaw puzzle. Sam's slip of the tongue about Freetown, for instance. Obviously, he and the rest had known that was not

247

their destination. Instead, they were off to some nameless land to bring back specimens from the wild and put them in iron cages. There was probably room enough in the hold for a whole menagerie.

Clues came at him, thick and fast. The confabulation down below when Tom and Sam—so insincerely!—had pretended that Monkey had followed them. They had dragged him into the hold, more likely! As for the branches, the beef, the netting—what could they be but animal fodder and the wherewithal for cages? And then the titles of the books —*Forty Effective Cures for Snakebite*—a zoologist would indeed need that, as well as *Gorillas, Wild and Captive.* And which of the seamen, he bitterly wondered, had sported with the Great Sea Turtle and whisked it from the Caribbean into some northern aquarium?

Mr. Linnet sighed aloud, reproaching himself for his lack of judgment. He had hobnobbed with his fellow sailors, respecting them for their seriousness—especially Chidwick and Throgmorton. But now these two—and Tom Locket and Sam—appeared to him in their true colours, as collectors, thieves, animal-snatchers, waiting to catch him off his guard and so make off with Monkey.

Monkey! Remorsefully, he met the eyes that, quick as ever to catch his mood, reflected his own distress. He longed to be able to explain, to say that he had done his best, in order that Monkey should be free—free of the world of Professor McWhirter and people such as Joe Boskin and the beautiful Mrs. de Quincey Belmore. And what had happened? He was here, with Monkey, on the *Southern Pearl,* hemmed in once more by that very world, and with far less chance of escape. Out of the frying-pan into the fire—that was his situation.

Well, what was he to do now? What, indeed, could anyone

do, in the middle of the Atlantic Ocean and at no known point of the compass?

He glanced about him anxiously, as though the night or the stars could help him, and saw the Captain coming towards them, followed by Mrs. Linnet.

"Ladies and gentleman," said the Captain, and paused as though hunting for suitable words. "Something has happened that concerns you all. The ship has sprung a leak!"

"Oh, Captain, no!" shrieked Mrs. Linnet. "Worse than my aunt who went to New York—she at least not shipwrecked—terrible thing to read in the papers—three young children drowned at sea—oh, my poor dear mother—!"

"But, my dear chap, isn't this rather careless? Why not plug the hole?" said General Post.

"Calm yourself, please, Mrs. Linnet. No one is going to be drowned. No, General, I have not been careless. The *Southern Pearl* is an old ship, and you can't plug rotting timbers. It's what we call a slow leak, which means that we have time to prepare. The lifeboats are new and in working order. And by dawn, I have reason to believe, the *Northern Star,* a sister ship, will be off our starboard bow. She will pick us all up and return us to London."

"I shall need to take my knitting, Captain," said Mrs. Post, decisively. "I am making the General an overcoat."

"Take what you must, all of you. But don't overload the boats. Lives are worth more than any possessions. So—I'll leave you to your preparations. The seamen will all be on hand to help you. We shall disembark at dawn."

Back to London! Mr. Linnet was stunned. As he watched the Captain stride away, distributing orders right and left, he could think of nothing else. The slow leak in the *Southern Pearl* became a minor detail. Back to London! Then all his efforts had been in vain. He might just as well have stayed there. The thought of the long homeward journey in the company of Professor McWhirter—not to mention Sam and Tom Locket—was horrible to contemplate. They were wily and determined men. To outwit them would need strength and cunning—qualities he himself lacked, as he knew only too well.

What could he do? Where could he turn? Was there any alternative to going back on his tracks?

Mr. Linnet prayed to his lucky stars and looked at Miss Brown-Potter. After all, she had mastered Kilimanjaro. She had snatched Stanley Fan from a crocodile on the banks of the River Tooma. A woman with such a past as that would surely have something to suggest.

And Miss Brown-Potter, on hearing the whole unhappy story, had, indeed, a suggestion.

Long after the General and Mrs. Post, with Uncle Trehunsey bemoaning his fate, had retired to their respective cabins, she and the Linnets sat in the starlight—Monkey and Little Louis asleep—discussing a possible plan.

Mrs. Linnet, every few minutes, dashed away to the side of the ship to see if it was sinking; then to the children to make quite sure that none of them had been kidnapped; and back to the hatch to exclaim and protest at Mr. Linnet's disclosures.

"Am struck dumb—simply cannot believe it—Winthrop and Percival so kind—giving Trehunsey piggybacks—and Bertram and Neville so polite—washing the dishes—how terrible—all of them whited sepulchres—just goes to show, as my grandmother said—"

Mr. Linnet patted her hand and continued with the discussion. And at last, after much cogitation, the plan was clear and complete. They would now have to make their preparations.

As they parted by the companionway, Louis lifted his head from his breast.

"Abide with me," he croaked. "Umtota!"

The three looked at each other in silence. Louis, each of them was aware, would have to learn a new word. They would never, now, get to Umtota . . .

11

"Hail, shipwrecked mariners!" called Chidwick, peeling the canvas from a lifeboat. *A Hundred Ways with Wire Netting* peeped over the edge of his pocket.

"Good morning," said Mr. Linnet, coldly, dragging Monkey away. He was not going to bandy jokes with a man who read such books as that.

Chidwick, looking mystified, continued with his work.

"All hands on deck!" came the Captain's order. And the seamen swarmed from everywhere. A big, broad sun came out of the sea, flooding the world with light. And the shadow away on the starboard bow resolved itself into another ship, swimming swanlike towards them.

The *Southern Pearl,* Mr. Linnet noticed, was now quite low in the water. And the dark blue smudge on the horizon had become a white palm-bordered shore with green hills rising behind it. How far away was it, he wondered. His eye measured the distance.

The deck now buzzed with activity. The seamen laughed and joked as they worked. Some of them even whistled. Indeed, far from worrying over the shipwreck, they behaved like men relieved of a burden, as though they had brought some difficult task to a favourable conclusion.

The Captain put his glass to his eye and trained it on the other ship.

"She's received our signal! She's answering! The *Northern Star* will stand by, and we'll be aboard by sunset! Are you ready, all you passengers?" He waved at the little waiting group.

"But, Captain—" Mr. Linnet began. The words, "We'll be aboard by sunset!" had given him a shock.

"You mean—you won't go down with the ship?" In cases of shipwreck, he had always believed, a captain saw his men to safety and then, standing on the deck—saluting, perhaps, or singing a hymn—disappeared heroically beneath the rising waters.

"What—me? Of course not! I never do."

"Never? You've been in *other* shipwrecks?"

"Dozens of 'em." The Captain grinned. "No, no, General Post, not you!" He thrust out a firm, delaying arm. "Women and children first, you know."

"My dear chap, that is quite out of date. No one observes it nowadays. I really mustn't be drowned, you know, before they have time to make me a field marshal. Now, where's that silly Bhima?"

A pile of trunks staggered along the deck. They toppled themselves into the lifeboat, disclosing at their base as they did so a slender knitted figure.

"Ah, there you are! Hop in, my boy. And you, too, Flora, my dear. Now, all we want are two good rowers. No, Mr.

Truro, I think not. There isn't room for you, I'm afraid. Well, no need to be rude, dear fellow!" The General smiled his kindly smile, as Uncle Trehunsey, foiled in his efforts, turned, snarling, from the boat.

The Captain sighed resignedly. He knew he was no match for the General, even in a shipwreck. "Chidwick! Throgmorton! Lower away!" The faces disappeared from view as the lifeboat swung over the side. Bhima's nose bumped against the bulwark as he put his two hands together and made a farewell bow to Monkey.

"Now, Mrs. Linnet, you and the children. Good heavens, you won't need all that stuff!"

Mrs. Linnet stood beside the Captain, festooned with bundles, cooking pots, the blackboard, and Little Trehunsey. Edward had his string bag and Victoria the doll's house.

"Must think of the children's education—and, of course, don't want them to starve, Captain—clothing also necessary, even in Equatorial climates—" Mrs. Linnet suddenly stopped, transfixed by her husband's warning eye. He evidently wanted her to be silent.

"But you'll find all you need on the other ship! Oh, well, if you must, you must, I suppose. But please leave room for the two sailors who will row you across to the *Northern Star.*"

"I think we can do that ourselves, Captain," said Miss Brown-Potter, quickly. "I have much experience of rowing —along the Congo River, you know. And Stanley, too, is competent." She glanced at Mr. Linnet.

"And so am I!" Mr. Linnet assured him. He thought it wiser not to add that the only rowing he had done was in Regent's Park where the lake water was only three feet deep. "I am sure we can manage, Captain."

253

"Very well. It isn't so far. And I need every possible man in the hold."

To do what, Mr. Linnet wondered. Poor deluded Captain Twice, sending his seamen into the hold to rescue a cargo of sandbags!

"And your uncle can take an oar, as well. In you go, Mr. Truro!"

Loudly groaning and resolved never to touch an oar, Uncle Trehunsey obeyed the Captain. Tinker and Badger with the eiderdown, and Stanley with Louis on his perch, followed Miss Brown-Potter.

"You and the animal, Mr. Linnet"—Captain Twice pointed at Monkey—"will have to use the ladder. We have to think of the weight, you know."

"See you soon again, Mrs. Linnet!" Bertram and Winthrop waved at her. "And thank you for all those splendid pies!"

"Yes, of course, I mean, no!—no trouble at all—oh, what can I say?" Mrs. Linnet was distressed. She did not like to be impolite to men who, however unprincipled, had washed the dishes for her.

"Lower away!" the Captain ordered. And the lifeboat, with a loud rattle, swung out and down to the sea.

Miss Brown-Potter and Stanley Fan seized their oars and steadied it. Mrs. Linnet and Edward, neither of whom had ever rowed, took another pair.

White-faced and frankly terrified, Mr. Linnet crawled over the side, put his foot on the swaying ladder, dragging Monkey with him.

"Undo his rope," Neville advised. "You'll find it easier if he's free."

"Oh, no, you don't," thought Mr. Linnet. If they hoped

that at the last minute they could get their greedy hands on Monkey, the animal fanciers were mistaken.

"I prefer it this way," he said, coldly, as he seized Monkey by the leg and planted his foot on a rung.

But Monkey seemed to have no idea that he was being rescued. This was, clearly, a new sort of game, and he was determined to play it. Up and down the ladder he went, pulling Mr. Linnet this way and that, while Little Louis, enjoying it all, repeated his breathless word.

The *Southern Pearl* gave a sharp lurch. The ladder swung out with a sickening swoop, and every watcher held his breath as the two figures, locked together—each trying to save the other—went hurtling through the air.

"Alfred! Papa!" Three voices wailed.

Down at the bottom of the sea, the lid of Davy Jones's Locker opened to receive the pair.

But suddenly a rope whipped out, caught the oddly assorted bundle, and swept it into the lifeboat. Percival, quick as any cowboy, had cleverly lassooed it.

"Row!" commanded Miss Brown-Potter, striking away from the ship's side.

"Pull on your right!" the Captain cried. "The *Northern Star* is to the *south*. You're going away from her."

Mr. Linnet seized an oar. Monkey seized its fellow.

Away went the lifeboat, jerking and bobbing. Mrs. Linnet, to her own surprise, proved to be an excellent oarsman, in spite of her one pair of hands. She and Edward bent and dipped as though they had lived all their lives in boats.

"MR. LINNET!" The Captain was shouting through a megaphone. "YOU'RE GOING IN THE WRONG DIRECTION. PULL ON YOUR RIGHT OAR!"

255

"Pull on your left," said Miss Brown-Potter. "All together! In! Out!"

The Linnet family and Stanley pulled.

"Alfred, have you gone mad?" Uncle Trehunsey banged with his stick. "The rescue ship is falling behind us. Do what the Captain says!"

"No," said Mr. Linnet, calmly, amazed at his own temerity. For the first time in his whole life he had said "No" to his uncle.

"*Mr. Linnet! Can you hear me?*" The Captain's voice was far and faint.

"Row!" commanded Miss Brown-Potter.

"Why won't you let us be rescued, Papa? I can't even see the *Northern Star!*" Victoria, holding Little Trehunsey, burst into frightened tears.

"You *are* being rescued. Just be patient."

"ALFRED!" Uncle Trehunsey roared. And now his voice held a note of panic. "We're going nowhere! You'll drown us all. We'll end up in Australia!"

The lifeboat was bouncing like a ball—plonk, plonk, over the waves.

Mr. Linnet had known the sea would grow choppy. Miss Brown-Potter had warned him last night when the three had made their plan. The nearer the shore, the rougher the water. He glanced back over his shoulder.

There it was, floating towards them, the land that only yesterday had been nothing but a smudge! He could hardly believe his good fortune.

"Ship your oars!" said Miss Brown-Potter. "The sea will carry us in."

And it did. The waves, as though they wanted nothing better, were rushing towards the shore. They lifted the lifeboat on their backs, heaving it from crest to crest, each wave bringing it nearer the land.

"Hold on, now!" cried Miss Brown-Potter, tightly linking her arm through Stanley's and gathering Tinker and Badger to her.

The Linnets held on to their children and Monkey, Monkey held on to Mr. Linnet. They were all trying to save each other.

Uncle Trehunsey held on to a rowlock, trying to save himself.

Bang, bang. Thump, thump. The boat plunged forward with the waves into a curdle of foam. It spun about like a spinning top, shipping the ocean, rocking and tipping.

Then Miss Brown-Potter and Stanley Fan leapt out into the swirling waters and hauled it safely to shore.

The plan, at least so far, had worked . . .

12

The little clearing by the shore, the green jungle beyond the clearing, and the lofty plateau beyond the jungle were waking to the morning sun. Out of the shadows came a pair of palm fowl, their feathers the colour of cocoanut leaves, and strolled among the grasses. A ripe fig fell with a thud to the ground. A soft wind stirred the tamarind trees. None of these sounds disturbed the clearing.

Suddenly, someone—or something—whispered. A twig cracked under a foot.

The palm fowl lifted their sleek heads, not afraid, but enquiring.

At the edge of the clearing stood a man, with a large black object on his head. Two children huddled at his side and a woman carrying a baby. Behind them stood another woman and a dark boy carrying a branch—or so it might have seemed to a palm cock—with a large white bird upon it. A second man, with a bandaged foot, had slumped down with his back to a tree, as though in a state of exhaustion.

Beside this little group of people and firmly roped to one of them, there was another figure. He stood there gazing at the scene, half as tall as a tall man, his wet fur edged with light. Upon his brow was a white spot. And round his neck, like a circle of flowers, were patches of white amid the brown. He wore a sailor cap on his head with *London Ex—* in gold on the band. And perched upon his right shoulder was a sulphur-crested cockatoo about six inches high.

The palm fowl pecked their way towards him, examining him with beady eyes, while he, in his turn, examined the clearing, as though drawing it into himself with eyes and ears and nose.

A noisy cry shattered the silence. On the tamarind branch above his head a black bird with a yellow beak was jabbering at Monkey. He made a leap as if to join her. But finding himself still held in check, he put out his paw palm-downward.

"Why is the bird so cross with him?" Victoria demanded.

"Mynah birds are very quick-tempered. Perhaps she's afraid he'll disturb her eggs." Miss Brown-Potter pointed upwards to a muddle of rags and twigs and palm strips. The mynah bird scuttled along the branch and settled herself on the muddle.

The palm fowl, taking this in their stride, came pecking over the strangers' feet, seeking for salty tidbits. And a small pink bird, the size of a wren, sat itself down on Edward's head, plucked out two of his long fair hairs, and bore them away in triumph.

Edward was surprised, but pleased.

"An Equatorial Plumper nesting," said Miss Brown-Potter, calmly.

"Well, do hope Equatorial Plumpers won't make a habit of it—don't want Edward to be bald—no, no, Alfred, come back, come back—!"

Mrs. Linnet emitted a shriek far louder than any mynah bird's. For her husband, prone upon the grass, was being dragged across the clearing at the end of his piece of rope. Monkey had given a huge leap and was now bowing to a friend and offering his paw.

It had never occurred to Mr. Linnet, in spite of his many imaginings, that one day he would find himself compelled to bow to a tiger. But this, in fact, was what he was doing. Transfixed by horror, unable to move, he bent before the yellow eyes and waited for the worst.

The tiger sniffed at Mr. Linnet. The tiger sniffed at Monkey. And then, apparently disgusted, he pushed the paw aside with his head and turned to examine the other strangers.

Mrs. Linnet thrust the children behind her and clutched Trehunsey so forcefully that he broke into a roar. The tiger, with a look of terror, hurriedly made a jump for safety and landed at Miss Brown-Potter's feet.

She gave him a little poke with her toe. "Don't be so silly. We won't hurt you. Get along!" she said.

With a nervous glance at Little Trehunsey the tiger got

259

along at once. He stalked away across the clearing, his hindquarters swinging from side to side, moving slimly inside his coat as though it were too large for him or he a little too small for it.

"W-was it a m-man-eater, Miss Brown-Potter?" Mrs. Linnet was shaken. Were her fears to be realised, after all?

"Clearly not," said Miss Brown-Potter. "He was frightened out of his wits."

Mr. Linnet untied the rope that had bound him and Monkey together. Tigers, apparently, did not like him and therefore would not eat him. Better still, tigers seemed to dislike Monkey and would not eat him, either. Best of all, he had a son—he patted Little Trehunsey proudly—who could frighten tigers out of their wits. What more was there to fear?

"I think I am going to like Umtota!" Edward bent and touched the grass, apparently putting down the dogs.

"But this is not Umtota, Edward—" If the truth had to be told at all, the sooner the better, thought Mrs. Linnet. They were strangers in a strange land, and the children would have to know it.

"Not Umtota? Then where are we?" Edward was looking agitated.

"We don't know, Edward," said Mr. Linnet. "All we know is that it's somewhere. And anywhere, it seemed to us, was better than going back to London."

"But where's somewhere? I have to know! It has to have a name!"

"Edward!" said Miss Brown-Potter, firmly. "When the little bird came and sat on your head, did it say to itself, 'I'm lost! I'm nowhere! Until I know the name of this place, I really can't accept it'?"

"B-but I'm a p-person, not a p-place!"

"For the little bird you are a place. She does not know you are called Edward. Perhaps she is telling her mate about you and suggesting he pay you a visit."

"Is s-she?" The thought of two Equatorial Plumpers discussing him in their cosy nest was interesting to Edward.

"I'm a place in a place!" He spread out his arms. "And that place is in another place, and the other place is inside a place and that place again is inside another—"

"All right, Edward, that'll do. And now we must build a house in this place!"

Mr. Linnet seized on a fallen branch. It was just about the size he needed. Four of such branches stuck in the ground, with thin green boughs to make the rafters and woven palm leaves for roof and walls—in no time he would have a house.

Edward looked into his string bag. The sugar clocks were all there, faithfully assuring him that the time was Ten Past Five. This, and the fact that he was a place, gave him a sense of security. He set to work to help his father.

"Need our house have a door, Papa? I don't want my soldier to be behind it."

"There will be no door and no soldier, Edward. We have left him behind in London."

Mr. Linnet, Edward, and Miss Brown-Potter set up the framework for three shelters. Everybody worked. The clearing rang with their human voices. And birds, delighting in the sounds, sat in the trees and listened.

Victoria, exploring the clearing, came upon a little spring that bubbled with fresh water.

Stanley Fan, with a bent pin, caught an unsuspecting Tropical Trout, straight out of the sea.

And Mrs. Linnet ran back and forth between the two

Trehunseys; shielding the elder from the sun by propping the blackboard against him; trying to persuade the younger to take some cocoanut milk.

"Perhaps we shall find a wild goat and then you can milk it," said Miss Brown-Potter.

But the thought of milking a wild goat was not to Mrs. Linnet's fancy. This new world was still too strange to her, too far from Belvedere Gardens. And the green jungle beyond the clearing filled her with anxious dread.

"Keep seeing little old men's faces peering through the leaves, Alfred—just like the ones on brass door-knockers—very unsettling—may be pygmies—!"

"Nonsense! It's just the flicker of sun and shadow. You'll get used to it." Mr. Linnet was tiling a roof with alternate banana and cocoanut leaves and delighting in his handiwork.

The little settlement was growing. Grass that had never known human footfall was bent this way and that. Little paths appeared in it, running between the houses. Something new was taking shape. The mounting sun took note of it as he strode up through the sky.

And Monkey, of course, helped everyone, no matter what it cost them.

He brought Mr. Linnet so many palm leaves that they shrivelled in the morning heat before they could be used. He seized the doll's house and leapt away, perching it on top of a tree to give the dolls a view. He helped Mrs. Linnet unpack her bundles, putting cough drops in the cooking pot and wrapping Little Trehunsey up in Edward's winter underwear.

And between these various acts of kindness he would

pause and gaze at the jungle curtain with an anxious, inquiring look.

"He's waiting for something," said Miss Brown-Potter, noting the ears pricked to listen and the eager, watchful eyes.

"What could it be?" Mr. Linnet wondered.

And, Monkey, at the sound of voices, forgot his own preoccupations and brought a spray of orange blossom and tried to make them eat it.

"Enough, enough!" Mr. Linnet cried, patting his stomach to indicate that he wanted no more flowers. Monkey, however, mistook this gesture for a sign of urgent hunger. So, he leapt into the nearest palm tree, hurriedly plucked a cocoanut, and then, to everyone's concern, dropped it on the prostrate figure that snored beside the blackboard. They had all hoped that Uncle Trehunsey would sleep at least till lunchtime.

The clearing rang with his shouts and curses. The listening birds stared in surprise. They had never heard anything like it.

"I don't know what you think you're doing—bringing me to this awful place. And what am I going to eat, may I ask? Grasses? Dandelions?"

"Veal patties!" cried Mrs. Linnet, fossicking in a bundle. "To be eaten on a piece of shell—and some of yesterday's apple pie—"

"And roast Tropical Trout, Mr. Truro!" Miss Brown-Potter smiled at him. "And one or two ripe figs!"

Uncle Trehunsey was disappointed. He had hoped there would be nothing to eat, so that he could continue to grumble. But here they were, like grandees, setting a feast before him.

"Well," he muttered, ungraciously. "I shall take a little rest first." He hobbled towards the largest shelter.

"No, not there, Uncle Trehunsey!" For the second time in one day Mr. Linnet was being recalcitrant.

Uncle Trehunsey turned upon him. "What do you mean —not here?" he demanded. "I'll rest wherever I choose to rest. Don't you say 'No' to me, Alfred. I mean to be master in my house as I have always been."

"Of course you do!" Miss Brown-Potter agreed. "That is what every man should be. But this is Mr. Linnet's house. Yours, Mr. Truro, is over there." She pointed to the smallest shelter. "We have made you a bed of leaves and grass and Mr. Linnet's jacket. I hope you will be comfortable."

She might have been a London hostess, pointing out to an honoured guest the way to the best bedroom.

Uncle Trehunsey glared at her, praying that Heaven would strike her dead.

But nothing happened to Miss Brown-Potter. She spread about him her luminous smile, and Uncle Trehunsey, in a moment of terrible clarity, realised he was beaten. His days of ruling the roost were over. There was no longer any roost to rule. He had become a poor relation.

A memory stirred in Mr. Linnet, as he watched his uncle—or his wife's—hobbling off to the modest dwelling, cutting off flower heads with his stick.

Long ago he had promised himself that someday when his ship came in, he would have a home of his own. Yes, and someone to help his wife with the many things no woman can do who has only a single pair of hands.

He looked at his large leafy shelter. He looked at his wife, bent over the fire, roasting the Tropical Trout. He

264

looked at Monkey sitting beside her, with Little Trehunsey in his arms, contentedly asleep.

And it seemed to him that the longed-for ship had, at last, come in. Here, indeed, was his own home, albeit a house of leaves and branches. And his wife, indeed, had someone to help her, someone inclined to overdo things but nevertheless with a willing heart; somebody clad in a fur coat with a sailor cap on his head.

"It's ready!" Mrs. Linnet exclaimed. "Wash your hands at the spring, children. This is yours, Miss Brown-Potter——" She handed them each a heaped-up shell.

Happiness flooded Mr. Linnet. They had food. They had shelter. They were together. And Monkey, at last, was safe and free. From today a new life would begin.

"Figs and troot! That's a bonnie luncheon! May Ah wish ye all a good appetite?"

A familiar voice, a voice they had hoped not to hear again, hailed them across the clearing.

There, under a tamarind tree, with a ferret round his neck, like a collar, and his pockets full of marmosets, stood the well-known animal fancier whose name was Professor McWhirter . . .

13

Edward was the first of them to recover from the shock. "The dogs!" he cried, anxiously, making a grab at the empty air.

But, alas, he was too late.

A couple of invisible somethings were apparently greeting Professor McWhirter, as though he were a brother.

"Good doggies! Bonnie doggies!" Professor McWhirter stroked the air with every mark of affection.

Mr. Linnet was disgusted. That any dog, real or imaginary, should truckle to such a villain!

"And how's the beastie?" the Professor enquired.

There was no time for anyone to answer. For a great roar sounded from the jungle and a long shadow of black and gold streaked across the luncheon party and fell on Professor McWhirter.

"A terrible ending!" thought Mr. Linnet, at the same time feeling it somehow just that a man who catered for zoos and pet shops should be eaten by a tiger.

But the tiger, he was surprised to see, far from making a meal of it, was hugging the shaggy kilted figure and tenderly licking its cheeks.

"Hee balou, Rajah laddie!" Professor McWhirter returned the hug. "Eh, but ye're lookin' braw and sleekit, forbye ye've had the moths at yer coat. Now, dinna be such a wild old clootie. Wait till ye see what Ah've brought ye!" The Professor glanced back over his shoulder. "Where's his lassie? Where's Ranee?"

Out from behind the Professor's cloak a tigress shyly sidled.

Mrs. Linnet snatched up Little Trehunsey. Mr. Linnet snatched up Monkey.

But the tigers took no notice of either. They were thinking of nobody but themselves.

"There now! Ye're together again! Away with the two of

ye! Shoo, shoo!" The Professor flicked his cloak at them, and the pair slipped silkily into the jungle.

Mr. Linnet looked on suspiciously. What was the rascal up to now?

"Come along, now. Dinna dilly-dally. What's the matter?" called Professor McWhirter.

"It's Flossie, sir," a voice answered. "Trying to nibble the grass."

"Shove her along," said another voice. "Algy's right on her tail!"

It was not the sight of a rhinoceros stumbling unwillingly into the clearing, nor the hippopotamus that followed, that made Mr. Linnet stiffen. He had heard those voices somewhere before. And Monkey, struggling in his arms, seemed to know them, too.

Two figures emerged from behind Flossie, one tall and seamanlike, the other a skinny, gangling youth.

Barley Hawkes and Young Napper! Mr. Linnet was horrified. That they, his old acquaintances—to whom, indeed, he owed Monkey—should stoop to Professor McWhirter's trade!

"Off you go, you patchwork quilt!" Barley Hawkes, with a slap on its rump, sped a giraffe through the clearing.

Mr. Linnet gazed after it. Tiger, rhinoceros, hippopotamus, giraffe—and all brought here by Professor McWhirter! What was afoot? What could it mean?

A horrible thought presented itself. Was this green clearing at the edge of the jungle a kind of collecting station; a place where wild animals were kept till the moment came to transport them abroad and sell them to various zoos? It seemed extremely likely. If so, he had built his new home on the worst of all possible spots, and he—and Monkey—were once again between frying-pan and fire. He ran round his mind, like a rat in a trap, trying to think of a way of escape.

His meditations were interrupted by a fearful peal of laughter.

"Careful, Young Napper!" said Professor McWhirter. "That's a verra, verra rare hyena!"

The hideous creature, noisily hooting, went streaking through the clearing. It was followed by a Persian goat, with two young kids at heel.

"We're nearly at the end, Professor. Now, now, Bruno, get down on yer fours. You don't have to go on two legs here!" Barley Hawkes urged on a grizzly bear, which in spite of his friendly exhortations, insisted on waltzing towards the jungle, bolt upright, as though in a ballroom.

"And you, too, Alf, in yer seven-leagued boots! Come on, then, give us yer paw."

A trunk wound itself round Barley's hand, as he led an elephant over the grass and hustled it away.

"And that's the lot, sir—barring Toby. Mr. Locket's urging him on."

"Well, lend him a hand. And you, too, Napper. We havena' all the time in the wurrld. Give him a wee bittie push, Tom!"

At that moment Tom Locket appeared with a leopard draped like a shawl round his shoulders. In front of him, being hustled along, was a very reluctant lion.

"Dinna be such a gawk, Toby. Ye're no' so unchancy as ye think. Barley, give him a heave!"

The three men heaved and pushed and tugged, and the lion, halfway across the clearing, gave a groan and sat down.

"Stop it!" cried an outraged voice. "Leave that lion alone!"

Mr. Linnet was surprised to discover, as four pairs of eyes were turned towards him, that this voice was his own.

"Barley Hawkes! And you, Young Napper! What are you doing here?"

"Hello, Mr. Linnet! Glad to see you again. We're working for the One and Only." Barley Hawkes nodded at Professor McWhirter.

"Then, I'm sorry to hear it," said Mr. Linnet. "Collecting animals for zoos—I wonder you're not ashamed. Look at that lion! He's panic-stricken."

"Would ye no' be panic-strruck yerself if ye'd lived all yer life behind bars and suddenly found ye were free? Ah doubt ye'd be doin' the Highland Fling, all mim and primsie and trig!" The brown eye of Professor McWhirter sparkled at Mr. Linnet.

"Tchah!" Mr. Linnet exploded with scorn. The Professor was not going to get round *him* with all that Scottish gibberish.

"But you've got it wrong, Mr. Linnet, sir. Topsy-turvy, as you might say." Barley Hawkes dug into a pocket, fetched up a little piece of pasteboard, and proceeded to read aloud.

The One and Only
Professor McWhirter!
Animal Fancier and Collector.
Zoos, Circuses, and Pet Shops Catered For.
Suitable Situations Found
For Birds, Beasts, Fish, and Reptiles.
Highly Recommended.

"I have read that card," said Mr. Linnet. "Highly recommended, indeed! By whom, I'd like to know?"

"By the animals!" Barley Hawkes declared. "All right, he

269

caters for zoos, etcetera. *Caters* for them, eh, Napper?'' He emphasised the word, with a grin.

"Oh, 'e does. 'E's deep, the One and Only.'' Napper winked at his mate. "Caters for 'em proper, I'd say. 'E empties 'em! Runs 'em out of business!'' He gestured downwards with his thumb.

"And as for suitable situations—well, this here place is a pretty good one—wouldn't you say, Mr. Linnet?''

"This place? I don't know what you mean!'' Mr. Linnet was mystified. What were the two men getting at?

"Mebbe, Mr. Linnet,'' said Professor McWhirter, taking a marmoset from his pocket and setting it carefully on a branch. "Mebbe it's a matter of prepositions.'' His bicoloured eyes had a wily look. "Ask auld Tom—he'll tell ye!''

"Well, you see, Mr. Linnet—'' Tom Locket grinned. "What the One and Only means is that he collects not *for* but *from*. From zoos, circuses, and pet shops. Someone leaves the cages unlocked so that he—and Sam—can get in and bring the animals out.''

" 'E's our man in London, is Mr. Locket,'' Young Napper put in admiringly. "And this 'ere cargo is all from there.''

"Oh, well—that's just the luck of the game. Another time it will be Chidwick, bringing a batch from Hamburg. Or Herbert, maybe, from Hong Kong. There's one of us in every zoo. The rest stand by to help Sam and the Only—getting the animals down to the docks and smuggling them aboard. And, of course, we all study seamanship—under men like Barley and Captain Twice, who navigate to this or that island and advise us where to knock in the holes and the proper moment to sink the ships.''

"Old vessels, of course,'' put in Barley Hawkes, "the ones

270

on their last legs, so to say, not up to making the journey home."

"Then, once the Captain is sure of a rescue, we get out the rafts, as we did this morning—if you look, you'll see them down on the shore—quickly land the animals, and sail back for another lot. It's very simple, really." Tom Locket peeled off his spotted burden and slipped it into the undergrowth.

Mr. Linnet stared at him. His mind seemed to be reeling. Not "for" but "from"—our man in London—cargoes composed of animals—holes knocked in sinking ships—somebody there to unlock the cages—somebody else to bring animals out—very simple, really!

Well, it might be simple to Tom Locket, but to him it was like some tricky riddle. When is an animal fancier not an animal fancier? When he's the One and Only.

Could it be true? Was he now to think of that artful rogue as more of a saint than a sinner? And Chidwick, Throgmorton, and the rest as our men in Paris, Berlin, Moscow—animal snatchers not from the wild but from cages with iron bars? He struggled with the proposition.

He remembered the sounds his wife had heard—the goat bleating, the bear grunting, the lion, the elephant, the hyena; and he himself dismissing them as a squeak of wind in the sails. The listening silence in the hold, Tom Locket with his knocking crowbar; the books that, seen in another light, could be evidence not of villainy but of serious dedication. *The Locksmith's Gazette,* after all, would deal not only with making locks but also with ways to pick them; and anyone rescuing a cobra would do well to familiarise himself with *Forty Effective Cures for Snakebite.*

He remembered the Captain's care for his cargo, so excessive—had it been pins and needles—so understandable now. His deference to the cabin-boy, unsuitable as it then had seemed, was really a proper attitude if Sam, indeed, was a leading figure in Professor McWhirter's enterprise. A mariner, however expert—if his cargo consisted of wild beasts—would need an animal fancier somewhere in the offing.

Oh, yes! The facts were all there, staring him full in the face. But what use is the right fact when the point of view is wrong? You might as well not have facts at all for all the good they did you. In his constant anxiety for Monkey he had missed the mark again and again, and grasped the wrong end of every stick. He blushed to think of it.

He stole a look at Professor McWhirter, who was plucking the last marmoset from his pocket and looking as villainous as ever.

Then he glanced at Miss Brown-Potter. Her smile was humourous and serene. Had she guessed? Had she known the truth for what it was when the animals entered the clearing? Of course she had, he told himself. She would never let facts bamboozle her. She would look them straight in the eye.

Sheepishly, he glanced at his wife, thinking of those shipboard sounds and expecting to hear, "I told you so!"

But Mrs. Linnet had no such thought.

"Am rendered speechless—so unexpected—Professor McWhirter a changed man—might as well say the sky is falling —everything now turned back to front—oh, please save my baby—!"

Little Trehunsey had crawled away and was now seated beside the lion, hitting its nose with his fist.

"Nay, dinna fash yerself, Mrs. Linnet. No creature that's known captivity would hurt a hair o' a human head."

"Nor an animal's?" Miss Brown-Potter enquired.

"Not one that has mixed in the human wurrld. Though Ah wouldna say"—the Professor winked—"that he'd turn up his nose at a wild pig. But dinna fear for yer pets, ma'am. Badger and Tinker are safe."

"I was thinking of him—" She nodded at Monkey. "I am not at all afraid, Professor."

Mr. Linnet, having digested his facts, suddenly made up his mind.

"Neither am I," he said firmly, and loosed his arms from Monkey.

"Ahoy, me old shipmate!" said Barley Hawkes, as Monkey leapt to greet him. "What you been doing since I saw you? Or *over*doing, I ought to say!" He winked at Mr. Linnet. "It was due to this here creature, sir—he's hard to forget, if you know what I mean—that I joined the One and Only. It's a better life, I said to myself, than a pub on the Dover Road."

Monkey now embraced Young Napper and then bowed to Professor McWhirter, stretching his paw, palm-downward.

"And the same to yerself!" said Professor McWhirter. And to Mr. Linnet's astonishment, he put his two palms together and made a deep obeisance. "Ah'm happy to see ye here, at last."

"But where is here?" asked Miss Brown-Potter. "Edward would like to know."

"Ye're on Three, Edward," said Professor McWhirter. "But dinna ask me for points of the compass. Ye're somewhere in the Atlantic."

"Three? But three what?" Mr. Linnet demanded. It had to be one of three somethings.

Tom Locket hurried to the rescue. "You're on Island Number Three," he said. "Two is in the South Pacific, for animals from the temperate zones. And One is somewhere

273

away up north—for polar bears and suchlike. They're just like any other island except that they come and go as they're needed and they can't be found on any map."

Suddenly Mr. Linnet remembered. The General had failed to spy out the land. And, until he had set his foot on the shore, Uncle Trehunsey had firmly believed that there was nothing there.

"But—if nobody knows just where they are, how does anyone find them? And why was I told we were making for Freetown? Why wasn't I warned that the ship would be wrecked?"

"Oh, Sam and the Only know where they are!"

"Ay, and we'll teach the younger ones. An' they, in turn, will teach others, till there'll come a time—lang hence, mebbe—when there'll no' be a thing behind bars in the broad stretch o' the wurrld."

Professor McWhirter removed his hat, uncoiled a grass snake from his head, and slipped it into the undergrowth.

"An' as for warnin'—" His smile was crafty. "Whaur's the man that would voyage wi' us if we told him he'd cairtainly be shipwrecked? We need the pliskie passengers to give us protective colourin'. An' if they don't like it—well-a-day! They must dree their weird like anyone else. Ah dinna care tuppence for passengers when weighed against our kind o' cargo—except when we get one like yerself who has something we want to save!"

The Professor made a mocking bow in Mr. Linnet's direction.

It was true, Mr. Linnet thought to himself. He would never have sailed on the *Southern Pearl* if anyone had warned him. Nor would he have heard—or played a part in—the story that was now unfolding.

Secret islands that came and went! A band of honourable men turning themselves into thieves and picklocks in order to set wild animals free! This was work he himself could do, if the honest thieves would have him. It was better, even, than checking cargoes. He saw himself, a watchful shadow, picking the locks in the London Zoo. He saw the creatures step cautiously out, lion and antelope together, innocent, humble, grateful beasts trusting him to help them. He would lead them through the sleeping city, down to the docks and a waiting ship. "Well done, Mr. Linnet!" someone would whisper, as he herded his troupe aboard.

A cry from his wife shattered the dream.

"Alfred, Alfred, the brass door-knockers—the little faces —they're coming nearer—!"

14

Mr. Linnet came to, with a start.

Dozens of little furry shapes were creeping towards the clearing. None of them looked at Mrs. Linnet. Each had eyes only for Monkey who was standing with his arms outstretched, as though he were waiting for them.

"So here they are!" the Professor exclaimed. "Ah kenned they'd approach him, sooner or later, to see if he's a ghost from the dead or his own true self come home."

"Is this his home?" asked Victoria. "Then why did he leave his friends?"

"Ay, lass, Ah think this is his home. And mebbe it was the other way roond. Mebbe his friends left him."

The brown shapes were pressing nearer, gazing enquiringly at Monkey.

And Monkey stood and looked at them, his dark eyes darkening with—what?

None of the watching human beings could know what Monkey was thinking. But they saw him, now, do a curious thing.

He took off his navy sailor cap and handed it to Stanley. He took Little Louis from his shoulder and set him on Stanley's hand. The falling sun lit his white patches as he swung his tail round and round in ever decreasing circles. Then the tail itself began to spin, rising into the air in a spiral, bearing Monkey up and up till he sat upon it as on a throne, stretching his right arm downwards.

At this, as though with recognition, the other monkeys surged towards him, each putting its palms together and bowing its forehead to Monkey's paw.

Mr. Linnet was startled. He was used to Monkey's loving gaze that sought out and shared all his own feelings, intimate, friendly, self-forgetful. But here was somebody all unknown, ancient as time, withdrawn and mournful, utterly alone. Were monkeys, then, so like to men that they, too, in their inmost parts, had a place where they were lonely? It troubled him to think of it.

"That's how Bhima bowed to him. Is he a sort of king?" asked Edward.

"Ah, Bhima is a Hindu, Edwarrd, and the Hindus have an auld legend—"

"Tell me!" Edward's eyes were shining.

"It's a story of a hero-god, wounded in battle, needing

276

herrbs. And a monkey lord leaping away and bringing back part of the Himalayas. A sprig o' green was all was needed, but—unable to do a thing by halves—he had to bring back a whole mountain! A mountain for one herrb—the gawkie! An' for that the hero rewarded him; a jewel to hang in the midst of his forehead and others to hang around his neck. And since that time—once in many a year—there's a monkey borrn wi' white on his brow an' a patch o' white aroond his throat to show where the jewels were. And the monkeys take him for their king—or so the auld wives tell us."

"And do you believe it?" asked Miss Brown-Potter.

"Ah didna say that, Miss Broon-Putter. Ah simply told the lad a tale. Ah'm hardly an auld wife, ye ken."

"Then you don't believe it, Professor McWhirter!"

"Ah didna say that either, ma'am." The Professor's brown eye had a foxy glint. "But Ah gang by what Ah see!"

He turned to Monkey, his blue eye blazing, and behind his back Miss Brown-Potter smiled.

The last little face had made its bow. The ceremony, it seemed, was over. For Monkey had leapt down from his throne, wound his tail again about him, and reached for his cap and his friend. He was his old familiar self, embracing each of his furry brothers, rushing to get them fruit and flowers; presenting Barley Hawkes and Napper with trails of jungle creeper; forcing a flower on Professor McWhirter who looked more scoundrelly than ever in his effort to seem to enjoy it.

"Well, if he's a king, he's also a sairvant, which mebbe is what a king should be. What's fidgettin' ye, Mr. Linnet? Dinna pull off ma arm!"

For Mr. Linnet had drawn him aside and was trying to find suitable words for what he had to say.

"Professor McWhirter, I—er—misjudged you. I thought you were—well, a villain, in fact! That you wanted him for a zoo or a circus or possibly a—er—pet shop."

"But Ah *am* a villain, Mr. Linnet. A clishmaclavering auld varmint, interfering wi' the wurrld's affairs. Dinna fit me out wi' a harp and a halo. Ah'm a villain, man, and prood o' it."

"Well, what I want to say is this—I offer myself, if you will take me—" The words came shyly tumbling out, and Professor McWhirter gravely listened, his blue and brown eyes alternately shining.

"Ay, ye're the verra man for us. Ah have no doots aboot ye, now. When we saw that ye wouldna agree to be rescued, that in spite of warnings ye ganged yer own gait, we knew that ye could see the island and that ye'd bring him"— he waved at Monkey—"over the sea to safety. But—" He was silent for a moment. "Mebbe ye have in front o' ye a harder task than that."

"Harder?" Mr. Linnet stared. What could be harder than picking locks and risking years in jail?

"Well, let me put it this way, Linnet. We others are no'—shall we say?—attached!"

"Oh, you're thinking of my wife and children. But they'd be all right. They have Miss Brown-Potter. And I would be back from time to time, helping to bring the new cargoes—"

"Ay, the wife and bairnies, as ye say. But Ah had another thing in mind. If a pairson owes ye a debt, Linnet, have ye no' a duty to let him pay it?"

"A debt? Of course! That's only fair. But nobody owes me anything!" A debt! The idea was ridiculous. He had never had anything to lend.

"Ye think not?" Professor McWhirter glanced at Monkey,

who was now looking up at Mr. Linnet, offering him a broken branch from which hung a comb of wild honey.

"Have ye no' saved him again and again and crossed the width o' the wurrld to do it? Saved him from me—" The Professor grinned. "Saved him from Sam—when all we wanted was to bring him here—saved him from ganging back to London?"

"Well, yes, I suppose so. But that was nothing. I couldn't do anything else, you see."

"Ye couldna, indeed. And that's not nothing, forbye it deepens the debt. And ye think he'll no' be wanting to pay it? Do you think he'll no' need to help and sairve ye—ay, and overhelp and oversairve—all the days of his life? If ye dinna ken that, ye dinna ken him. It's a matter o' lettin' yerself be loved—that's no' an easy thing!"

Mr. Linnet turned his head away. Was life to be always so uncertain, so full of changes and disappointments? Must he give up what he so much longed for, the work that would fill every crack in his being, the work he could do so well?

He glanced across at Miss Brown-Potter who was weaving a hammock for Stanley Fan from strips of cocoanut palm. Her face had the same contented look it had worn in Belvedere Gardens. All places, it seemed, were alike to her. She did not choose between them.

He looked at his wife and the two children absorbed in a quiet domestic task. They were trying to tidy the lion's mane with Victoria's comb and hairbrush.

And then he looked at Monkey. The dark eyes were watching anxiously. He could not disappoint them.

"You're right," he said, and took the branch. "I shall stay here, Professor."

"Ay, lad. It's the proper choice. A man must bide all

279

things, Linnet. Forbye, ye'll no' be so unchancy. You'll be Our Man on Three!" The Professor smiled his wily smile. "Now, Barley, Tom, and you, Young Napper! We must be off. The day's away down. And you, Fred, Ah'm bidding ye farewell!"

He pulled the ferret from his neck and sent it skittering off.

"Au revoir, Mrs. Linnet," said Tom Locket, as he and the others, garlanded with Monkey's gifts, rejoined Professor Mc-Whirter. "We'll meet again soon!" he told the children.

Soon! Soon! Soon! Soon! The clearing echoed with the human sound, round and soft, like the calling of doves, as the men went down to the shore.

There was now no sign of the *Southern Pearl.* She was safely stowed, presumably, in Davy Jones's Locker.

The oars resounded in the rowlocks as the oarsmen steered for the *Northern Star,* the line of rafts bobbing behind them, light from their lack of freight.

Mr. Linnet gazed after them. Some day those rafts would appear again, heavy with new cargoes. And Our Man on Three would be there to receive them, to lead the creatures from shore to clearing and restore them to the wild. It comforted him to think of that and to know that somewhere in the world there were men who knew where the island was and its latitude and longitude . . .

15

The tropical night was over the clearing. Light, like water, flowed from the stars. The little settlement was quiet.

Patches of white shone among the grasses, patches the shape of tombstones. Edward had evidently been busy.

Louis and the mynah bird were sitting side by side on a tree.

Stanley was cracking palm-fowl eggs. There would be an omelette for supper.

Mrs. Linnet, having bandaged Uncle Trehunsey's foot, bustled across to her own house to put the children to bed. Above the roof was a tangle of branches. Monkey, Mr. Linnet saw, had built his nest as close as he could to the nest of his human family. And in the doorway lay the lion, kindly but firmly showing Little Trehunsey that he was not to be bullied.

Miss Brown-Potter, with Tinker and Badger at her side, sat with her back against a tree, her hands crossed in her lap. Stanley's hammock was finished.

It was a peaceful, domestic scene.

Mr. Linnet stood at the jungle's edge, his ear to the sounds of evening. Up on the plateau, the hyena laughed, struck by some clownish joke. A piglet squeaked and something roared. The leopard had found its supper. Somewhere the bear huffled and puffled, making its way to the hills. The elephant gave a sudden trumpet as though it had only now discovered it was not in the London Zoo.

281

All these sounds, Mr. Linnet knew, would become his everyday familiars, as commonplace and unheeded as once the clop of hansom cabs and the twitter of city starlings.

He had dreamed all his life of far places, and now the far had become the near and what had been near was far. When he walked about on Island Three, keeping his tropical world in order, he would dream romantically—he knew it!—of Billingsgate market smelling of fish, of foghorns on the River Thames, the rain, the mist, and the snow.

Voices came drifting over the sea. The sailors were singing "Auld Lang Syne" as the *Northern Star* departed. Chidwick, Throgmorton, and the rest were sending him across the waters a fading message of friendship.

Away in the jungle, now here, now there, he could hear Little Louis on Monkey's shoulder, repeating his piercing cry. He would always know where Monkey was because of that vibrant word.

And close at hand, in his own house, Mrs. Linnet was singing with the children, Victoria out of tune, as usual.

> *"London Bridge is falling down,*
> *Dance over, my Lady Leigh!"*

and, later, with a sleepy fall,

> *"Now the day is over*
> *Night is drawing nigh."*

It did not seem strange to Mr. Linnet that here in this place beyond the compass these songs should seem as suitable as once they had done in Putney. A lullaby was a lullaby, wherever it was sung. Sleep was the same everywhere, men were the same everywhere, and the same sky over all.

282

He reached up a hand and took off his bowler—or rather, Mr. Perks' bowler—and flung it away as far as he could. Then he did the same thing with his boots. Perhaps some Equatorial Plumpers would make their nests inside them. And tomorrow he would weave some sandals, and a hat from strips of cocoanut palm—more fitting garments, he decided, for a man who, from this day forward, would be living on a tropical island unknown to any map.

Yes! Tomorrow he would set to work. He would find the Persian goat and milk her and clear a patch of earth for the seeds—corn, parsley, Brussels sprouts—that Miss Brown-Potter had remembered to bring. He would gather armfuls of green leaves to make into soft, receptive beds—so different from the furniture in Uncle Trehunsey's London home; and further strengthen the three houses against a possible storm.

He thought of the mud hut in Umtota that now he would never see. His present dwelling, on the whole, seemed preferable to that. Cleaner and easier to repair. And were there, he wondered, in Umtota, such quantities of delicious fruits, such treasures to be fished from the sea as Island Three provided? Probably not, he decided.

Indeed, Mr. Linnet was beginning to think, such was his optimistic nature, that he was a fortunate man. He felt like singing a song of praise but remembered, as the impulse seized him, that he, like his daughter Victoria, was unable to hold to a tune. Besides, it wasn't necessary. Little Louis would do it for him.

The piercing voice was nearer now. "Auld Lang Syne" had died away and "Now the Day Is Over" was coming to its close. The silence that followed was full of sadness, the sadness that comes at a song's ending.

"I'm a castaway!" he thought to himself, for a moment feeling lost and lonely.

But the cry from the darkness came again. And Mr. Linnet took heart. All songs that had ever been sung, he thought, were gathered into that single word. That was a song that would never end. The singing would never be done.

There! The sound was almost upon him. The dark screen of the jungle parted, and Monkey came prancing through.

But what was he bringing in his arms? Could it be—yes, it could, indeed! The starlight made no bones about it. Something that had been thrown away—lost forever, it was hoped—was now, with anxious, loving care, being restored to the owner.

Mr. Linnet sighed, not unhappily—too much was better than too little!—but simply accepting his fate.

The pair leapt joyfully towards him, Monkey carrying boots and bowler, and his jubilant friend upon his shoulder, throbbing with his word.

"Hallelujah! Hallelujah! Hallelujah!"

Mr. Linnet held out his arms . . .

A. M. G. D.